Côte Tales

from Walton Street Writers,
Oxford

Anglepoise
Books

Published by Anglepoise Books – an Oxfordfolio imprint (www.oxfordfolio.co uk)

ISBN 978-1-0687661-0-7

Printed in the United Kingdom by Short Run Press (SRP), Exeter, Devon

10 9 8 7 6 5 4 3 2 1

Cover illustration by Valerie Dearlove.

Designed and typeset by Freya Morgan

FSC
www.fsc.org
MIX
Paper | Supporting responsible forestry
FSC® C014540

WALTON STREET WRITERS

was founded by novelist Sara Banerji.

We meet regularly to share our writing and thoughts on love, mystery, life and croissants.

This collection contains short stories, poems, a memoir and a novella.

EDITED BY *Laura Callaghan*

ILLUSTRATION BY *Valerie Dearlove*

COORDINATED BY *Harold Roffey*

We thank Côte Brasserie for their generous hospitality.

CONTENTS

THE SETTING OF THE SUN

CATHERINE HURST

HOLDING HANDS, THEY SAT ON THE BEACH, silent, nervous, neither daring to speak at the end of what had been a hot July day.

Robert's heavy uniform felt itchy and uncomfortable as he and Daisy watched the sunset. She moved closer into Robert's protective arms, her floral dress fluttering in the cool of the summer evening breeze, praying this moment would never end.

The descending sun lit up the beach, casting a shadow of the couple onto the sand. The sea, a collage of silvers, golds, greens and greys, gently splashed onto the shore. The setting sun radiated a palette of dazzling colour, finally disappearing below the horizon.

The huddled silhouette of the couple sat alone on the beach. Daisy slowly slid her arm down Robert's back as he silently rose, shaking the sand from his uniform, before placing his service cap on his head. She couldn't look as he walked away from her in the chill of the evening. She put out her hand onto the sand feeling the shape and warmth where Robert had been sitting. Emptiness overwhelming her, she wondered whether she would ever see him again.

*****

Daisy was now living alone in a house she and Robert had rented on the south coast. The void in Daisy's life grew larger as each day passed. She stared at the walls of the two-bedroomed terrace house, recalling the row with her parents.

'We will marry after the war,' Daisy had promised them. Her father hadn't been convinced.

'You live with him in sin, you're no daughter of mine.'

His words echoed in her head, along with the final moments with Robert slipping away from her arms. To relieve her loneliness, she would walk to the beach, clutching the letters that came sporadically, reading and re-reading Robert's words.

> *I can't bear being without you. I need your warmth in this cruel world I find myself in. Your letters bring me such comfort, against the deafening noise of war. Today has been a good day, quiet and without casualties. The lads are a great help, and we keep one another's spirits up. I think of you constantly, yearning for the day we will meet again, when this crazy war is over. All my love.*

The newspaper headlines fuelled Daisy's anxiety. Customers of the local grocery shop, where she worked, talked only of the war. A day not going by when there wasn't a story of loss. The small income she received helped pay the rent. Occasionally, there might be oddments of food left at the end of the day, such as outer leaves from cabbages, or bruised fruit, that she could take home. This was vital as she was now pregnant.

It had been a shock at first when she received the news, but an inner strength comforted her. She was carrying Robert's child. She had not written to him about the baby, afraid he might get court-martialled should he try to leave the regiment and come and visit her.

Christmas came. Daisy's mother pleaded for her to come home for a few days, having been given the news about the baby. Daisy reluctantly agreed to visit. 'Come in, love.' Her mother kissing her on the cheek, taking her coat and bag. 'I'm so pleased you could come.'

Her father didn't stir from his armchair, coughing uncontrollably; her mother was resigned to the idea that he might not last much longer.

'The house looks very Christmassy, Mum. I hope you haven't worked too hard.'

'She's a good'-un, your mother.' Ernie, her father, shuffled to the kitchen to give Gertrude a hand, ignoring his daughter's advanced pregnancy.

'Mr Radcliffe from next door, heard you were coming.' Gertrude lowered her voice almost to a whisper. 'He gave us what we're eating for our Christmas dinner. He pushed it into my hands, wrapped in newspaper, warning me not to mention it to anyone on the street. Has a contact, was all he said.' Gertrude served them a couple of slices each of the black-market chicken.

'Have you heard from him then?' Her father spluttered out the question. Daisy, enjoying the chicken, didn't want to get into an argument, and remained silent.

'How are you going to bring it up on your own? I told you nothing good would come of him.'

'Easy on her, Ernie. I'm sure she's got it all worked out. Here, let's pull a cracker.'

Daisy pulled on the cracker her mother had made from old toilet roll centres covered with painted newspaper. Conversation was impossible with her father's incessant cough, but she tucked into her meal, consisting of a few roast potatoes alongside, turnips and parsnips which Ernie had grown on their small, garden patch. Daisy's thoughts were only of Robert, not knowing where he was. She wanted to be at home with him.

The next day, Daisy was packed ready to return to her lonely cottage. As she kissed her father goodbye, his eyes told her that this might be for the last time. He pressed a few shillings into her hand. 'Take this, you'll need it for the baby. Let us know of any news you get from him.' He turned, continuing to cough until he reached his armchair.

Daisy left with a mixture of sadness and anxiety. She felt the baby kick. She had no idea how she would manage the coming months.

*****

'You need to come quickly. The baby is on its way!' Daisy screamed down the phone, clutching her stomach in the phone box at the corner of her street.

'I'll get there as soon as I can.'

Midwife, Mavis Bains, looked at her watch, concerned she might not be able to pedal fast enough. Her years of long service as a midwife had taken a toll on her body. Her back ached and her knees were stiff. She knew they were warning signs that she must retire soon.

Contractions were coming quickly. The sirens had started up. Daisy heard in the distance the drone of aeroplanes coming towards the coast as she walked home in the early evening. 'I'm having a baby!' Daisy shouted, shaking her fists at the sky. 'Go back and leave us alone.'

A knock at the door came soon after Daisy had returned home. She waddled towards it, opening it a few inches, expecting the midwife.

'Mum!'

'I got here as fast as I could. Caught the last train out of Victoria, which was just as well, as the Hun are on their way.'

Her mother stepped into the house swiftly, so as not to let in light due to the blackout.

'What about dad?'

'Mrs Radcliffe, from next door said she'd pop by. She and Bert, who gave us that chicken at Christmas, have been so good to us.'

'Aren't you worried about leaving him?'

'We're not in the firing line, they're heading for the munition factories. I thought you would need a hand seeing as you're on your own. Besides, a new baby brings hope from all this horror.'

'You're just in time,' Daisy groaned.

'It's freezing in here, Daisy. You haven't lit a fire.'

'I haven't much coal. I didn't think I would need to light fires now. There's a shilling on the windowsill in the kitchen. Could you light the gas and put on a kettle and make us some tea, please Mum?' Daisy yelled, as another contraction engulfed her.

'It must be one of the coldest April's we've had.' While they waited for the kettle to boil, Gertrude went upstairs and pulled the bed away from the window, dragging it to the landing. She hoped it would be far enough away from flying glass, should a bomb drop.

There was a sense of relief when they heard a discreet knock on the door. Gertrude opened it carefully.

'You must be Daisy's mother.' Mavis Bains quickly pushed her bike into the hallway, the sound of sirens filling the outside air.

Mavis got to work immediately.

'There's nothing like a spring baby to cheer us all up.' Mavis chatted happily while examining Daisy. 'I've made it just in time, you're nearly there. Now give me a good push.' Daisy screamed.

'You'll wake the street up, Daisy.' Mavis laughed, then suddenly stopped, putting a finger to her lips. 'Did you hear that?'

A dull thud of a bomb hitting the ground was heard in the distance. Daisy tried not to scream as another contraction came. A few seconds later the explosion shook the house. A crack in the ceiling appeared, pieces of plaster falling onto the birthing area.

'Oh God, not now,' Daisy wailed. 'My baby!'

'It sounded quite far away.' Mavis urging Daisy to keep pushing. 'It was probably a rogue bomb. There's nothing for them around here.'

With one more push and a blood-curdling scream from Daisy, Mavis beamed.

'You have a baby boy.'

Mavis cleaned the baby as best she could, wrapped him in a blanket, and weighed him on her portable scales. 'He's a good 6lbs,' she smiled, then placed him against Daisy. The sight of a newborn baby never ceased to thrill her after all her years of midwifery, but she pitied mothers bringing a baby into the world under these circumstances.

Gertrude gently picked up her first grandchild, holding him close to her. For a few, blissful moments the world seemed at peace.

'I wonder who the poor blighters were who got that bomb.' Gertrude said, smiling contentedly at her new grandson, while remembering Ernie alone in their house.

'Your dad will be pleased it's a boy. He's been telling everyone he's going to be a granddad, Daisy. He's come around to the situation at last.'

Mavis washed her instruments in the stone sink, collected her belongings and left, leaving the two women alone with their newborn boy.

'Have you a name for the little fella?' Gertrude asked Daisy, stroking the baby's face.

'Jack,' Daisy replied. Gertrude could not conceal the look of disappointment on her face.

*****

I hope you receive this letter, Robert. I've been worried sick about you. It's been so long since I heard from you. In your last letter, you told me you lost your friend Pete. I can't imagine what you are going through.
We had a bomb drop not too far from here in April.

This is why I am writing to you Robert. It was while I was giving birth to our baby son, that we heard it. Robert, you have become a father. A little boy, weighing 6lbs. He looks just like you. I named him Jack after your dad who I know you miss so much.

My mother came down from London to give me a hand. I don't know what I would have done without her. I wished you could have been with me, as it's been so lonely. The grocer shop where I work has been very understanding. No one knows we haven't tied the knot, as I wear a ring to stop any gossip. When this war is over, I hope we will be able to be together as a family.

Write when you receive this letter, Robert. Jack has a small patch of dark hair, blue eyes and is smiling now. His little face lights up just how I remember you, when you smiled.

All my love.

Daisy pushed the pram down to the coastal path and sat on a bench looking out to sea. She rocked Jack gently back and forth. She had not received a reply to her letter telling Robert about Jack. She tried not to imagine the worst. The memory of their last time together still haunted her. She could not bear to think that Robert might never return.

Their little boy not ever knowing his father. She felt tears welling up. Through her misty eyes, she watched the sun momentarily appear, as it gradually moved down towards the horizon. Streaks of pale pink and blue lit up the grey clouds. Jack, fast asleep, lay peacefully in the pram. Daisy smiled at her little boy's resemblance to his daddy. She shivered as the sun set. Placing a blanket over Jack, she slowly began to push the pram back home.

In the dark, Daisy heard someone approaching, the irregular steps indicating they were walking with a limp. A half-moon shone onto a man who had a black patch over one eye, his face badly scarred. A shadow of a human being, crippled by war. They looked directly at one another.

'Robert? Robert is that you?'

'Don't be afraid. I won't hurt you.'

Daisy stepped back, horrified to hear his clipped German accent.

'I must be getting back.' Daisy turned to walk away.

'Can you help me?' His broken face pleaded with her.

'I can't be caught with you. I don't know who you are, or what you're doing here. I've got my baby to think about.'

'I'm sorry. I know what you think, but I need help. Do you know where I can stay for a little while? My food has run out and I need medical help.'

He was about the same age as Robert. Daisy was surprised how well he spoke English. Would the enemy help Robert if he was found wounded? she thought. She hesitated.

'I have a shed. You can rest there until I think of something.' 'Thank you.'

'Can you walk up the hill? It's not far.'

'I'll be slow.' They walked back in silence.

'Good evening.' A stranger doffed his hat as he passed the couple. 'Getting chilly now, isn't it?'

'Yes,' Daisy replied hurriedly, hoping her voice wouldn't tremble.

'You must be glad to be back in old Blighty.' The stranger directed his question at the wounded man.

'Yes, it's lovely to have him back.' Daisy continued pushing the pram up the hill, wishing the stranger would move along.

'I hope you recover soon, and that you gave the Hun what they deserved. Bloody war, bloody Germans.' The stranger disappeared into the night.

Daisy was anxious to move quicker, but the young man was struggling to get up the hill, having to stop for breath.

'We're nearly there. We'll go in by the back gate near to the shed. It's not much, but it's all I have,' she whispered, careful not to disturb the neighbours.

'Thank you. I'm most grateful. Daisy eased the man onto the floor of the shed. He looked exhausted.

'I only have tea and some bread, she told him.

'Thank you,' he murmured, drowsily.

Daisy prepared Jack's night-time feed. Once he was settled, she tiptoed to the shed. The German was asleep, slumped on the dusty, cob-webbed floor. She placed the drink and food inside the door, quietly shutting it behind her. Returning to the house, she fell into bed, longing for Robert to return. She was tired and confused as to what to do with the stranger. She hoped he might be gone by morning, relieving her of further responsibility.

*****

Robert Jennings' injuries were so severe, he lay motionless on a camp bed, alongside other injured men, on an open ward. He had been one of the few survivors from a bomb blast that had hit a train carrying troops. Beside him, on a bedside table, lay un-opened letters. He had recurring nightmares, a tangle of discarded body parts, mixed with Daisy's golden curls brushing against his cheek, her soft lips, warm, the gurgling of a last breath from a comrade. He would wake screaming most nights. A woman's voice interrupted the noise coming from the tinnitus that filled his head, holding him down gently, but firmly to prevent him from moving. Sudden movement could cause further damage to his eyes which were covered in bandages.

'How are you feeling today, Robert?'

'Where am I?'

'Hepworth Hall, in Sussex.' The voice replied. 'It's a country house that has been converted into a hospital.'

'Where are the others?'

'Try not to move. I will help you.' Robert clutched the hand of the person who was re-positioning him, to help relieve him of his bed sores.

'How did I get here?'

'We need to get you better again, Robert,' was all she would say. The conditions in which he and others were found would become apparent as the months went by.

'Who are you?'

'I'm Sarah. I am one of the nurses. You have a lot of un-opened letters, Robert. Would you like me to open them and read them to you?

Robert didn't want reminders of the past. His old life was finished, but in his helpless state he appeared not to have a choice. He heard the sound of an envelope being torn open.

'I'll start with the most recent one.' Sarah sat down beside him.

Robert lay quietly as Sarah read the letter from Daisy. Neither of them spoke for a while after she had finished, allowing Robert to absorb the information.

'What wonderful news Robert, you've become a father.'

'Daisy has had a baby? I'm a father?' He repeated.

Sarah wondered why he hadn't known of Daisy's pregnancy. She looked at the number of un-opened letters. Perhaps the news was in one of those, not understanding why he had left them untouched.

'I'll get you some fresh bandages.' There was urgency in Sarah's voice.

'We need to keep the area around your eyes dry.

Sarah took his arm and placed the letter in his hand. Her touch sparked a yearning inside, a feeling Robert had long forgotten.

*****

It was early when Daisy was woken by Jack crying. Her head was banging from lack of sleep and her reckless decision to take in the young German. What should she do with the stranger in her shed? Why had she not walked away from him last night? She picked up Jack, giving him a cuddle, making her way downstairs to give him his breakfast of a soft-boiled egg. She placed him back in his cot, then made her way to the shed. A putrid smell hit Daisy as she opened the door, making her want to retch.

'I'm sorry.' The German, tried to get up. 'I was unable to move to go to the toilet outside.'

'You need to come inside and get cleaned up and get out of those clothes.'

Daisy helped him up from the floor, placing one arm over her shoulder, almost dragging him to the house.

'I'm sorry. I am causing you much trouble.'

'I don't even know your name.'

'Franz. Franz Hoffman.'

'I'm Daisy, and this is Jack, my son.' Daisy eased Franz onto a chair, and began boiling water so he could have a wash in the basin.

'How did you get here?'

'My plane was hit. I was losing control. I opened the cockpit and parachuted into the sea, just before the bomb exploded. I was picked up by a fisherman, who looked after me for a while. He destroyed my German uniform and found me some civilian clothes, but I had to move as it was becoming dangerous for him.'

'When was this?'

'In April.'

'April? A bomb exploded near here when I was giving birth to Jack. The house shook. You can see there's a crack in the ceiling.'

'I'm sorry. I hate this war. I want to go home, but I will be arrested if I return.'

'I will have to burn these clothes.' Daisy gathered them up in newspaper. 'Robert left his only suit behind. It might fit you.'

'Robert is your husband?' Franz asked.

'Yes.' Daisy twisted her makeshift wedding ring around her finger.

'Where is he?'

'I don't know. I don't even know if he's still alive. I'll get it out of the wardrobe to see if it fits.'

She brushed down the double-breasted, pinstriped suit, holding it to her face. The memory of their last dance, when he had worn it, brought back painful memories of their love for one another.

Franz appeared wearing Robert's suit. Daisy took a deep breath. He looked young and vulnerable, particularly wearing an eye patch and having a scarred face. In the daylight, his hair was the colour of autumn straw. Daisy turned away quickly, hiding her neck with her hand, feeling it get hot, knowing her skin was going red. She hadn't felt this way since she first met Robert.

'You'll have to stay here, while I go to work.' She picked up Jack and put him in his pram. 'They're very kind letting me bring him. I don't know what I would do, otherwise.'

'You're taking a risk having me here, thank you.'

'When I'm gone, don't answer the door.'

Daisy looked behind her as she walked to work, making sure no one could see that she was sheltering someone in her house.

It was eerily quiet when Daisy and Jack had left. Franz, exhausted from months on the run, lay on Daisy's bed. The first bed he had slept in since the start of the war. He fell into a deep sleep.

*****

Queues had formed by the time Daisy had reached Wallace Grocer's.

'We've had a delivery this morning: we need to get the stock out onto the shelves quickly,' Fred Wallace told Daisy. 'The ladies are getting right tetchy at waiting outside, now it's raining.'

Fred was in a constant state of stress, never knowing when supplies might reach him. Once a congenial man, he had little time for niceties now.

The shop bell rang. Rita rushed in, eager to share her latest piece of gossip.

'Have you heard, ladies?' She didn't wait for a reply. 'They've arrested a fisherman.'

'A fisherman?' a customer asked. 'We need our fishermen.'

'He'd been harbouring a German, apparently. It turns out one of them had jumped from his plane on his way to bombing us. The plane had got hit by one of our men and the pilot parachuted into the sea. Don't you remember when that bomb exploded down the coast?' Rita looked around for assurances.

'I don't know where you hear all this stuff,' Fred Wallace commented.

'My friend, Liz, had to be evacuated.' Rita continued. 'She wrote to me with her new address, telling me she read about the arrest in her local paper. They haven't been able to track down the German.'

Rita looked towards Daisy.

'You OK luv?' Rita saw Daisy's hands were shaking.

'Yes, just tired. Jack kept me awake most of the night.'

'Must say, luv, you've gone awfully pale.'

Daisy stamped Rita's ration book, handing over her groceries with a fixed smile, and moved quickly on to the next customer.

'You be careful,' Rita continued. 'A woman on her own with a child. He could take advantage of someone in your state. He could be hiding under your bed if you don't watch out.'

The customers laughed, knowing Rita's imagination often ran away with her, though on occasions her gossip had some elements of truth.

'So, watch out, ladies,' Rita announced. 'If you see a stranger around, remember, "Careless talk costs lives."

'Perhaps you should be careful spreading rumours like that, Rita.' Fred Wallace didn't have time for gossipers like Rita.

*****

'Wake up.' Daisy was shaking Franz. 'We've got to get out of here.'

'What's happened?' Franz woke, dazed and confused. His wounds hurt as he got up from the bed.

'They know you're on the run. A customer who comes into the shop told us they've arrested the fisherman who sheltered you. It's in the newspapers.'

'I might as well hand myself in.' Franz looked defeated.

'I called my mother on my way home. My dad has gone into hospital, and she's offered to help us.'

'Why are you doing this for me?'

'Quickly. We have no time to waste. I'll gather Jack's things and I'll pack what I can. There's a late train going to London tonight.'

*****

Robert Jennings was wheeled into the garden of Hepworth Hall where he had been recuperating for almost a year.

'It's hard to believe there's a war going on when we're here, Robert.'

Sarah was on duty again. Vision had returned to Robert's right eye. Where previously, he had only ever imagined what the softly spoken, gentle nurse looked like, he could now see how beautiful Sarah was. He had grown fond of her, missing her when she wasn't on duty. They sat quietly watching the setting sun.

'The sea is calm today, isn't it?' Sarah realised she too, would miss Robert when he was to be discharged. She wondered where he would go.

'Robert was staring out to sea. 'I should have written to Daisy. I just couldn't write and explain what I had witnessed. I thought it best to let her go, as I didn't think I would survive.'

'We've tried contacting her, but we understand she's no longer living at the address you gave us.'

'Now I've lost her and our son.'

The sun dipped down, slowly a rainbow of colours spread across the horizon.

'It's getting chilly, Robert. I'd better take you inside.'

'Have you any idea where they might be?' Robert didn't want to go inside.

Sarah took a deep breath. She didn't want to be the one to break the news.

'We were told they had gone with Daisy's mother, who has relatives in Ireland, where they could be safe.'

'Ireland? Daisy never mentioned she had relatives living in Ireland. What happened to Daisy's father?'

'We understand he was sent into hospital for the critically sick. We assume he has died now.' Sarah was finding this more difficult than she thought.

'Daisy was safe in our cottage on the coast, away from the bombs. There was no need for her to move away.'

Robert was getting agitated, trying to get out of his wheelchair, but fell back, his legs still not ready for any weight-bearing.

'The relatives in Ireland were able to secure a passage for them all.' There was a long pause before Sarah could tell Robert the next piece of news.

'You see Robert, Daisy was sheltering another wounded person, like you. An airman.' She took a deep breath. 'A German.'

The last orange rays of sun gave out a final splash of colour, casting a shadow as Sarah wheeled Robert back to give him his medicine. She looked at Robert's broken body, which was slowly mending through her gentle, patient care. Could she be the one to mend Robert's broken spirit as well? She hoped she could. She had omitted the final piece of news she had heard about Daisy.

The British authorities had got information of a German pilot on the run. Franz Hoffman had been arrested on his way to Ireland, his current whereabouts, unknown.

GHOSTLY PLOTS

CATHERINE HURST

HE OPENED THE DOOR TO ROOM 101. Dressed only in the hotel's white towelling dressing gown, he ushered me in.

'I can come back later, sir.'

'You can clean while I get changed.' His tone was haughty, as he disappeared quickly out of view.

It felt awkward cleaning with a guest in the bedroom, but I went about my chores, singing happily, as I had always done.

'Do you have to make that noise?' He was hovering outside the bathroom door.

'Sorry, sir. There's not usually anyone listening.'

'I must have silence when I'm in the midst of writing up my investigation.'

'You should have put a "Do not disturb" notice on your door.' I was annoyed: he hadn't appreciated my singing.

'Everyone knows I can *only* operate from this room. You must be one of the new ones.'

He had changed into cords and an open-necked shirt, a cravat around his neck. He stood, clasping his hands behind his back.

'Do you know this hotel is awash with ghosts?'

'Don't believe in those, sir. If you'd excuse me, I need to continue my cleaning for the next guests.'

'Perhaps, the next guest will be a ghost writer.' His eerie laugh sent a shiver down my spine.

As I was bending over the bath giving it a good scrub, I heard heavy breathing behind me. Then something tugged hard around my neck. I began to gurgle, desperately trying to pull the dressing-gown cord away, screaming for help. Then everything went black. My life, my job – gone in a flash.

*****

I reside in this hotel, no longer as a living human being, but as a member of the spirit world. I may not be seen or heard, but I soon discover I have other powers.

It was when I was drifting through the foyer, I recognised him. The murderer from Room 101. He was wearing an expensive, tartan, cashmere scarf, draped across his shoulders, a deerstalker hat on his head.

He was having a heated argument with the manager. I'm shouting, 'Arrest him. He's a murderer!' but no one can hear me.

'I want my usual room!' he bellows.

The manager, firm, but polite, explains he hasn't booked, but he can offer him a room at the top of the hotel. 'It's that room or nothing, sir.' The manager points to the service lift.

Since my demise, I have made acquaintances with some of my fellow inmates. My murderer was right: the hotel has many ghosts. I occasionally float past one I'd read about in the days when I read books. They waft around, sizing me up, trying to decide if I might be an important character from a novel. Concluding that a chambermaid couldn't possibly be of any relevance, they ignore me.

Recently, I was introduced to the late Inspector Morse, often seen hovering around the bar named in his honour. He's taken a great interest in my case. I tell him I have seen my murderer entering the hotel and that he is now being shown to the service lift.

He's puzzled as to why no one was arrested. He looks pensive, as he contemplates the moments leading up to my death.

'He did it with a dressing-gown belt, you say?'

'Yes, I was pulling hard on it, but I didn't have enough strength to remove it.'

He quietly sips a drink, while viewing the surroundings, muttering something under his breath.

'The scarf. The scarf.' I hear him say. He immediately heads towards the service lift. I struggle to keep up with him.

'You know what to do, don't you?'

'No, Inspector. What have you in mind?' I'm clueless as to what he's going to ask me to do.

'Just follow my instructions. Grab one end of the scarf. I'll take the other end.'

'I thought you solved crimes, not committed them,' I remind him.
'I can't. I lost my strength when I died, Inspector.'

'Try tugging on his scarf.' Morse urges. 'You'll be surprised what you can do.

'Harder! Tighter!' Morse shouts.
Morse presses the top floor button. The lift doors shut, trapping the scarf. Morse rubs his hands, satisfied that he had rid the world of an unsavoury character.

We drift alongside the lift to the top floor. The doors open. My murderer lies lifeless.

'Welcome to my world,' I whisper to him.

'I've been dead for years,' he laughs, 'strangled by my own scarf while waiting for a lift. Your Inspector Morse should have known that.'

'How did you kill me if you were already dead?'

'I didn't kill you.'

He rises from the floor of the elevator, staring at Inspector Morse and me and begins quoting from a play.

'All the world's a stage, my dear, and we men and women merely players, or in our cases, fictional players, brought to life in books.'

'You mean, we're not real people?'

'Unfortunately for you, my dear girl, you too were an incidental character in a book. A crime I investigated and solved easily, with the aid of my esteemed assistant. You were killed by the hotel porter. The Inspector Morse could do well to take a leaf out of the books I featured in.'

'I was too young to die,' I sigh.

'Let's face it. You were in a dead-end job. I must go now to the only room they've allowed me to occupy. The hotel has had complaints about my violin playing – hence the servants' quarters.'

I perch on a windowsill, bereft that I had only ever been a bit player in a book long forgotten, while Inspector Morse drifts off into another chapter of his life.

THE IDEAL LOVE INTEREST

ANNE HARRAP

'YOU'RE SURE YOU DON'T MIND ME HAVING a drink with Carina?' (Actually, I was planning on champagne in bed with Carina.)

She raised her perfect eyebrows. 'Of course not, why should I?'

I felt relief – this was the freedom I'd always wanted. At the same time, I felt a stab of annoyance. How contrary is the human heart. Against all common sense I scratched the itch.

'I thought you might be jealous.'

Her periwinkle eyes were severe. 'Greg, you haven't read your technical spec. Jealousy has been programmed out as unhelpful.'

It was true – I hadn't read the 'hubot' spec. It was too complicated. I was just delighted to have passed all the tests and acquired a beautiful, compliant girlfriend tailored to my requirements.

Anyway, the Carina thing was next week. Tomorrow we were out on the town.

It was a lovely day as we wandered arm in arm near the Serpentine. I could feel the collective male gaze of the park slanting towards us. A famous pianist was playing at the Albert Hall – my choice of Prom of course. I felt uplifted by the whole programme, which culminated in some sound and fury by Liszt. Out of the corner of my eye I could see her flinch at the crashing of the keys – bit of a glitch there, then. Had I skipped the question on musical tastes?

Afterwards we went for lunch – a charming little terrace on a sunny side street, tastefully ornamented with flowers. On this occasion, she was the one to point it out.

'Let's sit here.'

'Use those blue eyes, gal. It says "Reserved".'

'I thought that would suit you. You can choose another if you like.'

I glanced over at the other tables. One said 'Extravert'. Another said 'Phlegmatic'.

'For heaven's sake! What is this?

I felt another dart of annoyance and sent a mental javelin at her lace-covered arm, which promptly fell off with a spurt of blood. The approaching waiter turned green and fainted.

'Now look what you've done! Technical spec, Greg, technical spec... The addendum, postscripted by popular request: "Modification via thought process".'

The periwinkle eyes and pearl-blonde hair were beginning to pall. And the contract was for two years, renewable. Oh my God!

REJUVENATION

ANNE HARRAP

In the year two thousand and twenty-two
The brilliant shade of YinMin Blue
Becomes available to you
Artists have known it since twenty-o-nine
An accidentally created hue

Of course the invention was overdue
The number of colours was just too few
But if you are over seventy-two
You'll not care how the tones combine
Just join the rejuvenation queue

Add the tincture to your shampoo
And create a magical witch's brew
To turn your scalp intensely blue
It will feel like a heady dose of wine
And you'll become intensely you

The flux is flowing through and through
You know it's turning out to be true
From the way you move to your choice of shoe
To the place you're going out to dine
To dance and never take a pew

And suddenly everything that you do
Is clear and strong, entirely new
Your stance is straight and not askew
Your skill is honed, your touch is fine
Your years rewound, dementia flew

Youth is upon us, thanks are due
To a certain tint of brilliant blue
How it works, we have no clue
Our colour's strange, the rest opine
What care we? Old age, adieu!

ADVENTURES IN GERMANY 1964

A School Exchange

ANNE HARRAP

I HAD BEEN PAIRED WITH MARGOT, a snooty blonde with slanting green eyes, out of my league linguistically and socially. In England she hit it off with her male equivalent, Reiner, from the German group, and they wanted to go off to London together, to the alarm of the hosting English parents. Arm in arm they would walk behind me making whispered remarks – derogatory ones, I felt sure. Margot's home was in Marxgrün, a small place near Hof, not far from the Czech border. The following is based on a letter written from there.

*****

Margot's parents have just come in. I haven't had the courage yet to give Frau her present. I'm sitting in the bedroom looking at a bottle for inspiration. It has the remains of a red and white candle in the neck, producing a pretty pink and white cascade of wax which has coated the glass.

The meals are more or less as expected – large, large and very large – and the funny old grandmother (Oma) keeps saying '*essen*, *essen*, *essen*'. She doesn't understand it's far more uncomfortable to eat too much than too little ...

Table manners are rather different here; with any bird up to the size of a goose you're allowed to yank the legs off with your fingers and gnaw away ... Breakfast means cornflakes – not as good as ours – and about half a pint of yoghurt eaten in a dish, with jam. Otherwise, there's little difference between breakfast and supper. You have slices of thick brown bread, and the idea is to load them up with cold meat, sausage, cheese, tomato, tuna and sauerkraut, as much as possible onto one slice. The midday meal is a large potato dumpling which you cut open and roll out like a carpet to find bits of bread in the middle. Veg and meat are heaped on top. Everyone chomps through about three of these while one leaves me gasping, which is unfortunate as they're Oma's speciality and it makes her very proud if you eat more than one.

The eiderdown – no sheet – is so heavy I invariably wake in the night, sodden with sweat, and spend ages shaking the thing like a rat.

My two years of German doesn't go very far and comes up against the Bavarian dialect, though they do try and speak the standard version to me. Oma is generally incomprehensible. I did once ask in the kitchen, 'Can I help you?' and understood her to reply that at least I'd learned something. (I already knew how to say that, thank you ...) I can however also now say: 'We're going to rescue beetles.' (From the pond – they keep falling in ... .)

Margot's brother-in-law is very dishy, claims to have limited English but then comes out with words like 'amphitheatre' and 'judgement'. Their little boy is curly-haired, hardly ever cries and is inclined to throw things. The scenery is beautiful, especially a lush green dell called Hölle or Hell. I suppose 'go to hell' must have quite a different meaning round here.

I wouldn't choose to do the journey again. The suitcase was impossibly heavy. It got very cold on the ship, and we were swigging whisky to keep warm. When we reached Ostend, we were still on the sundeck and there was a coagulation of bodies trying to get down the steps. Reiner, bright boy, led us down another way, dashing back and forth through the first-class restaurant. When we finally reached the lower deck, the coagulation was even thicker.

I'd lost track of my suitcase, and the label had come off, so finding it in the mêlée with the ship shifting to and fro was not funny. Nor was tearing down a Belgian railway platform lugging baggage, only, once settled in the carriage, to hear on the bush telegraph, 'wrong train'. All our stuff was thrown out of the windows while everyone wrestled with everyone else to get out of the train and pound along the opposite platform where the right one was about to pull out of the station. Luggage hauled through the windows again or thrown in after you – panic! panic! Nearly every seat was occupied, and the corridor was chock-full of bags reaching halfway up the walls. Of course, 80 seats had been reserved for 160 people.

I was at last shoved into a three-seater compartment with two boys, no idea again where my case was, and managed to doze between lights on and off and cries of 'Where are we now?' His having a charming smile doesn't help when a man hurls open the door with a thundering crash and says '*Guten Morgen*, tickets please' at 2.40 am. At the border one boy got stung for customs duty for a quarter pound of tea; another bunged four bottles of whisky, tea, coffee and cigarettes under the seat.

WITNESS: MURDER IN THE UNDERCROFT

ANNE HARRAP

I AM THE BYSTANDER, IMPASSIVE AS DREADFUL deeds are done, knowing they cannot affect me. I am there, pale but visible; I do not impinge.

It is late afternoon. Low light in the crypt. A priest is praying. Above us arch the splendours of the vaulted ceiling; enclosing us, the intricacies of pillars carved with angels, demons and botanicals.

Footsteps padding over the mosaics, slow with dark intent. A flash of steel, a scream, a rumpus. It is done. Who they are I do not know. Nor do I care.

Now I care. Someone approaches, fingers poised. I flutter and gutter. The flame of life burns low. The fingers, wetted in a vulgar mouth, approach me in a pincer, closer, closer. I gasp and all is black. I am transported, reincarnated as a wisp of smoke, spiralling upward to the vaulted ceiling, curling round the angels, demons and botanicals.

TO A GENTLEMAN MOVING FURNITURE BY PUBLIC TRANSPORT

ANNE HARRAP

To board a bus with wooden chairs
And carry a hat stand to boot
Shows a passenger who dares

Creates a question that is moot.
Will the driver give him hell
Or simply change the rules to suit?

Will other passengers rebel
Say the pole should get the chop
Can he reach to ring the bell

Through the furniture, over the top
When he arrives at destination
And needs to indicate his stop?

Or will there be expostulation
When they meet a deviation?
Driver, drop me at the station!

PARISIAN DAYS

ANNE HARRAP

I TOOK MYSELF OFF TO THE CINEMA yesterday to see Woody Allen's *Interiors* – different from his usual style and decidedly Bergmanesque – all grey, soft light and people flaying their souls.

I'm listening to a musical compilation provided by my brother – we've now got Pink Floyd with some howling in the background. I don't know whether he's been doing some mixing – or whether there are dogs somewhere. Shouts and fumes drift up from the street below, the Rue St Jacques, a thoroughfare which, followed through all its extensions, will lead to Santiago de Compostela. My miniscule flat, accessed via a seventeenth-century *porte-cochère* from the street, up perilous stairs and past a water fountain on each floor, is carved out of a single space. The bathroom and kitchen are tiny triangles knocked off either end; the intermittent whiff of sewage rising from the bidet wreathes its way through to the kitchen where I wrestle with the regulation tournedos, a steak as thick as it's tall; the accepted dish for entertaining a friend, accompanied by a bottle of cheap red plonk. I can't cook steak, and I can't finish the last half-glass. Perhaps I should try coq au vin and buy a *cocotte minute*, the pressure cooker that's standard for small flat dwellers, but liable to explode ...

A couple of weeks ago I went to Le Procope, reputedly the oldest restaurant in Paris, to eat a ball of cabbage with a partridge inside, in the company of a gentleman who looked and talked like an undertaker, but turned out to be one of those 'Isn't it a small world' people who did engineering at my university, lived in the part of Germany where I did my placement abroad, and nearly got a job where I grew up. We get on quite well but, as he talks at the speed of a hearse, I had an urge to produce a key and wind him up. He keeps clapping his hand to his forehead, complaining that his social life is overwhelming and making cryptic comments into space that he never explains.

I rang my friends Chris and Denise in Brussels, who are in the middle of an eternal decorating process. They spend their time moving to ever vaster mansions and filling them with plants. I, on the other hand, have just spent a fascinating evening at the launderette, reading about relativity and microwaves, explanations written for the scientifically obtuse like me. I'd determinedly hoiked home a new ironing board from Place Denfert-Rochereau. I find it easier to pepper Europe with cheap ironing boards than transport the original one.

Josie in London has been facing various contretemps. Her friend Mel is recently married and just before Christmas her husband disappeared for two days, returning merely to rush out of the house again, taking the wedding photos and ripping out the telephone on the way ...

Arthur, the 'undertaker' has just rung to say he will pick me up to go to Clare's tomorrow where there is to be a beanfeast to celebrate various birthdays. We are rather hoping Elspeth won't be there. She features rather too prominently in his social life, it seems, being one who batters company into stunned inertia through a constant 'ack-ack' of speech. He went to her for lunch on Saturday and didn't get away till 7 pm. I think she literally barred the door. It's all coming out now – she regularly invites him up for 'a bit of what you like'. He tells me he 'doesn't mind but she's an awful lay'. This seems unappreciative of a lady who is treating you to her charms. Sitting next to him, I become aware that his flesh has the sweet scent of freshly powdered baby. Perhaps that's the attraction. It seems Arthur's female friends fall into two categories: the 'frigid and fascinating' versus the 'randy and boring' ... As he's addressing himself to me, I'm presumably unclassified.

I went with Clare to the Bouffes du Nord theatre to see *Measure for Measure*. The only other time I'd seen it was at an open-air theatre in Germany when I didn't understand a word. I did get the story this time as we were nearer the players. It comes over very well in French considering it's Will's deathless prose. The wicked Regent had a hook nose and an annoying English accent, presumed assumed for the occasion. It's an interesting theatre – small, completely circular, with tiers of balconies and arches, very rough-hewn looking, as if the stonemason had just left for lunch.

At Clare's party was yet another Ricky. Imagine, if you will: tall and thin, a shock of red hair, Punch profile, the accent of the upper clergy in nineteenth-century Cambridge and a laugh like a bird of prey in a *Tom and Jerry* cartoon ... The eternal student, he studied Classics, moved on to theology and is now embedded in a mammoth treatise on mediaeval tile mosaics. He is actually very '*sympa*', as the French say, and presented me with a small book on 'Grave Humour', with epitaphs like: 'Here lyeth the body of Martha Dyas, always noisy and not very pious, who lived to the age of three-score and ten and gave to the worms what she refused to men.'

Dancing, on top of too much cake and champagne, seemed unwise, so I sat it out. When I arrived at eight, two French friends of Clare's were already leaving. Marie-Thérèse is a phenomenon from another century – delicately chiselled pale porcelain looks, dark eyes, dark bun; she wears retro lace collars and blouses, and basic owl specs. She's a fanatic of French literature and very amusing but seems to be heading for self-immolation on the altar of sobriety and early nights. No one can persuade her to stay out past 9pm.

Clare had overbudgeted for candles as well as cakes, so Sophie got the requisite 22 and I got the remainder – 37. They seemed to think this was a good joke, not realising perhaps it was nearer the mark than they might have expected. Never mind, I shall probably crumble nicely in a year or two ...

WHAT DID YOU SAY DEAR?

CHARLES BIDWELL

'I THINK I'VE LOST MY CARD DEAR.'

'What did you say Herbie dear?' said Maudie, looking up and blinking as he came in.

'I've lost my card dear' he said again as he lowered himself down into the chair opposite her.

'Oh no. Where did you leave it?'

'I can't remember.'

Silence, the type of deep, peaceful silence that can only exist between couples who have recently celebrated their diamond wedding anniversaries with hardly ever a cross word between them in all those years.

It was broken by the clock on the mantlepiece striking six. Herbie looked at it to make sure then pulled himself up from his chair and headed towards the sideboard.

'The sun's over the yardarm dear.' he said.

Maudie smiled.

'Good' she said. 'At last. It's been a long afternoon. Nobody dropped in and the telephone didn't ring apart from one nuisance call.'

'Oh dear.'

Herbie fussed around finding the gin bottle and two glasses. He poured two fingers worth into each glass, then looked for the ice bucket decorated with a Canaletto painting of Venice which their grandchildren had given them as a silver wedding present many years ago. He tugged off the lid and peered inside.

'There's no ice dear' he said. 'Only some rather mouldy-looking water with bits of something floating in it.'

'Oh Herbie, you know where it is, don't you?' she replied.

'Yes dear. In the top of the fridge. In the kitchen.'

'Good boy. Well done.'

He pottered off, and Maudie smiled to herself as she heard him muttering to himself as he banged the ice tray on the metal draining board to get some ice out.

She looked up as she heard him coming back.

'I forgot to take the ice bucket dear' he said and pottered back to the kitchen with it.

There was a short pause.

'I've got it dear' he said, putting two blocks into each glass.

There was a hiss as he opened the tonic and then a clatter as he threw the empty can into the rubbish basket. This was repeated as he filled the second glass. He carefully put the two glasses onto the little silver tray Maudie insisted he use for carrying glasses, as his hands were not very steady these days and she didn't like having to ask the daily lady to clean the carpet too often.

He tottered over to Maudie with a cheery 'Here you are dear.'

She gave it one sharp look.

'You forgot the lemon dear.'

'The lemon?'

'Yes, the lemon, you daft old thing.'

'Oh', and he tottered back to the sideboard.

'There isn't one dear' he announced, going through everything on the sideboard.

'There are plenty in the kitchen dear. In the fruit bowl.'

'Oh! yes'. He then pottered off again just as the mantlepiece clock was striking the half hour. It wasn't long before he was back.

'Look dear, I found one' he announced proudly, holding up a gleaming yellow lemon for inspection.

'Well done dear. Now put a slice in each glass and let's get on. I'm absolutely parched.'

Maudie took hers gratefully and when he had sat down, they solemnly raised their glasses to one another.

'God bless you, dear.' he said.

'And you too dear' she said and waited for him to take the first sip before starting her own ...

***

They drank in silence for a while, savouring the fresh taste of the drink. Then Maudie started racking her brains. She knew there was something important she had to say to him, but what was it?

She took another sip of her drink and thought hard. She prayed to St Anthony; the saint who helps find things that are lost.

It came to her. The car. She smiled to herself, wondering how to broach the subject, as Herbie had clearly forgotten, and she didn't want to upset him. She took another sip to clear her mind.

'Herbie dear' she started, but there was no reaction from him. She paused and said it again louder. He had clearly forgotten himself for a minute or so, as her mother used to say when she nodded off.

This time he looked up and smiled at her.

'Yes, dear?'

'What did you do this afternoon dear?'

He thought for a moment.

'Oh yes, I played a couple of hands of bridge at the club' he managed at last.

'That must have been nice for you dear.'

'Oh yes. We had a nice time. Everybody asked after you.'

'That's kind of them.'

She stopped and took another sip. This was going to be tricky.

'When you came in this evening, you said you'd lost your car, didn't you dear?'

He looked confused.

'Did I?' he said.

'How did you get home dear?'

He thought for a moment.

'On the bus.'

'Then you must have left it there.'

'Where dear?'

'At the club.'

He looked confused.

'I don't think so dear.'

'You must have, dear, if you came home on the bus,' she persisted.

'But I always have my bus pass with me. It's tied onto my keyring you know.'

She thought again.

'Have you any idea where you left it, dear?'

'Left what, dear?'

'The car.'

'The car?'

'Yes, the car.'

'It's in the usual place outside the house dear.'

Maudie looked at him in disbelief.

'Outside the house, what, here?'

'Yes dear.' He got up as smoothly as he could and walked to the window.

'Yes, I can see it clearly from here.'

After a moment's silence Maudie stated chuckling.

'Oh Herbie, you really are a muddle-headed old goon, making me worry like that.'

'Sorry dear,' was the only possible answer to that.

'Think dear, what is it that you have lost?'

'I can't remember dear' he said dolefully.

Maudie thought, and then a smile slowly spread across her face.

'Do you think it could be your card: card spelt C-A-R-D, you've lost yet again?'

'Oh yes. It probably is dear.'

'Listen to me, young Herbert, now that you are 94 it is about time you learned to enunciate clearly' she said, in her retired headmistress's stentorian tones – tones which used to frighten the life out of any child who dared to mutter or slur their words in Her School.

Herbie had heard this many, many times before. He just managed to stifle the usual schoolboy answer of 'Why don't you ever wash your ears properly?' in time and just uttered a contrite 'Yes Ma'am. I'll try harder in future Ma'am.'

They both laughed.

'Now supper, and when we've finished, I will go through all your pockets thoroughly and the drawers in your desk until I find it.'

'Thank you, Ma'am.' He pulled himself up and hurried across to help her climb painfully out of her armchair onto her walker and held her gently by the elbow as they tottered down the passage to the kitchen together.

CHANCING AN ARM

(Chapter 1 of a completed novel)

CHARLES BIDWELL

'I HAVE A PROBLEM, MOLLY,' said Michael Farrell, looking fondly at his friend. He was a lonely bachelor in his early fifties but looking and feeling years older, and the problem he had been struggling with for years was now really getting him down.

'The thing is' he continued, 'the pains in my chest have been getting worse, and Doctor Poole has told me, over and over again, that if I don't go down to the hospital and get something done about it soon, it will be too late.'

He leant on the low wall for support.

'I've come up with excuse after excuse for putting it off,' he continued, 'but I can't get out of it this time.' He shook his head sadly.

'He just booked the appointment for me himself, and arranged for Frankie, you know, his wife, who used to be the matron there, to take me down on Wednesday morning; and yous know that nobody ever argues with her.' He smiled at the thought and took a couple of deep breaths to steady himself.

'That's all very well.' he said with a sigh and thought again about his last interview at the hospital. 'They tell me I should only be there for a couple of days, but you never can tell what's going to happen, once that lot get their hands on you, can you?'

He rested for a moment then bent down and gently tickled her ears.

'I've nobody to talk to about it, except yous.' he said sadly, and I know at least yous care.'

But Molly didn't answer. She just snuggled contentedly in her bed of fine, fresh straw. She was busy looking after her first litter, and she grunted softly whilst her silky-skinned, day-old bonhams clambered all over her, competing for the best place to get a good feed. She looked up and smiled at Michael as he scratched the rough skin on her back with his stick, and Michael, having spent a lifetime looking after animals, knew that she was happy.

'But I can't help worrying about yous. I know I have explained to yous several times that Mick will be coming in every day to look after yous haven't I? And yous all know Mick. He's been great, helping me out whilst I was getting less and less to do much myself. But the problem is that he has to hurry home to look after his own animals the moment he's finished here, and he can't manage both places all on his own for long. I've had to find somebody to help him as I won't be much use myself for a while when I get back.'

He poured out his troubles to her again as he had so many times before.

He had a fair bit of money in the bank as he never spent anything other than buying the odd pint in O'Connor's in the village or on market days in Roperstown. He could hire temporary cover from an agency, but he had the true farmers' dislike of spending money unnecessarily, not that he had any dependants who needed looking after. He had never got on with his sister Bridget who was his only known relation, and anyway, she and her husband Dermot, a successful Dublin businessman, had plenty of money of their own. He used to enjoy having their children, Grainne and Guy to stay when they were young, but he hardly ever saw them, now they were townie teenagers.

He supposed the old farm would just be sold when he went up to the great abattoir in the sky himself, which he felt was a shame as there had been Farrells farming at Drumdangan for countless generations. Pushy estate agents called him from time to time telling him that city types were paying fancy prices for places like Drumdangan where they could keep ponies for their children and play at being farmers. He quite enjoyed chatting to them, but he had no intention of selling.

He had been born there and had farmed those good fertile acres all his life, besides; what else could he do? He didn't know any other way of life and had no ambitions to learn one.

'The thing is' he told Molly, 'I've had no choice but to call in Guy to help out. I know that he's a townie teenager but it's better than having nobody, and I'll get rid of him as quickly as possible when I get home.'

He almost laughed out loud as he imagined the consternation this arrangement must have caused in Bridget's household.

Bridget, brought up on the farm herself, had been horror-struck at the idea. She didn't want her precious, privately educated son to have to get his hands dirty. But Dermot had just laughed when she told him and reminded her that Guy had just finished his last term at school, and it was more than three months until his university term started. Helping out on the farm would be a great way of getting him out from under their feet for a while and save the cost of sending him travelling with his school friends.

Bridget thought about it for a moment then smiled.

'Besides' he added, 'we really ought to help your poor brother in his hour of need. Remember that although he looks and acts like an old man, he is in fact a couple of years younger than you. You've always been fit and healthy whilst he has had major problems of one sort or another, and now it's serious heart trouble. He's probably on borrowed time already and he has nobody else to leave the farm to but his only sister, and we could sell it for a good price if you and the children don't want it.'

Bridget nodded and it was all fixed up despite Guy's agonised protests.

Michael was still chuckling as he explained this to Molly when his thoughts were interrupted by the Angelus bell ringing on the Church down in Glencara. Six o'clock. Time to go in: a pity as it was such a lovely late March evening. He started saying goodbye to the pigs following the old tradition of never leaving animals, particularly pigs or horses, without saying goodbye and telling them he would be back soon so they wouldn't worry they were being abandoned, when he was interrupted by the dogs barking threateningly.

'Who's there?' he shouted.

He wasn't expecting anybody as few people called at the farm, particularly on a Sunday evening, so he grabbed a pitchfork and hurried out to see. But there wasn't a car, so it couldn't be the doctor coming to check on him. One of the neighbours looking for cattle that had got out. Perhaps. A tinker from the encampment down at the crossroads poking around? Michael bristled and hurried across the yard to the backdoor as he seldom bothered to lock it, and he didn't trust tinkers not to just wander in.

He was out of breath and his heart was thumping wildly from the exertion, so he sat down on the woodpile in the porch to rest for a moment. He listened. All was quiet and the dogs had stopped barking. This was a relief. It couldn't be serious, so he sat back and rested whilst his heart settled down a bit.

'Funny' he thought after a couple of minutes, 'why haven't they come back to report what's happening?' He couldn't see them anywhere. He called them but there was no answer, so he got up to have a look. Oh, there they were: Shep, the sheepdog, was sitting under the light by the gate holding up his paw to a figure Michael couldn't quite see, and Finn the Jack Russell was lying on his back whilst another figure was crouching down patting his tummy. He smiled; all was well. Clearly, they were with friends, and he strolled over to find out.

'Hello there' he called as he headed towards them.

The figures turned towards him as he got nearer. They were both so small Michael thought they must be children. 'Who are you?' he asked.

They came towards him slowly and stopped a yard or so away.

'Good evening, sir.' said the smaller one in a very foreign accent.

His dislike of anybody setting foot in his yard instantly rose to the surface and he clenched his fists.

'Who are you and what the hell do yous want?' he snarled.

He stopped. He realised he was speaking to a young girl, and she looked as if she was about to burst into tears. The young man beside her said something to her in a language Michael couldn't understand.

'What do yous want?' Michael repeated, as calmly as he could manage. He wasn't used to talking to strangers, and had hardly ever spoken to foreigners, apart from the New Zealanders who came every year to shear the sheep, and he found them difficult enough to understand.

'We sorry' said the boy very slowly, in an accent even thicker than hers. He thought for a moment.'We don't make you trouble' he got out eventually. 'We go' and they both bent down and picked up their tatty little rucksacks.

Michael's heart was now thumping so wildly that he felt he would collapse. He staggered towards the old milk stand where he used to put out the churns for the dairy to collect and grabbed it for support. He was panting for breath. His mouth was hanging open and he hugged his chest. He felt in his pocket for his glyceryl puffer to ease the pain, but it wasn't there. He must have left it in the fridge again. He needed it urgently.

The young pair turned and gazed at him. Something was clearly wrong, but they didn't know what to say.

'You ill?' asked the girl.

Michael tried to look at her. He was getting dizzy and leant heavily on the churn stand.

'We help?' she asked.

He started to panic as he felt his knees starting to buckle under him. He had to use his puffer urgently. He looked up at her gaunt face and tried to smile but felt too weak to move. He had to do something. The dogs had accepted them, and he trusted their instinct. He had little choice. He had to chance his arm with them.

'You help me back to the house please?'

They hesitated for a moment and had a quick discussion between themselves. They took him nervously by the elbows to keep him steady as he stumbled across the yard and into the house.

The security lights flashed on as they went through the back door, and they helped him down the passage into the kitchen and held him up as he got the puffer out of the fridge. He opened his mouth and sprayed three large doses under his tongue. His whole mouth felt on fire, and he shut his eyes as they led him to the old sofa at the far end of the room. He collapsed down onto it and took a dozen or so deep breaths. Finn immediately jumped up beside him and started snuggling into him and licking his face. Shep, who was too big to wriggle beside Finn, climbed clumsily onto Michael's feet and tried to get comfortable.

'Good boy Finn' Michael said, when he was breathing more easily. 'Good boy' and Finn rolled over onto his back for his tummy to be patted.

Michael smiled towards the two children, who were still leaning on the AGA trying to warm themselves.

'Thank you both, you've been great, he said, looking at them and seeing them clearly for the first time. He shook his head in disbelief. They looked so young, and there was no mistaking how frightened they looked. He read thc same desperate appeal for help in their eyes that he had seen so many times from injured animals. It was lovely and warm in the kitchen, but he noticed they were both shivering.

'You cold?' he asked, and they both nodded.

'I'm alright now, but you'd better have a hot drink.'

Their faces lit up.

'Tea?' he asked.

'Please' said the girl shyly.

Giving Finn a final hug, Michael heaved himself slowly off the sofa and put the kettle onto the hot plate. He busied himself getting out mugs and putting them on the table whilst the young pair followed him with their eyes without moving from their nice warm perches. The kettle was soon whistling, and he poured the boiling water onto the big heap of leaves he had put in the pot and gave it a stir.

He filled three mugs. 'Milk?' he asked. They nodded. 'And sugar?' and put the bowl on the table. 'Please.' they said together. 'How many?' but they just looked confused, so he piled two big, heaped spoons into each mug.

'Sit yourselves down' and he pulled out a chair and lowered himself onto it.

They reluctantly left the warmth of the stove and sat down at the other end of the table.

Michael noticed them both cradling the hot mugs in their hands before taking a swig.

So far so good, he thought.

'Hungry?' he asked, and he could see tears welling up in the young man's eyes.

'My brother not eat three days.' said the girl.

'Three days?' said Michael incredulously and they both nodded. 'Why?' he asked.

They didn't answer. They just hung their heads and looked down at the old wooden table. 'Well, let's see what we can do about that.' Michael smiled, then got up and went to rummage around the larder.

'There isn't much here as I live alone.' he said, coming back with a small loaf of soda bread, some butter and a pot of blackberry and apple jam. Their eyes followed him as he put it on the table. He cut two big thick slices and passed the breadboard across the table to them. They almost snatched it.

'Slowly' he said firmly, holding up his hands. After all, he was a farmer and knew only too well what happens when starving creatures gobble down food. They spread butter and jam as if it was gold dust and ate with as much restraint as they could manage. He poured them both another mug of tea and they looked longingly at the loaf. 'You must wait for that to go down before you can have any more' he said holding up his hand and patting his tummy, and even if they did not understand his words, they understood his tone and drank their second mugs of tea more slowly.

They had stopped shivering and relaxed slightly, so he gave them another slice of bread.

'Where have you come from?' he asked. This was a question they understood, but they looked nervously at one another without replying. After a pause the girl screwed up her courage. 'Syria.' she whispered, and her head sank into her hands.

Michael looked at them in amazement.

'Syria?' he echoed. 'That's an awful long way away, isn't it?'

They sat in silence for a moment.

'On your own?' he asked eventually.

'Yes.' the girl answered, wiping her eyes on her sleeve.

Michael shuddered.

'Where are your parents?' he asked.

'Dead.' she replied. 'Everybody killed in the bombing.'

Michael was stunned and the boy put his arm around her, 'My sister very brave.' he said. Michael had experienced very little emotion in his life. His own parents had been rather stiff and distant, and his sister was always hard and ambitious even when they were children, and never had much time for her rather dozy younger brother. True, he had loved his grandmother, who was always so kind and caring, and he smiled at the memory of her shouting at his easy-going, chaotic grandfather, who paid no attention and just puffed on his pipe and laughed.

There had not been many other children of his age around, so he had never had many friends, and had been too shy to have serious girlfriends. He had only really loved his dogs and his horses, and of course the pigs; they accepted him as he was, and never asked questions or expected anything in return. The sight of the boy putting his arm around his sister's shoulder moved him to some sort of emotion that he didn't think he had ever felt before, and, without thinking, he leaned over and patted their hands the way he patted his dogs or a horse.

'Thank you.' said the girl, drying her eyes on her cuff. They sat in silence for a moment and Finn, who had been watching jealously, took the opportunity to jump up onto Michael's knee for his turn.

'Good boy' Michael said again, as Finn wriggled for attention and licked his face.

He could feel his visitors' eyes on them, and when Finn had settled down contentedly, he asked them, 'Where are you going to?'

'We don't know.' said the boy slowly.

'It doesn't matter.' added the girl. 'We have nowhere to go.'

The silence was tangible. Michael looked at the clock. Nearly seven and almost dark already.

'Well, you can't just wander off into the night not knowing where you're going.' he said eventually.

The girl started to get up.

'We must at least get some proper food into you before you can even think of going anywhere.' He got up and headed towards the back door.

Brother and sister exchanged anxious glances reaching for their rucksacks in case they had to make a run for it.

They hadn't long to wait. He reappeared with a box of potatoes, which he put down on the table. He spread a couple of sheets of newspaper in front of them and a large saucepan of cold water. Smiles lit up their thin faces at the prospect of proper, hot food for a change.

'I have just realised, I forgot to ask your names. I'm Michael.' he said, pointing to himself and smiling towards them.

As one, they stood up. 'What are they doing?' he wondered. The boy gave a small bow.

'Zac' he said and gave another bow before sitting down.

'Leila' said the girl, holding out her hand. Michael shook it gravely. It was tiny and icy cold with the nails all broken and it was obvious that it hadn't been washed properly for some time.

'You are very welcome.' he said after a pause, and their smiles showed how much it meant to them.

'And I have just realised I forgot to show you where to wash' he added miming washing his hands when they looked puzzled. 'Come on, I'll show you.' He headed for the door. Leila picked up her rucksack, said something to Zac and followed him down the passage towards the back door. He turned on the lights.

'In here.'

When she was gone, Michael tried to say something to Zac, but he clearly didn't understand. Leila looked different when she got back to the kitchen. She had taken off her anorak and woolly hat, washed her face and hands and shaken out her long black hair. She looked even younger and more fragile than ever.

'She is only a child' thought Michael, as he told her to show Zac where to go.

She looked even more nervous whilst Zac was out of the room and stayed by the door with the table between her and Michael, but it was not long before Zac came back. He too had taken off his hat and coat and done his best to tidy himself up. He was so skinny that his clothes hung off him and Michael could see how young he was too.

'Better?' asked Michael, and they both nodded gratefully.

'You know the old rule. No work, no food' he said, smiling, and pointing to their chairs and the box of spuds. They sat down and looked at it.

'You know how to do it?' asked Michael as they were just sitting there. 'Look, I'll show you.' He picked up a spud. 'Oh, I forgot to get you any peelers' he said with a laugh and went to root through the drawer for some. Leila and Zac smiled and took them, selected a spud each and got on with it.

Michael went back to the larder to see what else he could find.

'This is the best I can do' he said, opening a carton and shaking the frozen contents out into a big pot, which he put into the bottom oven to start defrosting. 'It is the stew my sister made from the remains of the turkey last Christmas.'

They obviously did not know what he was talking about, but Michael thought how companionable it felt: the two young people peeling the potatoes whilst he fed the dogs and looked after the cooking. 'Vegetables' he said, getting up and fetching a cabbage from the rack inside the back door.

It didn't take them long to do enough potatoes.

'Well done' he said, and Zac picked up the saucepan and put it onto the hot plate that Michael had opened.

'That's right. Good boy.' said Michael, then suddenly, he started to laugh.

Zac looked puzzled, had he done something silly?

'Why you laugh at me?' he asked.

'Not laughing at you Zac. I just said, "Good boy". It is an expression of affection.' He stopped. 'It's what I say to my dogs to tell them I'm pleased with them, and you're a boy too, aren't you?

His visitors looked even more puzzled. Then Zac frowned and Michael felt he was getting angry.

'Dogs?' he asked aggressively. 'You speak to us like dogs?' Zac continued glaring at Michael.

Michael felt panic rising inside him. He realised he had said something which Zac had taken as an insult, and didn't want to make it at any worse. The language barrier made it very difficult.

Leila seemed to know instinctively that she had to do something. Nobody could fail to notice the close bond between Michael and his dogs and the loving way he cuddled Finn and talked to him quietly when he had jumped onto his knee. She was sure that she had heard him say 'good boy' several times when he was talking to them. It clearly meant something between them. The dogs were now curled up peacefully in their beds taking little interest in what the people were doing. She got up quickly and went over to Finn's bed and slowly bent down and spoke to him quietly. 'Good boy' she said patting him gently. He was snoring softly, and his mouth kept twitching as if he was having happy dreams, but he put up one ear, then opened one eye and looked up at her. 'Good boy.' she said again.

He licked her hand, yawned, then sat up to give her face a lick. Michael and Zac looked at her. She said something to Zac, but he looked suspicious. She said something else. Michael didn't know what to do, and Zac just stood rooted to the spot.

Leila said something urgent to him and gave Finn another pat. 'Good boy' she said again and walked across to Zac. 'Good boy' she said, patting him on the head and giving him a kiss on the cheek. He looked startled then his face broke into a wide grin. 'Good boy' he said patting her on the head.

'No, good girl.' said Michael, and they all laughed.

Leila went across to where Michael was standing. He towered over her. She stood on tiptoes. 'Good boy.' she said, patting him on the head, but he was too embarrassed to do the same to her.

'I'm sorry Zac' he said, 'I didn't mean to upset you.' Zac tried to say something, but Michael just patted him on the shoulder as he was so obviously trying to find words.

'Now for the cabbage' he said. 'Like this. I'll show you. Look.'

'It will take about half an hour' He stirred the big saucepan, then pottered towards the dresser to get plates. Leila realised what he was doing and hurried past him and picked up three.

'In the bottom oven to warm, Leila' said Michael, but she didn't understand and started to put them back.

'No, no.' he said, taking them from her and showing her what to do.

'Cutlery in the drawer here.' He pulled out the top left-hand drawer of the dresser, and it took Leila no time to find knives and forks and lay them neatly on the table.

The table was always covered with a jumble of old newspapers, junk mail, unopened bills, suppliers' catalogues for this that and the other, instruction books for bits of machinery all piled up together in no semblance of order. Michael started to shift the piles around to make more space.

'Here Zac, give us a hand with these.' Zac looked confused so just tried to copy what Michael was doing. Leila watched with a smile then tried to join in, but Michael soon lost interest and the piles were just re-stacked slightly more neatly and shoved to the far end of the table.

'Supper' he announced when they heard the clock strike eight. He got the heavy pot out of the oven and put it on the table. The children's eyes shone with amazement as he took off the lid and the lovely smell of the stew wafted towards them.

He ladled generous portions onto two plates for them and rather less for himself, and then the fluffy mashed potatoes and the cabbage. The children just stared at their plates, but didn't touch them.

Michael looked at them in amazement. They were obviously starving, so what was wrong? Had he given them something their religion didn't allow them to eat he wondered? He looked at their sad eyes and tried to guess their thoughts. Then he remembered that his mother had never allowed anybody to start before they had said grace.

'Let us say a little prayer for us all' he said at last. He hoped he could remember one, as it was so long since he had been to Church. He tried to remember what his mother used to say, then bowed his head. 'Bless us oh Lord and these thy gifts, and...' Then he remembered they had said all their family had been killed in the bombing, and quickly added 'Amen.'

He smiled at them. 'Now eat up' he said, as cheerfully as he could manage. They understood and didn't need a second invitation.

'Slowly' he said, holding up his hand. Leila got the message and warned Zac.

Michael wanted to be friendly and talk to them but didn't know where to start.

'How old are you?' he tried.

Leila stopped eating and looked down at her plate. 'I'm sixteen' she answered eventually, 'and Zac's nearly fifteen' she added so Michael didn't have to ask him too. Zac put down his knife and fork and stopped eating as a sad smile crossed his haggard face.

Michael was shocked and realised the question had upset them.

'You poor children' he said quickly, smiling at them. 'Now come on, eat up. There's plenty here.' He refilled their plates and tried to start telling them something about the farm, but it was difficult, and they soon lapsed into a companionable silence.

When they had finished eating and Michael got up to clear away, they both got up to help without being asked: what well brought up children, he thought to himself, and compared them with the horrors he saw on the rare occasions he went into town.

When everything was washed and put on the draining board to dry, Michael pushed the dogs off the old sofa to make enough room for himself and the children and sat down to think what to do next. They were such nice, polite children, he realised that had enjoyed having them, which came as a shock to him.

What could he do now?

He had to chance his arm again.

'Well, I really can't let you two just wander off into the night' he said at last, 'so I'd better find beds for you.' Leila and Zac looked worried and had an urgent discussion in their own language.

'Thank you, Michael,' said Leila. 'You very kind, but we must go.'

Michael's face fell.

'Don't be silly girl.' he said sharply. 'Where to, at this time of night?'

They looked baffled and started to fidget.

'We don't know' Leila said eventually.

'So why go then?' Michael persisted.

They looked at him in silence. He could see they were struggling.

'But you say you have nowhere to go. Where will you sleep? It's already dark, and it will be cold' he added. 'You can't just wander off in the dark.'

They looked sad but still said nothing.

'There are a couple of spare rooms upstairs you can have.' he persisted.

'We can't stay in your house,' said Leila eventually.

'Why not? I don't understand. Have I done something to upset you?'

'No, no.' Leila almost sobbed.

'We don't want make you trouble' she added.

'Make me trouble?' he asked, repeating her words. 'What do you mean?'

'Police looking for us. If they come, it make you trouble.'

Michael gasped with astonishment.

'Police looking for you. Why?' he asked incredulously.

'No papers' said Zac.

Michael was puzzled.

'No papers,' Leila said. 'We refugees. No papers.'

Michael's jaw dropped.

'Oh God' he said. 'I hadn't thought of that.' He shuddered.

'Two children like you,' he said, thinking of the pictures he'd seen on the television news of columns of refugees trudging across Europe, looking for somewhere to go and being harassed by police and border guards.

'You poor little devils,' he said with feeling.

Leila smiled at his obvious concern.

Michael thought for a moment. 'I don't suppose anybody chooses to be a refugee' he said. 'I suppose you're just unlucky people who have been driven out of your homes through no fault of your own and are now just trying to survive somehow.'

Zac put his arm around Leila as she sniffled quietly and wiped her eyes on her cuff. Michael got up, and the dogs quickly reclaimed their places on the sofa. 'Look here' he said striding around the room. 'Enough of this nonsense. Nobody's likely to come out here looking for you, not at this time of night anyway, and you need to get a good night's sleep. We will try to think what we can do with you in the morning. Right?'

They understood enough to look relieved but were still unsure what to do.

'We can't sleep in your house' said Leila at last. 'You kind to us.'

'Ah don't be silly, girl. What type of person would allow two little mites like you to wander around in the dark? You might catch your death of cold.'

They were all silent for a moment, and the dogs got up to remind them that it was getting on for the time for their biscuits and the final check around the yard.

'All right' said Michael eventually. 'If you won't sleep in the house, you had better bed down in one of the sheds.'

'Oh, thank you, thank you' said Leila smiling, 'We feel safer in sheds.' She explained to Zac. He seized Michael's hand and shook it saying, 'Thank you' again and again.

'No problem. We'll find you some blankets. Come on, let's see what we've got.'

He got up and led them up the stairs to the big cupboard on the landing. Piles of bedding tumbled out when he opened the door as he obviously hadn't stacked it very well when he put it away. They picked up a bundle and Michael led them downstairs and across the yard. He opened the door of what used to be the cowman's cottage years ago when they still had a dairy herd but hadn't been used since.

He found the light switch and was quite surprised to find the lights were still working. The old kitchen where they were standing seemed to be full of empty feed sacks, boxes of nuts and bolts, odd bits of machinery and other miscellaneous junk littered around any old how. Cobwebs were hanging from the ceiling and there was dust everywhere. But it was dry and felt reasonably warm. Michael tried the taps: nothing. Not even a trickle of water. It had probably been turned off years ago.

'Let's see what the rest of the place is like.' He led them to the stairs in the corner.

The wooden stairs creaked a bit under his weight, and he had some difficulty in finding the switches for the upstairs lights. They looked in the room on the right of the landing. Dust everywhere and there was an old black iron bedstead with a stripy mattress.

'I wouldn't sleep on that he said. 'There are probably mice nesting in it.' Leila and Zac obviously didn't understand.

They tried the room on the left. It was equally neglected, with another iron bedstead with rusty springs but no mattress, and an old children's cot in the corner.

He tried the taps in the bathroom but not a drop of water there either.

'I will show you the farm toilet where there's a wash basin with soap and a towel.'

'Thank you.' Leila said again.

'Have you got a torch?' he added.

They looked puzzled. 'Totch?'

'Light' he said, and mimed it, but they still looked confused.

'Don't worry, I'll get you one. Is there anything else you need?'

Leila looked embarrassed: 'A toothbrush please?'

'Let's go and see what we can find.' They followed him back to the house. He went to the dresser in the kitchen where everything was kept. He rooted around and found the toothbrush kit that he had taken off the aeroplane when he had gone to visit a cousin in Australia, more than twenty years ago. 'Sorry, I think there is only this one, can you share?'

'Thank you.'

'And now for a torch.' He unhooked the high-powered lantern that always hung by the back door, and they set off back to the cottage with the dogs following them.

'Totch.' said Leila as Michael showed them how to turn it on.

'You OK now?'

'Thank you.' said Zac.

'I think you can bolt the door from the inside.' he said. 'Now make yourselves comfortable and have a good night's sleep.'

Leila seized his hand and kissed it, and he felt it was wet. She was crying. Michael flushed with embarrassment.

'You very kind man.' she said, and Michael hurried out into the yard before she could say any more.

He called the dogs and when they all got back to the so-familiar kitchen, Michael glanced around it. Somehow it felt different. He couldn't put his finger on it. It was the only room in the house he normally used, doing the farm admin on the big table, sitting on the old sofa with the dogs when he read the paper or watched the TV. The only thing that had changed was that the pile of old newspapers was a bit tidier than usual, so what could it be? The atmosphere was somehow different. Friendlier?

Homelier? He scratched his head, sat down at his normal place at the table and thought about the evening.

He couldn't remember when he had last had other people sitting down to eat in his kitchen, apart of course from the occasional visit from Bridget and her family, but that was an ordeal these days. He smiled to himself as he went through what had happened from the moment the strange children arrived in his yard. Yes, it had been a pleasure to look after them. They obviously really needed the hot food, and it occurred to him that he had forgotten to offer them anything to drink with it. He very rarely drank anything himself nowadays but felt like a drop now and went to the dresser to see what he had. There was nothing, other than the bottle of malt whiskey Bridget gave him as a Christmas present every year and which generally lasted the whole year. He got it out, poured himself a small measure and swished it around the old Waterford crystal glass which his grandfather had won in a ploughing competition many years ago. He sniffed the malt and took a sip. It was good. Ah well, he said to himself, they wouldn't drink anyway being Syrians and he found himself wondering what type of life they'd lived there. They were so polite; they must have been very well brought up and educated. And they knew how to talk to the dogs. He smiled to himself, poured a refill and relaxed.

His reverie was interrupted by the dogs. They looked up expectantly and started whining. They sniffed the air then leapt out of their baskets and hurtled towards the back door. Michael knew they must have heard something. Then he heard it himself. A car was driving into the yard and the security lights had come on. He glanced up at the clock: a quarter past ten. Who the hell could it be at this time of night? he wondered.

GRAVE SOUNDS

HAROLD ROFFEY

MARGERY DIMPLEWAIT HAD, UNTIL RECENTLY, SLEPT WELL in her cottage in the small town in Idaho, not far off the Ponderosa Pine Route. Marge, or Doctor Marge, as she is known by local folk, retired soon after attending the birth of Angie Dreyfus fourteen years ago. Nothing connects the two events, and apart from being on nodding terms and the occasional exchange with Angie's family at the local stores, she didn't tend to socialise within the sleepy logging community.

There had been much speculation about Angie's death a month or so back. Angie had always been outspoken despite her parents' advice to be more discreet. Like most teenagers, she had a bee in her bonnet about something. In Angie's case it was about a girl of a similar age who'd apparently told a lot of world leaders at the UN that they had stolen her childhood. Every time Angie felt she'd wandered from her newly found obsession, she'd watch that girl on YouTube again.

Some folk agreed that a girl like Angie would grow out of her obsession and see sense, but when she walked out of the church on a miserable Sunday morning after a disagreement with the preacher, she brought disdain upon herself from most of the congregation, including the more tolerant among them. Perhaps if she'd left quietly, all would have been OK, but to say, 'This is rubbish!' as she walked down the aisle to the door and then to have left it open for all to see her striding down the path in the rain to the gate, was a step too far.

The magistrate agreed with the sheriff: the driver had done his best to avoid Angie. Those witnesses willing to give evidence had told the same story, while others appeared to be nervous when confessing uncertainty about what they had seen.

Apart from weddings and funerals, Margery rarely attended church and hadn't witnessed Angie's behaviour there, but within a few days she'd heard many versions of the event. Margery had also been out of town the day Angie was killed. However, she couldn't avoid hearing the gossip around the supermarket checkout justifying Angie's demise as a divine act. Angie had been alive after the accident and had choked on her own blood, whispered one.

That night, Margery dreamed of someone coughing. She knew she'd been sleeping on her back and had possibly been awakened by choking on her saliva. She had a similar dream the following night and had searched the house for possible causes. She'd gone into the garden and shone her flashlight over the nearby trees to see if their branches had been scraping against the house in the wind.

A week later, Margery dreamt she had been wearing her nightdress while visiting Angie's grave after hearing Angie crying and coughing. In her dream she'd fought her way through a tangled web of spiteful foliage to get to the headstone, only to find it badly weathered and Angie's name difficult to read.

The dream had been so vivid that Margery woke up crying. She went to the bathroom, rinsed her face with cold water and stared at her reflection in the mirror until she felt her stomach muscles relax and saw the lines of anguish fade from her face. In the hallway she slipped into her walking boots, put a coat over her nightdress, left the house and drove eight miles in her old Toyota to the cemetery, determined to put an end to her torment.

Using her flashlight, she soon found Angie's grave with its highly polished headstone. Satisfied, Margery walked back through the tree-covered churchyard to her car and sat quietly thinking. Half an hour later, she retrieved a stethoscope from her bag, which, out of habit, she always kept in the boot and returned to the headstone. Feeling very sheepish, she cleaned a patch of the stone and held the breast-piece of the stethoscope against it and listened.

She never dreamt about coughing again, but the sound of Angie crying for help between coughs remained with her for the rest of her life.

AQUATIC LOVE

HAROLD ROFFEY

SUNDAY. A SUNNY SUNDAY. ED SAT IN his car looking out to sea and occasionally dozed off. He'd had another two-hour swim and now he'd finished his sandwiches. His wife, Emma, would be back on Monday from seeing her brother in Paris. Each time he thought about the last few extraordinary days, he'd feel warm and content, and he'd self-consciously smiled, despite there being no one about.

His only concern was whether to tell Emma or not, and if he did, how would he go about it? He remained soporific, but once he dwelled on how he would tell her, a tiny spark of anxiety crept in. His recent experience was so deeply personal and private that he wanted to preserve it. The other thing that would need to be resolved if he told her was the evidence of the last few days. If he didn't tell her he would have to keep it a secret from her, and he knew that was too much to bear.

'Thanks for picking me up,' said Emma to Ed as they headed to their cottage on the south coast of England.

'You sounded excited, but you also said you were afraid I might not believe you. Come on, spill the beans – I'm itching to know.'

Ed had been going to wait until they were home, but Emma cajoled him into telling her within ten minutes of leaving Gatwick Airport.

'OK but promise not to ask any questions until I've told you everything.'

'Come on,' she laughed.

'You know where I love to park and look over the sea?'

Emma nodded.

'Well,' he said hesitantly, 'last Thursday it was low tide, and I took a towel and my snorkelling gear and went for a walk along the shore. There wasn't a soul on the beach.'

'You mean nobody on the beach in mid-September?'

Ed looked at Emma as if to say: One more question and I'll stop.

'Sorry,' said Emma, 'I promise.'

'I waded in up to my waist and was rinsing my mask in preparation for a few minutes of snorkelling, when I saw a huge octopus floating just below the surface. At first, I thought it was dead, but as I reached out to touch it, it swam away, then stopped and looked at me. I would normally have been afraid of something like that. I walked backwards to go to the beach, but the octopus swam towards me and stopped. I reached for it again and it moved away. I started for the beach again, but with one push of its tentacles it was near me once again. I must have repeated this funny little dance about ten times. I put my goggles on to look at it from under the water. I can't describe how beautiful it was. It then swam slowly away, but it hadn't gone far when it stopped and looked back at me. I had this weird feeling it wanted me to follow. So, I did. I felt totally at ease.

'I must have followed it for half an hour or so. I could no longer see the bottom, but I kept following as I was afraid I'd lose sight of it as it swam deeper. I took a huge breath and dived as far as I could. I must have gone down thirty feet. I thought I'd only be able to stay there for a few seconds, but I found I could stay near the octopus among the rocks for over two minutes. When I did go to the surface, the octopus came with me, and then it followed me to the beach. I was so distraught at having to leave it that I was close to tears.

'I went to the same place at the same time the following day and waited in water up to my waist. I was about to go for a snorkel when the octopus appeared. I can't tell you how happy I felt.'

Emma was looking at Ed's profile as he drove, but Ed didn't dare look at Emma while his eyes filled with tears as he relived the experience.

'I was in the sea for over two hours. It was beautiful.'

Emma remained quiet with an expression of concern until they arrived home.

After tea and biscuits Ed handed Emma a small box.

'Wow! Where did you find that?'

'I hunted through your jewellery things. I knew you kept all your old boxes.'

'I lost the ring that went with it at least thirty years ago while we were fooling around in the surf off that very beach. I was so sad. I know you always said you'd buy me another, but you shouldn't have,' she said as she opened the box. 'That is so sweet of you, Ed.' Her eyes filled with tears as she kissed him.

'Wow! It's lovely and so like the one I lost. That was very clever of you to remember the details.'

'It is the *actual* one you lost. The octopus found it.'

NEW YEAR'S RESOLUTIONS ARE GOOD FOR YOU

HAROLD ROFFEY

DID I REALLY ORDER A ROWING MACHINE costing £1,500? What on earth was I thinking about?

Oh, yes! I remember now. It was New Year's Eve, and I was filled with drink and virtuous thoughts. No time like the present, I thought then. And of course, that was the problem. My thoughts were converted to reality with a few keystrokes. Credit card details already stored in the bowels of some remote machine owned by an organisation eager to fulfil my whim like a fairy godmother, proving with her wand that immediate gratification is not just for the young.

I could hear the deliveryman's anxious voice asking where to put it, while my thoughts tilted towards total rejection. Then, once I'd recalled my New Year's Eve's thoughts without any sense of the virtuousness that should have accompanied them, I heard myself say, 'Anywhere.'

As he dumped it in the hallway, I tingled with terror at the thought of having to assemble it, and so I dragged it, rolled it and shoved it out of sight and out of mind into a corner of the garage in the hope that, if I left the door unlocked, it might just get stolen.

Back in the lounge with a mug of tea and a few biscuits, I realised I'd broken the no-snacks- between-meals resolution, but then I justified the misdemeanour by thinking of the struggle I'd had with the rowing machine and convinced myself I deserved it. Ten pleasant minutes passed before there was a knock on the door.

'Happy New Year!' I said to the ever-cheerful postman.

'And to you. Couldn't get this through your letterbox,' he said, handing me a thick cardboard envelope. 'Oh! and this one as well.'

'Thanks, Jimmy.'

Sure enough, both fat envelopes were for me. I tugged at the tag strip of one and read the envelope within. 'Speak Spanish in Three Months' was printed over a picture of a woman wearing black high heels, a red skirt and a white top clapping castanets above her head. I was exhausted just looking at her, until I recalled the enthusiasm I'd had when I promised myself a new language before the New Year was complete.

I frowned and sighed as I picked up the second cardboard envelope. Come on, I thought, pull yourself together. Surely you can remember ordering this one. No, it sat on my lap while I finished a fourth biscuit and then got carried to the kitchen and, propped up against the biscuit jar, watched me pour another mug of tea without shouting its contents at me.

I grabbed another couple of biscuits and took the whole lot back to the lounge. Off came the pull tag and out came a book and a digital guitar tuner. I won't pain you as to the whys and wherefores of those items, as I'm sure you can guess.

Now to open the normal mail: bills for me, cards for us both (leave them for her), letters for her and advertisements (she can have those as well). Then a letter for me. I read the first line. 'Thank you for offering to volunteer two days a week. We greatly appreciate you giving your valuable time to such a just cause ...'

I could tell them the truth, I thought. I'm feeling a little off-colour at the moment.

UNDAMAGED TALENTS

HAROLD ROFFEY

JOE SAID SHE WAS PRETTY. ED SAID she was very good looking. Dianne described her as beautiful.

Amanda had heard these comments about herself many times. People laughed at her jokes. They smiled when she came into a room. She seemed to grasp the nub of situations and arguments and people listened to her opinions. Did she frighten men off? Possibly. Did she even want to attract a man? She never discussed it, and nobody asked. That's how it remained until she let slip to Dianne.

'It was his voice,' she said. 'There were lots of people in the room. Hardly anyone knew each other. It was a gathering of fellow anthropologists. I needed to find him. I nearly panicked when I couldn't locate him. When the crowd dispersed, he remained talking with a small group. I barged in and they made a space for me. I waited for him to say something I could respond to, then I butted in, but I didn't care. They listened and he replied in that same beautiful voice. I thought I would crumble. I asked him if he would like to have a drink with me afterwards. If he'd said he couldn't, I think I would have screamed.

'We found a bar. He asked me lots of questions, which I quickly brushed aside because I wanted to know everything about him: his work as a scientist; why his wife left him; how he survived a fire; when was the last operation on his face and body; how he'd protected his eyes with his hands, which had only become functional again after surgery and physiotherapy; could he hear easily without the external part of his ears; when will they finish reconstructing his nose? I felt free of all inhibitions as I asked him.

'Eventually I asked if I could touch him. Did it still hurt? I asked. I think he would have said it didn't even if it did. I melted as I touched him, then I took those hands and held them against my face. We have so much common ground and, despite all he's been through, he's amusing and fun to be with.

'Occasionally, when I've forgotten where I've put something, he'll make a joke of me being blind. "As a beautiful bat," he'll add quickly, before I throw a pillow in his direction.'

A SECURE PLACE TO WRITE

HAROLD ROFFEY

ALONE IN AN OLD HOUSE AT THE end of a five-mile-long single-track road, where the forest is at its thickest, I sit at two in the morning in the only room with a light bulb and a power socket and type the first line of a short story, in the hope that any reader of that story will never wish to be alone again.

White words on the computer's black screen seem raised enough to feel with closed eyes, and I can sense by the telltale flickering of the table lamp that I will soon be in the dark and will need to use the torch of my iPhone.

I was in the process of inventing a balmy wind to pass through the room for my story, when the curtain over the window on my right moved imperceptibly along its track. I'd rented the house for a week and, not being familiar with its idiosyncrasies, I took it for an outside breeze or possibly a mouse playing with the curtain's hem. Whatever it was that caused that, it also succeeded in spoiling my concentration, and rather than sit with a nagging feeling and achieving little progress, I investigated. Sure enough, the window was not only open, but there was also no window stay or latch, only a piece of string tied to what was left of the stay. I reached out of the window to grab the string in time to see the bushes along the path move as some creature or other passed between them. I pulled the window closed and, for extra security, tied the end of the string to the radiator below the window.

You've probably guessed by now that my story had barely started, and time was of the essence. To start afresh, I switched on my iPhone and went to the kitchen to make myself a cup of tea, with the intention of calmly getting myself back into the story. Now, I know with absolute certainty that I had closed the kitchen door to the back garden.

However, there it was, gently swinging on its hinges. I left it like that until I'd made a mug of tea with two sugars, then I took my tea to the doorway and stood looking at the waning moon being switched off and on by passing clouds.

I glanced up the pathway as I turned towards the house and saw what I took to be the faint glow of the rear lights of a car about 250 yards away. I studied the lights but could not make out any shape that supported them against the blackness of the forest. I then heard a bark that echoed throughout the trees. The lights seemed to dance up and down and get closer before disappearing with the noise of breaking branches. I slammed the door shut behind me, and there being no key, I jammed the back of a chair firmly against the door's handle and forced its legs into a gap in the floorboards. As I did this, I could see by the light of my torch that there were deep scratches in the floor, which indicated that the chair had been used many times for the same purpose.

I was in no state of mind to carry on with my story as I returned to my computer. But then a shudder ran through me. I looked at the screen and realised someone had completed my story for me.

ARRESTED AFTER PAYING THE BILL

HAROLD ROFFEY

THREE AM AND THE SUN WON'T RISE for at least another two and a half hours. A police car cruises through the centre of Oxford with a female officer driving while a male officer sitting next to her half turns in his seat to address two handcuffed occupants on the rear seat.

'What made you do it?' he asked, without being specific as to the subject or whom he was addressing.

'I needed to get it in,' replied Ken from his bent-over position.

'Why don't you sit up? You'll be more comfortable,' said the officer.

'Someone might see me,' replied Ken.

'Don't tell me you have friends walking the streets at this time of night,' said Tina, who until then had not said a word.

'Now you're finally talking,' said the officer, addressing the other occupant of the rear seat. 'So, what made you do it?'

'Do what?'

'You've been arrested for causing an affray. I'm asking why cause it?'

'Cos I felt like it, and besides, you don't find a bloke like Ken every day. He's a laugh a minute.'

Ken sat up and glanced at Tina while tilting his head away from her with sufficient disdain to strike most people dumb, but not Tina.

'If the alarm hadn't gone off, we could have had a good time, you and me, Ken.'

'I've no idea what you're talking about. I've got a wife at home who'll be worried stiff if she wakes and finds me gone.'

'Stiff. I like the sound of that, Ken. You need to get out more. Do you know what a blow job and a crayfish thermidor have in common?' she asked, inching her bottom along the seat towards Ken.

'That's enough!' said the officer, turning back towards the front of the car and looking at the driver, who'd turned her head away to smile without being observed.

'He's telling us to be quiet because they know the answer, Ken. I wouldn't be surprised if that's what they get up to in this fancy car of theirs.'

Ken was now squashed against the door of the car with Tina against him.

'OK, you two, move further apart otherwise I'll have the car stopped and I'll sort you out.'

'You don't often get either at home,' laughed Tina as she moved away from Ken.

The female officer coughed to hide her laugh while the male officer remained silent.

The car stopped at the police station and the officers handled Ken and Tina through the police station to the desk.

'Attempting to break into a property is a serious offence,' said the charge officer while eyeing Ken. 'Have you anything to add to that?'

Tina started giggling.

'And is this woman with you?'

'Certainly not,' replied Ken.

'Oh, yes you are, Ken,' she piped up.

'Perhaps you can tell me all about it,' said the officer.

'I saw him park his car on the pavement and I knew what he wanted—.'

'She's got nothing to do with it,' Ken interjected.

'One at a time. You tell me what happened,' he said looking directly at Ken.

'I woke up at about 1.30 this morning,' Ken said while looking down.

'Please speak up. I can hardly hear you.'

'I woke up at 1.30 this morning with something on my mind—'

'I bet you did,' Tina piped up.

'That's enough from you!' said the officer.

'I woke up with something on my mind, but I couldn't figure it out. Then I realised I hadn't paid the bill at a restaurant I'd been to last night. I felt so guilty that I couldn't go back to sleep, so rather than toss and turn, I got out of bed, typed a letter and put it in an envelope with a cheque for what I thought would have been more than the bill. Then I crept out of the house without changing or waking my wife and drove to the restaurant to put the envelope through their post box, but there was this scantily clad woman in the doorway. I couldn't find the post box and while I was pushing the envelope under the door, this creature—' he said, nodding towards Tina, 'started pulling my pyjamas down and laughing. Then the alarm went off, and while I was struggling to pull my pyjamas up, a police car arrived.'

'That's not how I remember it,' laughed Tina. 'I think Ken's a bundle of fun.'

MY UNIQUE AGENT

HAROLD ROFFEY

THERE SHE IS, AGATHA PRINTWELL, MY AGENT, at the Book Fair. I half expected her to be at the November Fair last year. I sent an invitation, along with a manuscript of my latest book, to her PA, but Agatha failed to acknowledge my invitation. In the PA's reply, she said that Agatha knew exactly where to put my last brilliant piece of writing. She has such a sense of humour, that woman. I had to laugh. I immediately replied. Fortunately, I have a copy of my reply with me. I'll have a quick read to refresh my thoughts before springing a surprise on Agatha. I know she'll be pleased to see me.

My dear, dear Agatha,

It was so good to hear from you after all this time and thank you so much for sending my printed manuscript back. You'll be pleased to know I managed to sort the pages out and Sellotape the torn ones together again.

I studied your covering letter with my heart in my mouth because, as you know, I value your opinion. I just loved the way you expressed yourself on the second page by repeating the word 'crap' twelve times after the brief sentence, 'This is complete —'. To me, your clever use of repetition sounded like someone running down a staircase at high speed. If only I had such a way with words.

I thought I caught your eye at the international book fair in San Francisco last month. However, by the time I'd pushed my way through the crowd, you'd gone. What a pity as I know you and I could have chatted for hours about my literary work, and to be honest, I was looking forward to receiving the odd piece of guidance.

Never mind. There will be another time – perhaps in November in Oxford – who knows?

As you well know, one of my articles was published in a national paper three months ago. They'd made an error by placing it in the comedy section when it was obviously a serious observation of our government, but hey ho, that's the lackadaisical attitude we've come to accept nowadays. Also, as you're very much aware, I made sure your name appeared as my agent – no point in hiding your light under a bushel, I always say. Your modesty shone through a week later, and I admired you for it, when you said in the same journal that my brilliant piece had absolutely nothing to do with you.

You'll be pleased to know my next novel is nearing completion and should be with you within a month. I've already primed your secretary, and she lifted my spirits by saying you'd know exactly what to do with it.

Yours as always

I'm now bursting with excitement knowing that Agatha Printwell, *the* Agatha Printwell, is but a few metres away. I'll give her time to peruse our table before I spring from behind our poster. Yes – yes – yes, she's seen my name on one of the books. Oh dear! She looks as though she's suddenly remembered something. Where is she going? She's obviously caught up in her own thoughts and is making for the door. I'll run after her. I hope she's all right.

'Agatha – wait for me! Agatha – it's me! Agatha – Agatha – Agatha –'

A VISIT TO FRIDA KAHLO

HAROLD ROFFEY

HELEN WOKE UP AT FIVE O'CLOCK, FEELING uneasy without knowing why. She lay on her side and stared into the dark, searching her mind for items she'd left off the Sainsbury's home- delivery order. Then she thought about her daughter's visit the previous evening. *Had she really agreed to keep herself restricted to the house as much as possible, even though the pandemic was over?* It had seemed so easy at the time. Catherine, thirty-three, wine glass in hand had toasted her mother. 'Good health!' she'd said in a manner that was, now that Helen thought about it, not smug exactly, but somehow happy with the arrangement, as though giving it more significance than it deserved. And now that Helen really thought about it, *Catherine had had an unwarranted, contented look.* Helen had replied by repeating the words without too much thought. In fact, no thought at all.

Catherine's father, Helen's ex-husband, had left Helen five years ago, when he was sixty and she had been fifty-eight. *Hope he's happy with the bitch*, she thought. It was a bit more than a thought. She silently mouthed the words and then reflected, as she often did, on his spiteful words, 'I'll divorce you and perhaps I'll stop masturbating.'

While Helen lay awake and afraid to move in case she reverted to thinking about that Sainsbury's order, John, Catherine's twin, popped into her mind. 'Make sure you look after yourself,' she remembered him saying last Thursday. *Did he have the same look on his face as his sister?* she thought. *Yes, he damn well did.*

*****

'Are you OK, Helen? It's only ten to six. Do you need me to do something?'

'I'm OK. In fact, I'm more than OK, Charlie.'

'I hope you're not phoning about the other evening after the art appreciation lecture. I shouldn't have kissed you goodnight like that. I do apologise. I've thought about it a lot since then. I'm so sorry.'

'Stop wittering on, Charlie. You surprised me, that's all. I want to know how you would have responded if I'd been less resistant.'

'You've put me on the spot, Helen. I don't know how to answer, and I don't want to spoil our friendship.'

'Charlie! Just tell me the truth.'

'You have my total respect, Helen.'

'Stop it, Charlie. Did you hope to sleep with me or not? Yes or no. I don't want any beating about the bush.'

'This is so difficult, Helen.'

'I'm giving you one last chance to answer, Charlie.'

'Well – yes.'

'The other night you said you'd love to go to Mexico City to see Frida Kahlo's house. I'm booking this morning. Are you coming with me, or do I have to pay a premium for a single room?'

ANNE AND JOE TAKE A BREAK

HAROLD ROFFEY

'I KNEW WE SHOULDN'T HAVE COME. NINE hours in the bloody car and what is this place? A hovel in the middle of nowhere. Are you sure this is it?' Before Joe could answer, Anne carried on. 'I didn't think you'd manage the last, how many miles? On that dirt road in the pitch dark. I'm surprised the lights work. And as for the bedrooms. Just look!'

'We're here in one piece. You sort out the food box out and I'll get the rest of the luggage. We'll explore in the morning.'

'The morning's only three and a half hours away. You've really fucked up this time, Joe.' Joe didn't want to hear any more. He had already switched on the torch on his phone and was walking down the long garden path to the car, leaving Anne in the kitchen. It wasn't cold, and the air was still and silent as he lifted their hanging clothes from the hooks above the rear door and manhandled the remaining bag from the boot.

Anne, although she would never admit it, was feeling nervous, and carried on talking to herself for comfort in front of the kitchen window. She watched Joe's light swaying back and forth as he struggled with the luggage towards the steps leading from the drive to the garden gate. She was still watching when she heard the front door close. She turned her head immediately and stared at the door leading to the hall. She and Joe had looked in every room and although she was confident there was nobody else in the house, she couldn't help shouting, 'Who's there?' In fact, it didn't come out as a shout, it was more of a rasping sound from her dry throat. She couldn't see Joe's light as he ascended the steps hidden by bushes. *Relax, for God's sake,* she said to herself as she turned to the table and opened the food container.

'Good night sweetheart. I've locked up. Sleep well.'

Anne's arms, neck and the backs of her legs tingled as a man's pleasant voice ended his sentence. She went to the unlit hall. The doors of the rooms were closed, and no light crept from underneath. 'I switched on all the lights to make this place as homely as possible. What the fuck is going on?' she said aloud. She turned the handle of the front door, but it wouldn't open, and Joe had the key. She returned to the kitchen to look for Joe through the window. There were no lights, and she could see no further than the glow from the kitchen. She thought of turning the kitchen light off to get a better view of the outside, but she couldn't bear the thought of being in the dark. She was shaking and near to tears.

'Milk and butter to the fridge,' she said aloud as she grabbed the items from the box. 'You can follow them,' she said to the cold meat, the cheese and the fruit juice carton while she threw them onto the table. 'As for you, tomatoes, you can go in that green bowl.' She looked up at the kitchen clock as it struck three. Another glance out of the window. Pitch black. *Where the fuck is he?* she thought, making as much noise as possible as she emptied the box and laid the table for a snack.

'Pull yourself together!' she shouted and went into the hall and down to the first of the two bedrooms, opened the door and switched the light on. 'What the hell is going on and who the hell are you?' she screamed at a small mound of blankets, over which long, white hair lay. Getting no response, Anne gently prodded the mound. Still no response. Anne went to the other side of the bed to avoid having her back to the open bedroom door and to have a better look at the person in the bed. The woman's cheek had caved in against the skull and her eyelids were half shrivelled and opened to holes where eyes had once been. Anne screamed and started crying uncontrollably as she hurried to the other bedroom where she found an old man in a similar condition. The front door slowly opened as Anne went into the hall.

'Give me a hand with these things,' said Joe as he pushed the door open with his back. Anne ran to Joe and hugged him tight, which caused the clothes to fall on the floor.

'Eh, what's up, love?' Anne was choking on her tears and they both got a fright when the kitchen clock struck three for the second time.

MASKED STRANGERS

HAROLD ROFFEY

I'D NOT KNOWN THE WEATHER TO have emotion, and I don't believe it has, but when she, on the TV, pulled a long face while describing the weather as miserable, I took no notice. In fact, it looked good for three in the afternoon in November so, despite the wind and slight drizzle, a quick walk to catch the last of the light was just what I needed.

I'd shared that sort of feeling with Susan for twenty-five years. When she died two years ago, I had to drag myself to my office. However, I now spend most of my spare time pottering about, reading and talking to myself between brisk walks.

Within half an hour I was standing in long grass by the side of the canal and saying 'Good afternoon' through my mask to a stranger. I'd seen her anticipating the passing distance between us as she approached. At one point I thought she'd hesitated as if to turn back, but I'd subtly signalled to her by walking off the path and stopping long before I needed to. She'd responded by walking slightly faster towards me.

'It's Tony, isn't it?' she asked when she came close.

I looked at her face as she lifted her rain-hat slightly with a gloved hand, but before I could reply, she said, 'It's me, Amrita. Amrita Anand.'

'It's lovely to see you,' I replied while desperately searching for a clue to her identify among Susan's many friends. 'How are you getting on? Everyone well?'

'It's lonely since Adarsh died, but of course, you know all about that.'

'And the family?' I asked.

'This is the problem nowadays, they're scattered throughout the world, and I can't see myself being face to face with them for a long time because of this wretched pandemic.'

Amrita and I flicked snippets of information back and forth like a shuttlecock, both eager to keep the game in play.

'Enough of me,' she said. 'How are you getting on?'

'It's been lonely, but I'm coping reasonably well. I think we must get going before it's too dark to see our way.'

'I guess so,' she replied.

'It's a pity I can't give you a hug,' I said.

'Yes, I'd like that, Tony. Please ring me, it must be over a year. Goodbye and keep well.'

I walked on for about ten yards feeling strangely bereft. I then turned back and called out to Amrita.

She stopped and waited for me to get to her.

'I feel really bad,' I said.

'There's no need to feel bad, Tony. I feel the same. I know how difficult it is to talk to someone who has lost their partner. I must face the world at my age and learn to treasure what I've known and hope to see my children from time to time.'

'It's nothing to do with that. Would you like to have a coffee and a snack or something in a café next Thursday at about eleven o'clock, when Covid is officially over?'

'I'd love that, Tony.'

'I'd love that too,' I said. 'But, before you commit, and what's making me feel bad, is that I'm not Tony and I've not met you before.'

OH! HOW I LOVE MY WIFE

HAROLD ROFFEY

THE ARROGANCE OF THE MAN TO TELL *me* to stop bragging. 'Bragging?' I barked at him for trying to keep me caged up. 'You must be joking. I'm showing you lot how to look after yourselves in the bush, and you're not interested. Remain ignorant – get killed and eaten for all I care. I'm sure you'd make a reasonable snack for something bigger and stronger than you.'

Do you know what he said then? 'If you don't behave, I'll lock you up in a concrete pit. Then you'll stop.' I stared at him with my best 'Just you try it, matie' look, and then he walked off.

'And stop calling me "Stoffel!" I shouted after him. *Where did he get a name like that from?* I thought, as I walked back to my wife and four children. The wife, with two kids either side of her, looked a bit bored, I thought. But there again, she'd heard it all before, and she's just as good at telling the kids how to look after themselves as I am, only she rarely gives a live demonstration.

I once showed them how to walk through a pride of lions. The wife and kids were watching from behind some boulders. When I got back to them, I was more afraid of my wife's anger than the lions' claws. 'You are irresponsible!' she screamed. I had to laugh a few days later when the kids were complaining about feeling hungry. I pretended not to have seen a huge black mamba making its way from some bushes across the scrubland to a tall tree.

She saw the snake, then looked at me as if to say, 'Well? What are you going to do about it?' I decided to show more interest in something much further away, knowing that the snake would soon be out of reach. My wife then ran off, leaving me with the kids, and arrived at the black mamba in time to grab its tail and pull it backwards into the open. She leapt out of the way of its head as it attempted to strike, and then had to fight off a hyena, which had been asleep under some bushes. The kids were looking concerned until I started laughing at my wife leaping about avoiding the hyena's jaws and the snake's venomous fangs.

My wife was determined not to share the meal with the hyena. Each time the hyena attacked the snake from her left, she pulled the mamba's body to the left, which caused the snake to strike at the hyena before it leapt over the snake and was therefore on its right. She then pulled the snake to the right and it responded by striking right. When the hyena had done this fifteen times, it turned on my wife, but my wife, bless her cotton socks, opened her mouth to show off her teeth and then screeched so loud that the hyena returned to dancing over the snake. All the while, my wife had been dragging the snake towards thick undergrowth where the hyena couldn't fight her. By then, the snake was nearly dead, and my wife, with one bite to the back of its head, rendered it lifeless and then chased the hyena away.

The kids and I strolled into the bush to congratulate her and have a late afternoon meal. She was so pleased with herself that she forgot about our earlier tiff. I think she's the most capable honey badger I've ever met. No wonder I love her.

(Honey badgers are one of the most intelligent and fearless animals in Africa.)

FISH AND WATER ARE FURTHER DOWN

HAROLD ROFFEY

HETTIE VAN NIEKIRK HAD TOLD JOHANNES SHE wanted to go in her own car, but then she succumbed to his persistence, put her mother's Nissan back in the lean-to carport and climbed into Johannes' old Ford truck. This time, however, she said no to his amorous persuasions and meant it. Perhaps he wouldn't have been so hurt had it not been the first time she'd said no in six months. Perhaps it was the image Hettie had of her mother's look of disapproval becoming clearer with each kilometre that Johannes Opperman drove east out of Windhoek and into the Namib Desert that made her so adamant, or perhaps it was because Hendrick, her father, had threatened to give her a hiding if she continued seeing Johannes. Hettie valued her parents' opinions the more as her desire for Johannes faded. Hettie had planned to talk to Johannes at their favourite spot beneath a lone camelthorn tree. She had hoped to tell him she loved him but wanted to set their relationship on a less passionate footing.

The dirt road on which Johannes drove follows the Avis River. However, the riverbed, although wide in places with steep sides, rarely sees water from one year to the next, and the catfish that remained after the last flood had buried themselves deep in mud below the sandy surface on which it is too hot to walk, especially in January when the sun is at its highest.

Time had passed quickly for Hettie during the ten-mile drive to the shade of 'their' tree. When she viewed the shimmering Namib as Johannes drove off in a rage, she felt angry that he'd left her to walk home but satisfied with herself for clarifying her perspective of their future.

A few hours later, Johannes was overcome by a feeling of guilt, and within ten minutes of frantically driving back along the road, he discovered Hettie's body by a hole she'd dug with her bare hands in search of water in the dry riverbed.

A YOUNG MAN'S ASPIRATIONS

HAROLD ROFFEY

JAMES HETHERINGTON-SMYTHE knew he was severely hyphenated, but it didn't stop him from founding the party that made him a legend in his lifetime, one that became associated with the poorest in the land.

'The people need protection,' he said at the start of his inaugural speech on the steps of Clacton's town hall in front of a row of people consisting of his mother, three aunts, four uncles and a vast array of cousins stretching for yards either side of his father and one deep.

When they all clapped at the end of James' delivery (and had forgotten every word he'd said), James knew he was on his way to greater things. He also felt that fortune was already in the bag, as his father, dressed in Joe-the-chauffeur's cap and jacket, saluted James while holding the rear door of the family's Bentley open. His elder sister, Hortense, curtsied to James, waited for him to be settled on the back seat and then climbed in after him.

The car slowly pulled away and the Union Jack pennant, made by Beatrice, James' other sister, was soon flapping in the light breeze. Four other cars, especially cleaned for the occasion, took up positions behind the Bentley for the one-mile trip to the fully reserved Franco's restaurant for an early supper.

James' mother, Lady Cordelia, said that James was never quite the same after that day. 'In fact,' she said, 'I think that launched him into politics.'

Everyone, except James, laughed when James first presented a bound copy of his declaration at dinner in 2020 on the twenty-first anniversary of his birth. It wasn't the content so much as the gold leaf title on the leather cover:

The Feudal Party Manifesto

Know Your Place

Be Safe and Protected

It didn't happen overnight. Happiness throughout the country diminished with the decline in material wealth and low expectations. More of 'the People' listened to James as taxes rose and food and fuel became more expensive. The government stepped back from its responsibilities, leaving charities to fill the gaps, and the NHS curtailed its services.

James finally took his party into the Palace of Westminster in 2030.

DAUGHTER DOROTHY DOES WONDERS

HAROLD ROFFEY

DOROTHY LOVED EVERYTHING that nature had to offer, and we, Kate and I, being her parents, indulged her. What else would one do for an only child after ten frustrating years of failing to give her a brother or a sister, or anything in between for that matter?

'I don't give a damn, so long as it's healthy and capable of becoming the prime minister,' said Kate, my long-suffering wife.

'I agree, Kate,' I replied. 'But aren't you aiming rather low in your ambitions for our offspring?'

'What would you suggest?'

'Not given it much thought.'

'Well, you should. We only have one Dorothy, and time is of the essence.'

I'd not thought of it that way before, and Kate's prodding gave me a bit of a jolt.

'Instead of sitting in your study staring out the window every day looking for inspiration for your short stories, I think you should do something. And do it soon,' she said, pushing her chair back from the breakfast table.

Feeling a trifle impotent with regard to guiding Dorothy to heights beyond that of a lowly prime minister whose innate values must eventually be sacrificed, I rang the bell.

'Ah, James! I feel like a ride to the hills on the eastern side of the estate. Please saddle up Jessy and tell Mary to prepare a small lunch to take with me.'

It's not a large estate. In fact, on a clear day if one had had a good pair of binoculars, fifteen years ago one could have seen another house on the horizon. Had it not been for Kate's dislike of close neighbours, it would still be there. She told me to make the owners an offer they would find difficult to refuse.

'Get rid of it,' she said when I asked her how we could use it.

I was surprised at the high cost of having the old twenty-roomed mansion levelled, but they assured me that the rubble would be removed within a month, in time for the delivery of the thirteen hundred new trees and too late for the pests from the preservation authority.

'We're doing our bit for climate change,' Kate reminded me.

After steadily riding for an hour or so, I arrived at the bottom of a waterfall where I'd often spent many a time contemplating life, and what's more, often reaching very reasonable conclusions.

I'm glad to say that that day's contemplation bore such good fruit that I couldn't wait to infect Kate and Dorothy with my enthusiasm.

I enrolled eleven-year-old Dorothy at an after-hours computer study facility. She loved it. She'd lock herself away for hours in the special annex we built for her with the latest equipment that money could buy.

I must hand it to Kate. She persuaded Dot, as she calls her, to join 'The Political Party'. Dorothy then added psychology to her repertoire to understand what the mass of people want to hear, rather than what they should be told. She developed an algorithmic computer program with an artificial intelligence interface that continually monitored the electorate and wrote speeches for her whenever she wanted them. I shouldn't be telling you this, but she says that becoming prime minister will be a wonderful stepping stone to great things. As an offshoot, she's written ten bestsellers under my name. She's such a darling.

ALL THE BETTER TO DECEIVE YOU WITH

J.M. KENNEDY

ONCE UPON A TIME, in a rose-covered cottage on the edge of the woods, lived Grandmother Riding Hood. Grandmother's cottage was always filled with the smell of baking, and if the wind blew in an easterly direction delicious wafts of cake would reach Little Red Riding Hood's cottage on the other side of the woods, where she lived with her husband, Richard.

One morning, Grandmother got up early, keen to try some new recipes; she hoped 'Cakes You'll Wolf Down in No Time' would be as good as the magazine promised. With two of the new cakes in the oven, she was just weighing out the ingredients for a traditional coffee sponge when Richard burst into the kitchen.

'What big hands you have, Grandmother!' exclaimed Richard, as he shoved his briefcase onto the table. 'All the better to sign these papers with.'

Grandmother smiled noncommittally. 'What papers, dear?'

'Nothing you need worry about,' Richard replied with an odd little laugh. 'Just so I can help take over your finances.'

'That's very thoughtful of you.' Grandmother carefully poured batter from the mixing bowl into an old round cake tin. 'I see you're finding your feet again after that nasty fraud allegation.'

Richard paled, and sat down heavily, his bulky frame causing the delicate wooden chair to creak alarmingly.

Grandmother looked at him in concern and brought over a glass of water. Suddenly Richard slammed his hand down on the table, making Grandmother jump, and almost sending the glass tumbling to the floor. Scraping his chair back, Richard stalked over to the worktop and seized a kitchen knife, stabbing it into a loaf of bread which was cooling on a wire rack. Grandmother felt the hairs on the back of her neck stand on end, and she retreated to the other side of the table.

Richard turned abruptly, brandishing the knife. 'Just sign those documents, then I'll leave you in peace. Resting,' he added under his breath.

Grandmother suppressed a shiver, and wondered if she could buy some time by distracting him. 'Where's Little Red?' she asked, hoping her granddaughter was safely far away.

'She's staying at home for a few days – she walked into a door and doesn't want to go out until the bruises fade.' Richard was still attacking the loaf, but as the delightful aroma of gently baking cake reached his flared nostrils, he visibly relaxed.

Putting the knife down, he took his mobile phone from his pocket and walked back across the kitchen to sit at the table. Carefully positioning the phone, he quietly stated the date and time, and then said in a louder, rather patronising voice, 'I've tried to explain that I'm going to record our discussion, but Grandmother just doesn't understand, the poor dear.'

'What *are* you talking about Richard? What don't I understand?'

But Richard just ignored her. 'What big eyes you have, Grandmother! When did you last get your eyes tested? Not forgetting to go to important appointments, are you?'

Grandmother briefly considered the question. 'As a matter of fact, I went to the optician last month.'

Smiling to himself, Richard continued dictating. 'Hasn't been to optician for five years.'

As Grandmother started to correct him, Richard talked over her. 'No concept of time, clearly confused.'

Grandmother frowned at him. One of them seemed to be going mad, and she was fairly certain it wasn't her.

'Would you like a cup of tea?' She strived for a friendly tone, secretly hoping he wouldn't accept. She'd never really liked Richard, as he always seemed to be enjoying a private joke at other people's expense, and her distrust of him had only increased since Little Red had become strangely accident-prone when she was on her own with Richard. It was all most concerning, but Grandmother fought to keep her face neutral, suddenly frightened that he'd take it out on Little Red if he realised she was suspicious.

Richard stared at Grandmother. 'Tea? Um ...' Remembering that the recording was still in progress, he tried to undermine Grandmother's polite offer. 'I'd rather not. I, er, it's awfully dirty in here!'

Grandmother folded her arms. 'That's simply not true! My new butler, Wolfric, keeps the place spic and span.'

Richard muttered into the phone, 'Imaginary butler.'

Grandmother drew herself up, but she didn't tower over Richard in the way she had hoped. Hands on hips, she tried to speak in a calm but firm manner. 'He's around somewhere – you can meet him for yourself! Why do you keep muttering into your phone like that?'

A smug expression crossed Richard's face. 'Just a little recording to add to the file.'

'What file?' Grandmother was now thoroughly vexed, and she took a deep breath. *Think of Little Red*, she reminded herself. *Don't let Richard know that I can see through his lies.*

'Never mind, I'm sure you know best! Would you care for a bite? I'll just ring for the butler. Oh, Wolfie!'

Wolfric strolled into the room, his claws making a pleasant clicking sound on the wooden floorboards. As Grandmother glanced up with a smile, the telephone on the hall table started ringing, and she got up to answer it, motioning to Wolfric to sit.

'Oh hello, Red, my darling, how lovely to hear your voice! I was going to pop round later to bring you a basket of treats ... Wolfie, do stop licking my hand – it tickles! ... Sorry darling, Wolfie gets rather affectionate once one gains his trust ... yes, he's a very good judge of character, terribly loyal ... Richard said you'd walked into a door ... Yes, he's here, brought some papers for me to sign. Wolfie, stop that growling, at once! ... Sorry darling, I don't know what has got into Wolfie!

... I see. Well, thank you for the warning, darling, but I should imagine Richard won't be bothering us again!'

'Aarrgghh!' Richard shouted, wielding his briefcase as he tried to back away.

But it was too late.

'Get away from me Wolfric! What big teeth you have!'

PATIENT A

J.M. KENNEDY

Disempowered, but determined to make decisions, despite what the doctor said: *dying, dementia.*

Exasperated by the railings on your care home bed. Pyjamaed. Patronised. Infantilised. Imprisoned.

M*uddled. Befuddled.* Whispered cryptic messages. Scribbled notes, hidden from 'the guards'.

E*vidence of your lack of capacity*. Eccentric. Engaging. Eloquent. Charming. Unbroken.

Noble war hero. Spitfire pilot. Adventurer. Now wrapped in cotton wool. Not allowed home to die.
T*oo confused to understand the risks*. Tenacious. Victorious in your final flight. *Troublemaker.*

I*nconvenient. Insignificant*. Important. Irrepressible. Indefatigable. Indelible.

Arthur.

ELUSIVE STRENGTH

J.M. KENNEDY

GNAWING ANXIETY TIGHTENS ITS CLUTCHES, and she wishes she could close her eyes to shut everything out. Escape to a soothing, warm lagoon, gently shaded by fluffy white clouds. But the reality is not relaxing; the lights are unbearably bright, the small seat uncomfortably hard. A momentary lapse in concentration would be catastrophic. She takes small, shallow breaths and tries not to move.

She feels a single tear making its way down her right cheek. But he seems oblivious. In a detached part of her mind, she thinks of matinee heroines presenting an outward insouciance, a single tear the only indicator of an internal crumbling.

A soft click brings her back to the cramped room. A sharp metallic tang cuts through the warm smell of faded coffee. A second tear trickles down the same path.

This time, he notices the tear, dabs at it, before handing her a tissue. His avuncular manner is comforting, but his small, exasperated exhales are a warning.

'I'll be back in a moment,' he says quietly.

She needs to find a way to control the panic. Forces herself to take slow, deep breaths. A measured rhythm to calm the nervous system. 'Sniper's breath,' the instructors called it.

He comes back, and she has a horrible sense of déjà vu as they resume their tense positions on either side of the machine. She can feel her composure seeping away, and desperately seeks distraction, grateful for the air-conditioning unit blasting out cold draughts between mechanical noises.

She tries to focus on the feel of her feet against the ground, another calming technique. But there's no flexibility in the sturdy boots with their unforgiving soles.

'Right.' He sits back, and she feels a huge weight lift from her shoulders.

'That didn't work.'

The weight returns, tenfold.

Outside, the held-back tears coagulate with disappointment and fear, flooding her defences. She needs to retreat and allow the river to run its course. Needs solace to soothe her beleaguered, bruised resilience. Perhaps tomorrow will bring strength.

THROUGH CRUMPLED GRIEF

J.M. KENNEDY

As I recall your voice, your face,
They briefly fill that bleak dark space
Where deep despair and sorrow trawl,
And hopes and dreams and wishes stall –
Protect me from that hollow place.

Bereft and lost, I slowly trace
The picture of your carefree face
There's comfort there, however small
And I recall your voice.

You cherished me, you gave me grace
I yearn for you; I seek, I chase
You still give strength when I would fall
And fervently, I beg, I call
Come back, my love, to my embrace
As I recall your voice.

THE WRONG VIOLINIST

JANE SPIRO

'SO VERY KIND OF VIOLET TO OFFER hospitality to the visiting violinist, and of course, her cottage being detached from the neighbours and surrounded by a walled courtyard garden, a perfect location for practising without causing a disturbance.' She set a bunch of powdery pink roses with large drooping heads on the hall cabinet and popped a tray of flapjacks in the oven.

What a charming guest the violinist proved to be, so gracious in his demeanour, so kind about her cooking and so very appreciative of all the small touches in her home.

'How charming, these flagstones, Violet. Are they the original ones, do you think?'

'Yes, I imagine so, Martin. See, they are shiny with all the footsteps over the years.' 'How many years, do you think?'

'Well, a good deal more than me, and that's for sure and me nearly eighty!'

'Well, you're terrific, Violet, I must say, I wouldn't put you a day over twenty-one!'

Oh! he made her laugh.

She had said no to the complimentary ticket, then yes when he appeared like a maestro from the back bedroom. How smart he looked, sharp as a brush in black and white, his violin swinging in its black case as she walked with him the two streets to the church hall. How proud as Punch was Violet as he played with his ensemble, all fury and thunder one minute then soaring like the heavens at another, and you could never tell what was going to happen next. When it seemed everything was in a frenzy of anguish, the clouds would suddenly part and snowflakes would sprinkle down in a silvery shaft of light. Violet swung on the storm of these moods, as the violinist's bow stroked and skittered on the strings.

'Well, Martin, that was quite something,' she said as they walked home. 'I must say, I feel as if I have been on quite a journey, but for all you can see, here I am and haven't gone anywhere.'

'That describes it very well,' said Martin. 'We have done our job if you feel like that.'

He slept well in his cottage bedroom, in a high wooden bed with a long bolster pillow. Well, it's very nice, Violet thought, to have someone there breathing in Harry's room as if he's still in this world, our Harry, at last another living soul here in the house. How safe she felt with this Martin with his violin case. How well he filled the absence of Harry, long-departed.

'I hope the quartet come back to the village,' she thought as she drifted off to sleep, 'I hope he comes to stay again.'

*****

A year later, to her delight the quartet were again scheduled to play at the village music festival.

'Martin has asked if he could stay with you again,' said the organiser, Mathias.

Oh, Violet was delighted. There would be yellow roses this time, and he liked the flapjack especially so there would be more of that, perhaps with ice cream this time. The sheets were crisp and turned down for his arrival, and she stood in the doorway only five times that day, viewing the room proudly, so glad it was able to welcome guests such as Martin in his black and white attire with his swinging violin case.

*****

The doorbell jangled, bright and perky just as it should, and in her mind, she saw him on the doorstep, with his pointed chin and combed brown hair, perhaps with a light rain jacket open at the neck and an overnight bag on his shoulder. But when she opened the door, that's not what she saw at all. This person had a fedora hat pulled down over his eyebrows, and a shadow from the hat's brim over his face.

He was wearing a long herringbone coat as if for a much colder day than today. Instead of his violin swinging in his hand, she saw it hanging on a strap over his shoulder, with a small bag on wheels at his feet, the size of a small dog.

'Hello Violet!' he said brightly, stepping forward to shake her hand.

She stood widely across the doorway to block his entrance.

'Oh no, you're not Martin,' she said.

The man on the doorstep laughed nervously, not sure if this was a joke or a local form of greeting; for a split second he wondered whether perhaps he wasn't Martin and if not, then who was he? In any of these cases, the moment was awkward, and as sure as Violet was, so equally the man on the doorstep was unsure. He reached to remove his fedora hat, briefly considering it may have confused his hostess, but as he lifted his hand, she gasped and stepped backwards.

'Don't you threaten me,' she said.

He stood frozen, with his hand touching the tip of his hat, and to save the futility of this gesture, did clasp the rim and remove it. Here was a pointed chin like Martin's, but the hair wasn't combed sideways across his forehead, and there were signs that the hair was not entirely brown but had speckles of silver.

'You are not Martin,' she said again.

*****

Martin sat in the village pub, a hardly touched half pint of Kingfisher in one hand, his phone in the other.

'She says you are an imposter,' Mathias said. 'Nothing will convince her.'

'Well, what next?'

'I'll get you a B&B sorted, don't worry. If you can hold out at the pub until I sort that. God, really sorry. This is just the weirdest thing.'

'Yes, pretty weird. Maybe I'm not Martin. She seemed pretty sure.'

They both laughed, Martin a bit less convincingly than Mathias.

He sat at the round table in the corner of the pub, his box of chocolates for Violet sitting on the table forlornly. Both the chocolates and his pint of beer seemed as useless as each other at offering him a bed for the night.

Despite this setback, and his late arrival at a much less congenial bed and breakfast where he was at least allowed through the door, the concert went well. The hall was packed, with followers from last year as well as new audience members from further afield who had heard the good reports.

Violet decided to stay at home.

'Well, I'm hoping to see Martin again,' she said to herself. 'I'll show that imposter who the real Martin is.'

She pulled the flapjacks out of the oven, warm and golden brown.

'If Martin isn't coming, I'll eat them myself,' she thought.

She ate the first one, licked her fingers, then ate the next one.

'I'll leave the last one for Harry,' she said to herself. 'He'll be back soon.'

COMPULSION

JENNY BURRAGE

HE WAITED FOR THE BANGS ON THE ceiling overhead and for the usual shouting.

'For Christ's sake, what time do you call this?'

'Shut that row up.'

'I'm calling the police.'

Yes, that would be flats number 13, 14 and 15, up above.

It had happened every night, but not tonight. Ellery supposed they'd heard he'd been given notice to quit after all the complaints. They'd won and he had a month's notice. He wasn't sorry to be leaving this monstrous block of concrete with its paper-thin walls and an ancient lift and stairwell which smelt of wee. But where would he go?

The only good things about living there were its nearness to the school of music and the fact that it was cheap. His parents had spent loads of money on him at uni. He couldn't ask for more. He wouldn't't tell them anything about his eviction. He had two weeks to find somewhere new. He did have a little money left but it was definitely time to move and find a job.

He picked up his clarinet, kissed it and began playing again. He hadn't meant to be a nuisance. It was just that whenever he woke up in the night (which was often) he had a compulsion to play. His fingers itched to hold his clarinet, and his body trembled. Must play. Now.

'I wish you would find a nice girlfriend, Ellery.' His mum rarely gave advice.

It was all she seemed to say when he visited home, but the truth was, he didn't want one. Yet if he did, he could get one instantly.

His parents were elderly, and he had been a surprise baby and an only child. He supposed they'd thought that he was a normal boy.

Teachers had told them he was bright and imaginative but didn't mix well with the other children. Mother had told him about all those early comments recently.

But it was true what school had said, and here he was at twenty-three, still a loner.

As a child, his parents let him do exactly as he liked. They were both scientists, obsessed with their work, and to them, young children were an enigma. Even as a youngster, he had read books about a fantasy world and watched similar programmes on TV. He was obsessed too.

His clarinet now meant everything to him and music was his life.

He had begged for a clarinet at nine years old and his parents had been pleased. He listened to music all day long. And he joined the school orchestra, even though the other players were mostly eleven.

Studying music in Oxford had been amazing and here he was in limbo. He had to move. He had to earn money.

His mind turned back to his mother's question about a girlfriend. Did he need a woman in his life? Maybe he did. He thought about it for ages, like always. The words tumbled round in his mind. Yes. He needed someone.

Somehow, he knew it was the right time for what he must do.

He lay down, stretched out on the floor, closed his eyes and began to concentrate ... Gradually he could see the shape of a girl in front of him.

*****

The next evening, after playing Gershwin's *Rhapsody in Blue*, he heard a faint tap at the door. This was it. Hopefully it had worked. It was exactly 6 pm, as arranged. It must be his girl.

A young, stick-insect-thin girl stood outside, her dark hair hanging in straggly ringlets and her eyes large and conker-brown.

'Sorry if I disturbed you,' muttered Ellery. He had to pretend she might be an intruder to make her visit seem normal?

'Oh no. Quite the opposite. I wondered if I could come inside and listen. I do so love your playing. Gershwin, isn't it?'

'Yes. Do you play?'

She shook her head.

'I'm Ellery, a musician' he told her.

'I know,'she said, 'I'm Eliza, named by my mother after the famous Eliza Doolittle. George Bernard Shaw. You know him, of course.'

'Yes.'

Ellery had read the play and enjoyed it. So different from his usual choice of genre. The name Eliza was perfect for this girl he had dreamed up.

He pointed to the sofa, but she chose to sit on the floor, her wispy white dress billowing around her as she sat.

'I will continue playing?' he asked.

'Yes please.'

She smiled as he played, swaying to the rhythm. Occasionally she would get up and dance about the room as if she were alone. It was so good to watch. Ellery felt his heart and his clarinet sing.

That was the way it all started. Whenever Ellery played, whatever the time, whatever the day or night, he would conjure her up. He got used to her being there over the days he had left. But as the time for him to move came nearer, he wanted to be alone. His clarinet lay idle for a moment. He didn't need the girl there.

'I'm sorry, but I don't want you to come here anymore,' he said. 'I shall be leaving this place soon. I have to find somewhere new.'

Eliza stood, her mouth open but making no sound, and then she began to sob loudly. She rushed to the door, wrenched it open and hurtled down the stairs. Ellery knew it had been a brutal dismissal. How could he have been so cruel? He followed, trying to keep her in his sight as she ran ahead down the road. He could just make out her shape in the darkness. She had almost become a living girl. His mind had played a trick on him. He had lost control.

'Eliza. Eliza. Stop!' His voice was choking in the coldness. There was no reply, and then he saw her standing on the bridge over the river, a white butterfly, her arms outstretched as if she were about to dive into its depths.

'No! Please no! I love you, Eliza.' He knew in that instant he did. She was his perfect girl, an audience for his music, one who understood.

As Ellery almost reached the bridge, he saw her jump into space.

A white butterfly.

There was no sound, no splash, no ripples on the water. No body. Nothing. Absolute silence.

How could it have been otherwise? Her spirit had deserted him. Of course she had been in his imagination all along. He had invented her, as he always did when he felt the need for someone's company. So far it had always been someone different, simply a character, someone he could forget. Not this time.

His punishment was that he couldn't bring her back instantly. He would wait until he knew the time was right and he could summon her up once more. He would work it out. Ellery was determined.

'I shall bring you back, my Eliza,' he called into the wind. 'Soon.'

He walked slowly back along the bridge, unsure what to do about moving out and finding work. Unsure about everything.

As he reached the place he could not call home, he went in and gloomily climbed the stairs. He really wanted to go in the opposite direction. And then he heard music coming from his room. He recognised it as a favourite, Bartok's *The Miraculous Mandarin Suite.*

His clarinet was always there for him. His spirits lifted.

He would work it out.

ANNABEL'S ATTIC

JENNY BURRAGE

ANNABEL DELANEY SMILED, A SECRET SMILE, A satisfied smile, a smile of total happiness. She had lived all her forty years in the wooden three-story house on the mountainside in Arizona. After her father died, she and her ageing mother Evelyn had lived together.

Her brother Randy had made no attempt to share in the looking after of their mother.

'What do I want living on a goddamn mountain?' he'd said, 'You and Mom get along fine, sister dear.' After that he'd disappeared, no word now since last fall.

He'd abandoned her. Left her looking after her witch of a mother for whom nothing was ever good enough.

'Your supper's nearly ready, Mom,' she called upstairs as she stirred the corn chowder soup. Same meal every night. Had to be prompt otherwise the stick would pound on the floor, endlessly drumming in her ears and making her hands tremble so she often spilled the soup on the way upstairs. At least her mother never came downstairs anymore.

Evelyn's bedroom was on the second floor, but it was on the third floor that Annabel had followed her dream. Her mother had grudgingly let her turn it into a workshop. Silks, satins, brocade, cotton, velvet, rolls of every coloured material filled the attic where she created scarves and shawls and skirts and collages. This was her world.

She was well known in the area and had recently secured a contract with Macy's to add to her local ones. Annabel's Attic. People had heard the name now.

'Why couldn't you be a doctor like your father? 'Her mother despised her choice of work, but she'd never said anything like that to brother Randy, and he was a layabout. Evelyn expected to be looked after by her daughter. It was her duty.

'You're lucky to have somewhere to live and no rent to pay.'

Annabel's smile vanished as she heard the front door chime. She liked the peace and stillness of the mountains. She wanted to be left alone in her attic, Annabel's attic.

It was one of her neighbours, Richie. They were a small community, living among the cactuses in their wooden houses and shacks. Annabel didn't mix with them, but Richie was a frequent visitor, probably because he lived alone.

'Evening, Richie. I'm just making Mom's supper.' She'd hoped he would go away, but he stepped inside.

'Oh, that's just why I was calling on you, Annabel. I was only saying to Mrs Mendoza, we haven't seen Mrs Delaney about recently.'

'No. I'm afraid she's confined to her bed now, Richie.'

'Oh, that's a great shame.' He suddenly called up the stairs.

'Sorry you're not too good, Mrs Delaney.'

There was no reply.

'Her hearing's not too good, Richie. I'll just go up and tell her you're here and asking after her.'

She hurried up the stairs. It was lucky she had expected these enquiries by Richie.

'Mom, Richie's here. He's been worried about you.'

'I'm just fine.' The old lady's voice was reassuring.

'Oh, that's so good, Mrs. Delaney,' he shouted, and to Annabel, who had appeared again, he waved goodbye and left.

Annabel breathed again. She carried the chowder upstairs and placed it on the bedside table next to the old woman. Never a word of thank you. She stared at her mother.

'That Richie is a pest. I don't know what to do about him interfering in our lives.'

She smiled. The blood had congealed in red patterns all over the white body. It was lucky she had recorded her mother speaking on an audio voice recorder. Just the press of a button. Just three words.

She'd needed that recording as part of the careful plan.

'Eat your supper, Mom,' she said.

ARMS AND A MAN

JENNY BURRAGE

HAROLD HOPKINS COULD HARDLY BELIEVE IT. THE room, if you could call it that, was smaller than his toilet at home. The walls were stainless steel, and his naked body was reflected on all sides. There were holes around the walls which looked like small tunnels. The ceiling was low, with fiercely bright strip lighting. He had almost to bend his head when entering. The door closed automatically.

There was nowhere to sit so Harold stood there, surrounded by four huge images of his grossly exaggerated self.

'Bloody ridiculous,' he said to his reflections. 'Must be magnification. I'm not that big.'

It smelt of mothballs in there, not the usual disinfectant. He decided this seemed odd in a clinic claiming to improve body impairments by alternative methods.

There was a message beeping on the wall.

HAVE YOU SIGNED THE CONSENT FORM? IF NOT, PRESS THE EXIT BUTTON.

'Of course I bloody have!' (Harold had been given to swearing lately.) He shouted into the silence and his voice echoed back. It had become slow and drawling, sounding rather like a diver from a thousand fathoms.

'Of ... course ... I ... bloody ... have!'

Two larger holes like portholes on a ship appeared in opposite walls. These were at shoulder height. Harold peered through one of the holes, which looked dark and forbidding. A second message flashed red overhead.

INSERT ARMS ... NOW.

He shoved them through as though he was putting on a suit of armor. In a flash he could feel an iron grip clutching his skinny arms and pulling. He felt his arms stretch as if they were being wrenched out of their sockets.

'Bloody hell!' The pain seared through him.

*****

Harold wished he hadn't come. He wished he'd been able to forget about a stupid short-sighted old woman in the reality supermarket, who'd thought his arm was a gherkin and wanted to put it in her trolley. He wished he hadn't been wearing a green long-sleeved T-shirt at the time he was shopping. He wished his new partner Lizzie hadn't insisted on him doing something about his 'pathetically small arms', as she so unkindly put it.

'Go to the AI Osteo Clinic,' she told him. It's what everyone does now.'

'I'm seventy-nine,' he'd said to her. 'Middle-aged. Everything's getting shorter and thinner What do you expect in 2044?'

Of course Lizzie had won.

*****

The door suddenly slid open and there stood what he assumed was a woman who must be a doctor or nurse. It was the first human he had seen in the clinic. Or it could be a humanoid. You never knew these days. This place was mainly AI-run, according to the adverts. She handed the quivering Harry a fluffy white towel as he staggered out.

'How do you feel, Mr Hopkins?' she asked.

'Bloody awful,' he told her.

'But do look at your new arms, Mr Hopkins,' she simpered.

Harold looked. Two cream-coloured limbs hung from his body like long, long, plump sausages. He twiddled his fingers and stretched out his arms, like Worzel Gummidge.

He had done it. Lizzie was right. Harold Hopkins was a desirable man now, with a new part of his body.

'Bloody amazing,' he said.

She smiled. 'We can do your legs next if you like, or any other part of your body which needs lengthening.'

POTATO

KEITH MCCLELLAN

My name is Maris Piper; I'm a dainty little spud,
I'm very pale and smooth of skin,
When Cook cleans off the mud.
I am a royal potato,
King Edward is my name.
I have a red complexion
I'm often served with game.
My name is Désirée
And that's my nature too,
I'm a little red girl,
For chips or mash or stew,
I'll even keep my jacket on
With prawns and mayonnaise
I also make some good pommes frites
People love the little bits,
So many different ways.

LOCKED DOWN AND OUT

KEITH MCCLELLAN

Today is.. ... today is. What is today?
The days go by so slowly,
They also go so fast.
I never know what day it is,
Or how long this business will last.

I was going to sort out my study,
I had some sensible plans,
But that was many moons ago,
And still, it remains as in stands.

We go for a walk around the track,
But the cold bites into my face,
Or the rain drives into everything
And we can't wait to get back.

Oh, for the lovely summer days
When we sat outside with our beer
We listened to the bird song
And the blossom brought good cheer.

But ... on a sunshine day
We can walk down to the ford
Pass about twenty dog-walkers
And we will not be ignored.

It gives a chance to speak to friends,
And perhaps the end is in sight,
We've had our jabs, I've had two
So now there is a bit more to do.

VALENTINE'S DAY

KEITH MCCLELLAN

She loves me, she loves me not.
Dare I ask her? I think not.
And yet, and yet,
Do not forget,
All those years
That people spend in shedding tears
Of deep regret.

Does he love me? He doesn't show.
How am I supposed to know?
And yet, it's true, he seems to care,
Perhaps there really are signs there.
He takes me out, and there was that night,
I knew I shouldn't, it wasn't right.
But, that night, the spark was there.

'Hello darling, here's some flowers,
To mark this special day of ours.'
'What day is that then, mystery man?
Explain yourself, that's if you can.'
'Well, I have waited long enough
With all this lovely-dovey stuff,
So now I'll ask on bended knee,
If, my love, you'll marry me?'

"Yes, I will, I'll marry you.
And I promise I'll be true to you,
If you in turn are true to me,
Then no one happier could I be."

"I'll be true, so wear this ring.
You're my queen, and I, your king."

JEEZ WHAT A TEASE

KEITH MCCLELLAN

I lay on the grass
In the cool summer breeze
Making passionate love
To my gorgeous Louise,
When all of a sudden
From the small clump of trees,
Came a choking something
That caused me to sneeze.
This led my beloved suddenly to freeze.
'Get off me,' she said,
'I don't want your disease.'
I rolled away and
Rose to my knees,
And said to my darling,
'Forgive me, please, please.
Come with me to lunch,
I'll buy fish, chips and peas,
Or if that's too much
We'll have cakes and teas.'
Then I picked up her knickers
And said, 'Don't forget these.'

OUR VISIT TO NGORONGORO CRATER

(Memories From My Time As A Teacher In Kenya From 1968 to 1973)

KEITH MCCLELLAN

IN JULY 1971 WE DECIDED TO VISIT the Serengeti game park and the Ngorongoro Crater in Tanzania. We spent a day exploring the crater. It was full of wonderful wildlife, elephants, giraffes and lions. Next morning we packed up and left for Lake Manyara, but as we were driving downhill towards a bend, a large truck came towards us, cutting short the bend on our side of the road. I thought there was some space on the roadside on our left and pulled half off the road to allow the truck to pass. Our VW Beetle tilted and rolled slowly sideways through the tall elephant grass that had seemed to constitute the roadside verge. We watched in silent horror, the trees, the steep-sided crater and the sky turning slowly before our eyes as the car rolled over, bounced on its roof and hung momentarily upright before plunging nose-first through the treetops to thump into the stream coursing down the slope of the Ngorongoro Crater. Amazed to be alive and conscious, we twisted round to check the children. Lisa, at three and a half, was crying lustily, still in her car seat, which hung at a crazy angle. There was no sign of baby Lee.

'Are you O.K?' I asked Carol.

'I think so, but my foot's stuck. Can you get out?'

'I'll try.'

'It's all right, Lisa love, Daddy will get you out in a minute,' said Carol.

The car was wedged at an angle with the passenger side hard against a rock. My door handle was almost above me, but the hinge was lower down, so I tried to force the door upwards and sideways. Eventually I dragged myself out. Some Africans were clambering down towards us. They had seen us from their minibus, which was now parked at the bend where we had come face to face with the truck on our side of the road.

'Sorry, sorry, sorry,' they said.

One man leaned in and scooped the tearful Lisa out onto the dry grassy bank. Carol slid her feet out of her sandals, levered herself up and clambered out. Her foot was badly bruised but otherwise she was unhurt.

'OK, we go now, we'll send askari.'

'No, wait, there's a little boy in there.'

'No, no one there now.'

'Yes, a little boy, a baby.'

The African pulled the seat forward and began passing out pieces of camping gear, a potty and a nappy bucket. Eventually he pulled out a bemused Lee and held him aloft.

It was after 4 pm when the police arrived. Friendly and efficient, they carried all our belongings up to the road, leaving the empty car abandoned in the stream.

'Take what you need for the night. I'll lock the things in the store and keep the key myself. They'll be quite safe here,' said the police inspector, 'Then we will take you over to the Lodge. You can get cleaned up and have a meal.'

*****

'I'm sorry, we cannot serve you,' said a hard-faced man at reception.

'Why not? I've got the money.'

'You are not respectable in appearance. Our clients would object.'

'But we've just had a serious car accident. We'll be all right when we've cleaned up.'

'I'm sorry, sir.'

'Can't we just have a meal in the restaurant? My family are very hungry.'

'I'm sorry, sir.'

I turned away and walked towards the door, followed by my bedraggled family.

'Say, would you two care to join us for a hand of bridge this evening?' asked an elderly American.

'I'm sorry, we've been thrown out.'

'Oh my,' he exclaimed to our departing backs.

The police inspector took us round to the kitchen, where the cooks ushered us in and made us sandwiches. It was dark as he drove us down to the youth hostel and explained our plight. We were welcomed and shown some of the preparations for the Masai celebrations the next day. The warden opened a door, and a huge, skinned ox lay on its side oozing blood.

'For the roast,' said the warden.

Next morning we stood in the red murrum courtyard in the full heat of the sun. We were very hungry and felt trapped and frustrated, not knowing where our car was or how we were ever going to get to Lake Manyara.

'Is there any food we can buy?' I asked the warden.

'I'm sorry, tonight you can have some roast ox, they are setting up the spit now, see, over there,' he said, pointing across the yard.

'What about our car? Do you know where it is? How can we find out?'

'They will come.'

'Who? When?'

'Maybe today, maybe tomorrow, they will come when they are ready.'

He was clearly preoccupied with preparations for the coming festival and walked away to speak to some tribesmen gathering at the end of the compound.

*****

'Look daddy, look at that man,' said Lisa.

We saw a young warrior resplendent with his red ochre hair sculpted into a waved mound and bound behind his neck. His ear lobes, pierced in early childhood, now extended almost to his shoulders and held large, beaded ornaments. He wore a red blanket cloak and carried a pointed metal spear. He walked into the compound looking handsome and threatening until, seeing a friend he smiled broadly and went over to greet him. Others were arriving in dribs and drabs, unhurried, enjoying the day. As well as the warriors there were elders in their cloaks, women and unmarried girls with their broad collar-like necklaces of brightly coloured beads.

Enchanted, we wandered round asking permission to photograph. The warriors posed proudly, the unmarried girls giggled, and the elders strongly disapproved, although one or two succumbed for a cigarette or a shilling. A pick-up appeared in the courtyard, and after a word the warden directed the driver to us. 'We have your car. I'll take you.'

In the garage forecourt we were met by a burly Sikh in a turban and fawn overalls.

'Your car is working. Come and see.'

'How did you get it out?'

'We cut a road through the trees and towed it up to the main road. Then we drove it. It started first time. But it is dented in every panel, even the roof.'

'Can you do anything about the roof? We have a roof rack at the police station.'

'Wait, wait,' he beckoned to an African in overalls and spoke to him in Swahili. The African called other mechanics and four of them sat in the seats and bounced up and down, their heads hitting the roof in unison. The dent pinged up.

'Good as new, good as new,' smiled the Sikh, . 'Now we'll pull out the right wing and she is OK.'

One of the Africans crouched and pulled the front mudguard into approximate alignment.

'How much?' I asked.

'Fifteen shillings.'

'O.K. Thanks very much.'

We drove to the police station. We were now very hungry.

'We need to get our things.'

'I'm sorry, the inspector is at the other end of the district chasing cattle thieves, He'll be back later.'

'But we need our things now, we need food.'

'I'm sorry the inspector has the only key.'

'Have you got a screwdriver I could borrow?'

He returned with a screwdriver, and I began to unscrew the hasp on the door.

'Excuse me, sir,' he said.

'Yes?'

'In Tanzania it is not good to break into the police station.'

'But this store has all our things in, and we need them.'

'It is not good to break into the police station.'

'O.K, O.K. here's your screwdriver.'

We drove to the local duka and bought a tin of corned beef with its own key opener and a spoon. The children, taking it in turns, scooped ravenously at the corned beef. It was now late afternoon, and we drove back to the youth hostel where we were met by the police inspector.

'How are you, my friends? I have been looking for you. Now we can enjoy the celebrations.'

'Can we get our things please?'

'Later, my friends, later, there is no hurry. You will enjoy this evening celebration.'

The low -level drumming increased in pace and volume as the Masai began to dance. The warriors, arrogant and threatening, stood tall: their red ochre hair sculpted above their aquiline features; their red cloaks draped over their shoulders and their spears at the ready. As the drumming got louder, they began their dance, bouncing on the spot with ever higher jumps, competing with each other. In front of them the unmarried girls bounced and sang, naked from the waist up save for their broad multi-ringed necklaces, which bounced, out of time, on their breasts. The inspector had been right.

*****

We went on to Manyara Game Park, famous for the lions sleeping in trees. We drove round and came across a pride of lions all in trees near each other. It was an impressive, if somewhat frightening, sight.
That night we camped in the game park campsite in woodland similar to the lions' habitat. We thought it best to put Lee to sleep in the car in case scorpions or other creatures invaded the tent. During the night elephants approached. They inspected the site, held the car roof rack and rocked it vigorously. Lee did not wake up. Later, after a filling dinner at the park restaurant, I felt an urgent need for the toilet. I emerged from our tent and walked down to the toilet block, torch in hand. To my horror an elephant stood with its rear wedged against the toilet door. It was clearly impossible to access. Reluctantly I wandered deeper among the trees, relieved myself and covered the result with dead leaves.

THE STOLEN BEDS

(Memories From My Time As A Teacher In Kenya From 1968 to 1973)

KEITH MCCLELLAN

IT WAS QUARTER PAST EIGHT ON A THURSDAY morning when a tall young African appeared in secretary Alpoim's office. Assembly was over and I had just come up to the office in the hope that Paul, the office boy, had brought the mailbag up from the station, when Alpoim called me in.

'This is the deputy headmaster,' Alpoim said to his visitor impressively, 'Tell him what you have just told me.'

I looked at the man curiously. I had not seen him before. I judged him to be in his early twenties. He was simply but smartly dressed in a dark green short-sleeved nylon shirt and lightweight dark brown trousers. He wore sandals rather than the ubiquitous flip-flops. He was clean-shaven and well groomed, his hair cut short.

'Good morning, sir,' he said, extending his hand.

'Good morning,' I replied, shaking his hand firmly. 'What have you got to tell me?'

'Certain students are stealing beds from the school,' he said,' 'they are sending them to a certain village along the Busia Road. From there they are taken to another compound across the main road and carried away from there to many places.'

I looked at Alpoim in amazement.

'Are you sure about this?' I asked.

'Oh yes, sir,' he said. 'I have seen the beds in the village.'

'Have you reported this to the police?' I asked, knowing the answer before he replied.

'That is not possible, sir.'

'Why not?' I asked.

'These people can be dangerous,' he said.

'That's OK,' interjected Alpoim quickly, 'can you just write down the name of the village and of the other compound.'

The young man did so and took his leave, our thanks following him through the door. I sat down and looked at Alpoim.

'I'd better see the head,' I said.

Alpoim nodded and handed me the slip of paper the young man had written the details on.

Father van der Werf was still the head at that time. He was a tall, slim, handsome Dutchman in his fifties. He had short greying hair and wore the full-length white cassock of his order. I respected him greatly although he exasperated me at times.

'Ah, Keith, come in, come in!' he said as he answered my knock.

'But Father, it is rather urgent,' I said.

'I've no doubt,' he said, 'But come in and sit down and tell me about it calmly and we will deal with it all the better.'

I followed him through to his lounge and sat down as he pointed to a chair. He took out his pipe and tobacco pouch, sat down and began to fill his pipe. I knew better than to try to say anything before his pipe was being puffed to his satisfaction. I had seen and admired this technique for calming down hot heads too many times. At last, he invited me to explain my concerns.

'Well, Father, you know how some students have complained lately about beds disappearing?'

'They are always complaining about something,' he replied. 'I haven't seen any evidence for it.'

'Well, that's just the point, Father. I usually check the dormitories but there are always a few spare beds in there and Brother Hoos doesn't record the numbers in each dormitory, so I assumed, like you say, that it was just another thing the boys had picked on. But now I am not so sure. I have just been talking to a young man in Alpoim's office who says some students are stealing the beds,' I said, and continued to give him all the details.

'What do you want to do about this, Keith?' he asked when I had finished.

'The thing is, Father, when do they remove them? It would be very risky at night because the students are all in the dormitories and should be in their beds. During the day people in the staff room or the office overlook the gate, and absence from lessons would be checked. The only time I can think of when everyone is out of the way is during assembly. All the students and staff are round the flag and Alpoim and Paul haven't started work until towards the end. So, I thought, with your permission, I would miss assembly tomorrow and conceal myself in your garden overlooking the road and see what happens.'

'Good,' he said, 'Then if you see anything worth following up you can go down to the police station and get them to deal with it.'

Next morning at sunup, I pulled on a light sweater against the early morning chill and made my way up from the lower compound, where we lived, to the school compound. I came out of our small back garden and crossed the field behind diagonally; avoiding the cowpats and the cows as best I could and passed through the gate onto the school playing field. I skirted the top edge of the field and made my way to the garden area behind the head's house and the admin block. A pomegranate bush provided useful cover. It was about seven feet high, and its foliage was dense. I could see right down the track that led up from the dormitories and turned right at 90 degrees in front of me and then past the admin block where it joined the main drive out to the gate about 25 yards beyond.

Ten minutes later the assembly bell clanged to summon the whole community to raise the Kenyan flag, sing the national anthem and pray for school and country. I saw teachers and Fathers from the nearest houses make their way down. Father van der Werf followed, carrying his Bible and prayer book. I could see the top of the flagpole from my position behind the bush. The flag had just reached its position there when I became aware of movement on the track. To my amazement, I saw three students walking up the track with bed frames on their heads. They were Year Three students whom I knew quite well.

Instead of turning to the right with the track and going out of the main gate, they continued straight ahead across the garden, and I had to move silently round my bush to avoid being seen. They reached the hedge which bordered the main road and passed the bed frames over to some strong black arms raised to receive them. They exchanged a few words with the unseen helpers and strolled back towards the dormitories.

A moment later a bus roared up and stopped at the bus stop, sending up a choking cloud of red murrum dust. Soon the conductor was climbing up the ladder on the far side of the bus, taking the bed frames from an a still-unseen helper and placing them on the roof among the bicycles, hen coops and other bundles of various shapes and sizes. He descended and the bus roared off, sending up another cloud of red dust.

I hurried into the admin block before assembly finished and told Alpoim what I had seen. then I drove down to the police station to report the matter and ask them to look into it. The policeman noted the details carefully. I thanked him and was turning away when he said, 'If you want us to deal with this matter now you will have to take us in your car.'

'Why can't you take your Land Rover?' I asked, 'this village is off-road apparently, and I only have a VW Beetle.'

'We have an allowance of 44 gallons a month,' he said, 'and we used it up last week.'

'So how do you get about?' I asked.

'We walk,' he said.

I was so angry about the beds and the blatant theft that I agreed to take two policemen in my car. The man at the desk called into a back room, and two very burly policemen appeared. He briefed them in outline and then one of them took a key and a big ledger from under the desk and turned to a strongly reinforced cupboard on the wall behind him. As he opened it, I saw it was full of guns. He took a handgun out and turned to the ledger on the counter. I was aghast.

'What do you need that for?' I asked, trying to keep the fear out of my voice. 'These people can be dangerous,' he said. 'It's best to be safe. Do you want one?'

'No, thank you,' I said, backing away.

The two policemen squeezed into the back of my Beetle, and we drove off. The bigger of the two carried a very shiny knobkerrie made of a very dark hard wood, possibly ebony. The less burly one had the gun, and I had nothing. We drove along the main road towards Busia for two or three miles. It was a busy road with buses of many colours, lorries and the occasional car all sending up clouds of red dust which made it difficult at times to see the cyclists and pedestrians, both of whom were plentiful.

The policeman with the knobkerrie leaned across and indicated that I should turn off the road to the left. I found myself driving along a grassy track, hard and true beneath the grass thanks to the long dry season. After about half a mile the track passed through a narrow entrance in a thornbush hedge into a grassy compound with a semicircle of African huts. The main hut in the centre of the semicircle was rectangular and built of local brick with a corrugated iron roof. The rest were circular mud and thatch huts.

We stopped in the middle of the compound, and I let the policemen out. They told me to stay in the car for the moment. Then the bigger one leaned in the window and blew the car horn three times.

Africans began to appear from the various huts. The policeman leaned conspicuously on his knobkerrie and summoned them. They came slowly and reluctantly towards him, forming a rather pathetic group about halfway between him and the huts. He addressed them fiercely in Doluo and ordered them to bring out all their beds. Reluctantly they turned and went back to the huts. Soon beds and bedding were dragged out into the compound. The policeman indicated that I should identify any school property. This posed a difficulty because the school beds were not marked in any way. There was no record except for the original invoices, so I could not prove the beds belonged to the school. An elderly man had struggled to drag his bed and bedding out. His sheet was torn and grey and the springs stretched. I told him to put his things back. I selected about half a dozen newish looking beds and relied on the owners to protest if they were genuinely their own. No one did.

The policemen told the owners to bring out the mattresses and told everyone to search their huts for anything else belonging to St Mary's School. When I saw the mattresses, I felt more confident of my choices. They were in good condition and were clearly the same make as the school ones. Several piles of textbooks were also brought out. He then gave them a further lecture about receiving stolen goods, particularly from the school.

'What are we going to do with these?' I asked, pointing to the beds, bedding and books.

'Take them back to St Mary's School, of course,' he replied.

'Yes, but I mean, how?'

'In the car.'

'But the beds won't fit inside the car, and I don't have a roof rack.'

'We'll tie them on,' he said, and went off to commandeer some rope.

We put a mattress on the roof and lifted a bed on top of it. The roof sloped away on all sides, and it was as much as two of us could do to keep it in place. The larger policeman appeared with some thin rope and told me to wind down both windows in the back. He threaded the rope through and tightened it across the bed. I was not convinced, but he assured me it would work if we drove slowly. He realised we could only take one bed, so he called over some men and told them to take the other beds up to the chief's camp. This was on the main road about 200 yards from where we had turned off. We put all the bedding and books in various parts of the car, squeezed ourselves in somehow and drove very slowly out to the road and up to the chief's camp.

We could see the African men strung out across the fields carrying the remaining stolen beds. When they arrived, the beds were locked away, to be collected, and the men sent back to the village. At this point I wanted to get back quickly to the compound from which the beds were distributed. Word would pass very quickly, and the dealers would disappear into the bush before they could be arrested. The policemen, however, wanted to get the bed and other items back to school and arrange for the other beds to be collected from the chief's camp.

We drove slowly back to school with the policemen stretching their arms through the windows and clinging on to the bed to control its slipping and sliding.

Back at school, much to my exasperation, Father van der Werf welcomed the policemen into his lounge, offered them cups of tea, which they accepted with alacrity, and asked for a full account of the morning's activities.

'Father,' I said in exasperation, 'we will miss the chance to arrest the real culprits.'

'Don't worry, Keith,' he replied, 'you can't rush these things.'

I bit my tongue till it hurt.

Eventually we drove back to the compound, and I swung the Beetle into the dry, dusty yard. By now it was midday, and the light was at its most intense. There were three huts at triangular points of the yard. The larger policeman raised his knobkerrie, grasped it firmly and allocated huts to himself and his colleague, who immediately drew out his handgun and moved off towards the indicated hut.

'You can search that one,' he said, pointing to the third hut.

'Me?' I said in alarm, . 'But ...'

'Just be careful,' he said.

I watched them enter their chosen huts and moved reluctantly towards mine. I stood in the doorway and called in tentatively,

'Jambo.'

No reply. I stepped inside and found myself in complete blackness. I began to feel my way along a wall. Gradually my eyes adjusted, and I could see a source of light low down on the left. I remembered how round huts often had inner curved walls cutting off areas within them for storage or even sleeping. This proved to be the case, and rounding the end of this inner wall I saw the light came through some closed shutters. I threw them open and winced as the sunlight hit my eyes. Turning away, I saw there was a bed beyond the window. I lifted it out and carried it out to the door. It clearly resembled a school bed, but again had no markings. I re-entered the hut and searched the rest of it but found nothing more of interest except a few schoolbooks.

The policemen emerged from their investigations, and I indicated the bed.

'Anything?' the larger one asked.

'Nothing,' the other replied, 'they have gone running away.'

We drove back to school with a bed on the roof again, and after another cup of tea I took the policemen back to their station.

A TENDENCY TO STICK IN WET WEATHER

M.S. CLARY

WHEN TOBY WAS FIFTEEN, HE ASKED IF he could paint his room brown. When he'd finished, frankly the walls resembled the colour of dung. Not wanting to discourage, I merely told him to make sure he cleaned his brushes properly.

That's probably the main difference between Helena and me. She never holds back from expressing her opinions. When she first saw my staircase, she said it would have to go. But I liked its airy, open-tread effect, and the banister rail was handy for drying the washing. Another thing was the front door. I had become accustomed to its tendency to stick in wet weather. It pleased me hearing its perky slam as I left in the morning, and I welcomed the secure thud as it closed behind me at night. But to Helena, these objects were architecturally incorrect. When I ventured that this was a matter of taste and convention, she dismissed the suggestion, saying that post-modern Scandinavian and a faux Georgian front door just didn't work in a nineteenth-century worker's cottage. She'd written a paper on it. It was not a personal issue; it was simply wrong and should be changed. She even offered her brother-in-law's carpentry skills for the transformation.

I valued her friendship in many ways. When Toby went into depression in his first term at Uni, she came over at once and recommended a therapist. A Mr. Borodino. Toby came home for Christmas but spent most of his time in his room. (I'd redecorated it by then, off-white with an eau de nil border, and some nice pictures of dolphins.) But despite his sessions with Mr Borodino, I became very worried when Toby announced he wasn't going back for the start of the new term.

Helena had the answer. She believed the furniture was interfering with our creative energy. She could feel a particularly hostile element coming from one piece (I believe it was the sideboard) and she knew just the person to advise.

One weekend in January, Sasha came. We heaved everything out onto the front lawn and swept the empty rooms with a sage-brush while chanting. Actually, the supermarket had run out of sage, so we had to use parsley instead. Sasha wanted to go into Toby's room, but I persuaded her otherwise. Just as well, because I found out later, he'd started painting his walls again that day. It began to rain before we finished, so a lot of the cushions got wet, and the lacquer on one chair started to bubble up. Sasha didn't think it would matter, as she could feel positive energy starting to flow through the room again. She lit a lot of candles and put everything back differently. It looked alright, but I found I could only get into the kitchen by going out of the front door and through the garden, and the smell of parsley lingered, upsetting the cat.

Mr Borodino telephoned one morning to speak to Toby. I called up to him, but he said he was asleep (he seldom left his room) so I went back to the phone and Mr Borodino and I had quite a long chat. I told him I had enjoyed talking to him and he asked me if I'd like to make an appointment to see him in his downtown office. He said he wouldn't charge me the full rate, as Toby was already a client. As an afterthought, he asked me if I'd seen Helena lately. I hadn't realised she was his cousin.

That night, Toby came downstairs saying he felt hungry. Instead of going straight back upstairs with a plate, he lingered while I scrambled some eggs. It was the first time we had sat down together at the table in a long time. He said he quite liked the new arrangement of the furniture, apart from the obvious difficulty of accessing the kitchen, especially on a frosty day, so he helped me move things around a bit, until we realised it was more or less back to where it was before.

He told me he'd caught a glimpse of Sasha in the garden dancing round the sideboard and surprised me by saying he wished she would come back and readjust his energy flow. I got straight onto Helena the following morning.

Mr Borodino had a very smart office in a new block down by the railway station. He offered me a cup of coffee, which he made himself in a rather impressive machine, then he lay down on the couch. I complimented him on the attractiveness of his surroundings, but he told me the rent was very high, and he was worried he may not be able to keep up the payments due to unsound investments. Worse than this, he told me, he was in despair because his wife had left him for another woman and was writing a novel about it. He was so easy to talk to. In fact, I found I had to say very little. After fifty minutes, he got up from the couch and suggested another session next week.

Sasha came back on her own to purify Toby's room. They were closeted up there for several hours. I think they must have skipped the bit with the sage-brushes, although they did ask me for a bottle opener. Later, towards evening, the house became filled with the sweet scent of vanilla candles, and I heard them both singing softly along to one of Toby's favourite CDs.

Mr Borodino and I meet regularly now, and he is gradually getting over his difficulties, but I don't see so much of Helena. Not since she took a course on wedding planning. Toby and Sasha were her first clients, and now she helps them out in their design consultancy. It has become so successful they have started mixing their own colours and selling them on the internet. Toby tells me the most popular shade this season is Rustic Brown.

DO YOU KNOW ABOUT RAKU?

M.S. CLARY

'MOVING HERE WASN'T JUST MY IDEA, YOU KNOW.'

She's thrown a pile of books roughly down onto the seagrass mat. Those mats were a hundred and ninety quid each, as I recall. We bought two. Laughed a lot like a couple of kids that day. Must have been celebrating buying the house, or a rise, something like that. Had lunch at the Fox, probably drank too much and no doubt she ate tuna.

'Hey, careful what you're doing with those books!' I say.

'Yeah, like one day you might actually pick one up and read it.'

She always knows what wounds me most. Though it's true, they were bought in bulk, without much thought of content, to fill up the wall of bookshelves that came ready-fitted in the barn conversion. It was those shelves that sold it to us. Well, mainly me. I thought of the dinners we would give, how the guys would drift in here to smoke their cigars, while the women swapped recipes. Not that Shelley ever let anybody smoke inside the house. She's not keen on cookery either.

'You know, I reckon we could sell some of this stuff.' Now she's picked up a hand-thrown pot. The potter had told us he was using some kind of ancient technique. 'Do you know about raku?' he'd asked. It hadn't made sense to either of us, but it sounded good the way he told it. An investment, we thought. I hadn't hesitated to hand over three hundred notes. In those days, and not so long ago, I always had cash in my back pocket for an impulsive purchase like that. Didn't think twice about it. Looking at the pot now, with its nacreous interior and ashy streaks, I'm not even sure I like it.

'If you're looking for something to sell, sweetheart, just look inside your wardrobe. There must be at least a couple of hundred handbags.'

There's no response. I glance over – perhaps she didn't hear me. I think she's looking a little fatigued. Her hair is pulled back with a thin orange band and she's wearing a pair of old running shorts. I glance down and reckon I'm not looking that great either.

Outside the big windows the sun is beating down. I love that view across the countryside. I hear the sound of Frank's tractor starting up in the field across the way. Before long, he'll be sitting up there wondering how long it will take before he can finish and go for a beer. Once upon a time I'd have gone out to join him. We'd have a man-to-man about life and lawnmowers. Not sure I'd know what to say to him today.

'Anyway, while we're on the subject of wardrobes, what about those cashmere sweaters you bought in three different colours because you couldn't decide between navy blue and navy blue?'

She's got me there. I seem to recall we had one of our first little contretemps that day. We were in town just before the banks went bust. Saw an exhibition, did a little shopping. It's true I didn't need any more sweaters. I just liked the feel of the store. It was the way they piled the old leather suitcases around, just so. Something about the framed cigarette cards of old sportsmen on the walls and the old-fashioned games like marbles on the counter. It was class. You knew you couldn't go wrong buying a couple of sweaters in a place like that.

'What about if we give ourselves a break from all this.' I say. 'Fix ourselves something cold to drink and sit out in the shade for a while.'

She doesn't even look up. 'You've got to be joking. There's far too much to do in here.'

She carries on clearing the books and knick-knacks. She's taken down the photographs, and the shelves are looking bare. Now she's holding up a painting, looking at it this way and that, like it's some old master. It's a watercolour of Bliss Mill we bought one afternoon in a consignment shop soon after we moved in. It's not by anybody you'd know and it's a bit old-fashioned if you want the truth, but it appealed to both of us at the time.

'I suppose you'd like to sell that too,' I say. I remember we couldn't agree on the best place to hang it. She won, of course. Well, she's good at that sort of thing. Still, it surprises me when she says, 'No, I'd like to hold on to this one.'

We've nearly finished in this room. We'll be moving out in a few days, moving on, as they say now. It's for the best. Shelley's going to her sister's place for a while, but she says it's only temporary. I'm not quite fixed up yet. I cross the room and pick up a couple of books from the floor. Dan Brown sits next to Dickens. She's right. I've read neither.

'Well, I need a break,' I say. 'I'm going to send out a few more CVs.'

I turn on the computer and sit staring at an empty screen for a while, before opening up the job sites. I try to put in a few hours each day. It occurs to me that I can't hear Frank's tractor anymore, so I reckon he's finished for the day. If I opened the window now, I'd be able to fill my lungs with the sweetest smell of summer grass, just cut. I get this mad idea, that it's Frank and the sound of his tractor we're going to miss the most.

I USED TO LIVE HERE ONCE

M.S. CLARY

'THAT WOMAN WAS HERE AGAIN TODAY.'

'Woman?'

'That one you thought came to collect for Donkeys?'

Raymond thought his wife wasn't looking her best. Looked like she could do with a bit of chicken. 'How about an eat-all-you-want buffet for ten pounds tomorrow night was on the tip of his tongue.

'I hope you didn't give her anything.'

Sandra was peeling an onion. 'She wasn't collecting for donkeys.'

'What was it then, llamas?'

'She says she was born in this house.'

'So?' He started for the door, assuming the conversation had ended. The smell of frying onions began to fill the kitchen.

'I told her to come back in the morning and she could have a look around.'

Raymond paused. 'I don't like the idea of a stranger looking round our house,' he said.

'So, you'll need to take those engine parts out of the spare bedroom.'

'Where am I supposed to put them?' he grumbled.

'This won't be ready for half an hour, so you've plenty of time.'

'Why does she need to see the spare room anyway?'

'That's where she was conceived,' she replied, starting on the cabbage.

*****

Saturday morning, they woke to a sky heavy with rain. Sandra put out the second-best mugs and a packet of hobnobs. At precisely eleven o'clock, the bell rang. On the doorstep stood a stout middle- aged woman in a raincoat holding a bunch of flowers.

'I'm Rosalind,' said the woman. 'These are for you.'

'Chrysanthemums,' said Sandra, noting drooping petals already turning brown. 'How thoughtful.'

'It's all I could find.'

'Lovely,' Sandra said, juggling the flowers. 'Do come in. I'll put these in water ...'

The woman ignored her outstretched hand and walked past her down the hall to the kitchen. She clearly knew her way around.

'I expect it's changed a lot since you lived here,' said Sandra, searching for a vase. Why is it you can never find the right vase. 'My husband Raymond built the extension himself.'

'Vandals,' muttered Rosalind. Sandra thought she must have misheard.

The woman turned and swept into the lounge. Sandra, unable to find the right container, left the flowers on the draining board and followed. 'We knocked these two rooms together,' she explained 'to give us more space. Was this where you did your homework?'

'Wicked,' muttered Rosalind.

'I'll call my husband,' said Sandra, confused. 'He's in the shed – these men and their sheds. ...'

Ray entered the room, a whiff of engine oil clinging to his denims. He was not happy. It had poured overnight, and the shed roof leaked.

Sandra felt uneasy. She hoped Rosalind might say something pleasant to Ray about the extension that had taken him two years to finish, but she was staring out of the French window.

'What's happened to the sycamore?'

'There was no sycamore when we moved in,' replied Sandra. 'We put in the decking and the acer,' she offered.

'Vandals,' the woman muttered again.

This time Sandra knew she'd heard correctly.

'Would you like to see upstairs now?' she asked.

The woman stared past her. 'I don't think so.'

All that effort to rearrange the spare room and she wasn't even interested. Ray had been right all along. This was a big mistake.

'We used to have bookcases in here,' said the woman. 'Daddy was an intellectual.'

'That's a shame,' said Sandra. What else could she say?

'Daddy was a very special man. Of course, so was Mummy.'

Sandra wondered if that's how her children would have described her and Ray, if they'd been blessed. Perhaps not the intellectual bit.

'Where's the standard lamp?' Rosalind continued.

The woman's lost it, thought Sandra. We should get rid of her quickly. She glanced to Ray for support, but he had already gone back outside. The rain continued to fall. Rosalind strode back to the hall. 'I've seen enough,' she said, walking to the front door, opening it and slamming it shut behind her.

Not even a thank you, thought Sandra, seriously ruffled. Ray found her in the kitchen, her head bent over *World of Interiors*, nibbling a biscuit.

'Well, that went well,' he observed.

'Don't start.'

'Who did she think she is?' asked Ray. 'Acting as if she still lived here. What did she think of the spare room?'

'We never got that far. She acted so strange.'

'There's rainfall all over the bike.'

'You need to fix that shed roof. Have a hobnob.' She picked up the chrysanthemums and tossed them into the bin. The lid snapped shut.

*****

Sandra had set aside Sunday morning to clear the hall and study some colour charts. They were freshening up, as she liked to call it.

'I favour the grey,' she said.

He eyed her as she bent over in her baggy dungarees and wondered if he could suggest going back to bed for an hour.

'But perhaps Ghostly Whispers is a bit too pale?'

Ray was happy to leave such decisions to his wife. They had agreed he would spend a half hour testing his bargain recycled tyres while she cleared out the hall cupboard. Outside, the wind was gusting falling leaves down the street and into the gutters. She was deliberating the fate of a pair of Ray's old trainers when the doorbell rang. A young man stood on the doorstep.

'I'm sorry, I have no need of more dusters.'

He held out his hand. 'I'm Ralph, Ralph Harris.'

She took in his shiny brown shoes and thought the name sounded familiar.

'I think you met my mother. You kindly let her look round your house.'

Sandra hoped he didn't want to look round too. 'I'm a bit busy at the minute,' she said.

'I'm sorry to trouble you, but my mother left her bag behind.'

Sandra frowned. 'No, I don't think so. I've found nothing.'

He was glancing past her as she spoke, as if expecting to see his mother's bag among the old magazines and broken umbrellas.

'She had it with her when you went upstairs.'

'We never went upstairs,' said Sandra.

Sandra didn't like the way the conversation was going and was relieved to hear the sound of Ray's bike blasting down the street. 'My husband's here now,' she said.

'Ray, this is Rosalind's son. Rosalind,' she said with emphasis, 'who came here yesterday.' Ray, sensing trouble, removed his helmet.

'Rosalind says she left her bag behind. Ralph's come to collect it.'

'Well give it to him, then.'

'The point is, the bag's not here, she didn't go upstairs.'

'No. She never went upstairs.'

'See?' Said Sandra triumphantly. 'My husband agrees. She must have left it somewhere else.'

There was a short silence and for a moment she thought Ralph was going to argue.

'Sorry to bother you then,' he said turning.

'Tell her to look in the last place she saw it,' Sandra called out helpfully as he walked away down the path.

'Well, the cheek of those two,' said Ray. 'You didn't find her bag, did you?'

'Of course not! The whole thing has been ridiculous from start to finish. I wish I'd never asked her in.'

'Those new tyres are no good,' said Ray. 'I'll have to get back to Eddie. What time's lunch?'

'I wasn't planning on lunch,' she replied.

She looked round, trying to remember where Rosalind had stood. Some of her hurtful words came back, but nothing looked out of place. Satisfied and about to leave the room, she glanced behind the sofa and saw a grey cloth shopping bag bearing the logo Go With Flo.

'All I can say is, Ray, it wasn't here yesterday.'

Ray ran to the front door and looked down the empty street. The strengthening wind sent a clutch of leaves into the hall. He came back shaking his head.

'No sign of him. What are you doing?'

Sandra was looking in the bag. 'There might be some identification,' she said.

They saw a large crumpled brown envelope held loosely together with parcel tape and an elastic band. As Sandra pulled it out, a large number of fifty-pound notes fell onto the carpet. Ray knelt and swiftly tried to calculate but stopped at nine hundred. Both sensed the heady, unfamiliar thrill of finding themselves in proximity to a large sum of money.

'There's a lot here,' he said faintly.

'We'll have to go to the police,' said Sandra

Ray was having difficulty articulating his thoughts.

'People don't usually carry that sort of amount around with them,' said Sandra.

'Unless they've robbed a bank. Suppose it's not above board. And why did she send that man to pick it up?'

'That's for the police to decide.'

Together, they carried on counting, putting the money into separate piles of five hundreds. It soon spread across the floor. When they'd finished, they counted again and agreed the sum came to just over nine thousand pounds. The notes had begun to topple and merge, so they stuffed them back into the bag, not bothering with the envelope. It took longer to replace them than it had to tip them out. Exhausted by the effort, they sat back on the sofa, eyes drawn, as if hypnotised, to the bag, which seemed to have doubled in size.

'Do you think it's legal?' asked Sandra.

'Probably not. Let's not be hasty,' said Ray. 'She might come back. We don't need to get involved in something ... you know ...'

Sandra nodded. Cradling the bag as though it were a newborn, she carried it upstairs, pushed it to the back of her wardrobe and covered it with a skirt. 'In case somebody breaks in overnight,' was her silent reply to Ray's unspoken question.

*****

Ray slept well, despite the roar of Storm Brenda battering the trees against the windows. Sandra woke several times in the night. Once she fancied she heard the stairs creak. Later she saw Rosalind climbing into the wardrobe. She knew she was dreaming but was glad of Ray's comforting bulk beside her.

Next morning they woke to the persistent tip-tap of dripping water coming from the spare bedroom. They placed a couple of buckets and a saucepan under the leak. A brown stain was already forming on the ceiling.

*****

Rob the roofer was up on the roof for at least ten minutes. 'Storm damage,' he confirmed. Several tiles cracked and a few dislodged. It would cost around fifteen hundred to fix. He had a lot on but would prioritise for a mate. What's more, he could start immediately. He added casually that for cash, he needn't charge VAT, and he'd like an advance to cover materials.

Ray and Sandra looked at each other. 'This is an emergency,' they said. Ray went to the wardrobe, opened the cloth bag and withdrew nine hundred pounds. For an extra couple of hundred, Rob would make good the damaged ceiling and help them lift the ruined carpet. His brother Bob could get them a lovely wool tufted at a special price.

A few weeks later, the work complete, they stood in the doorway admiring the finished effect. 'I think this room needs something, Ray.'

'It's just been painted, Sandra.'

'These mattresses must be ten years old.'

Only that morning, by chance, a flyer had come through the door advertising an Opportunity at Wiggins, their local Department Store. They decided to treat themselves to a spot of lunch and a quick look in the furniture department. Once or twice, over lunch, their eyes met, aware what the other was thinking. Sandra voiced it first.

'What are we doing, Ray?'

'Having a nice lunch. How's your chicken?'

'You know what I mean.'

'All that cash lying around just encourages burglars.'

'What if they go to the police?'

'We'd have heard by now. Why didn't they come back? If anything's ever said, we'll pay it back. Or say we never found nothing.'

Sandra went cold as she felt a shadowy presence at her left shoulder, but it was only the waiter asking if everything was alright. They ordered another bottle of Prosecco.

'Drink up,' said Ray. 'Wiggins closes at five.'

*****

Christmas could be difficult for Ray and Sandra, with no children to visit or grandchildren to entertain. Sometimes they went to friends, but this year the friends were away.

'Can't we go away somewhere?' asked Sandra. 'What about a cruise?'

Ray pondered. He'd always been wary of water.

'We could go to the Med. See the Canaries.' She showed him the brochure that had come that morning.

'The ship leaves Southampton on the 23rd. It's been reduced to nine-fifty for the two of us'

Hmm.'

'Well, if you're not interested.'

'Don't be hasty.'

Sandra knew what Ray was thinking as he disappeared upstairs. He was in charge of Operation Wardrobe, as they called it.

'There's exactly seven thousand left,' he said, coming back into the room.

That settles it, thought Sandra, already online checking out details. The discussion had taken less than three minutes. The girl in the travel agency looked surprised when they offered payment in cash. They said they'd been saving up and had recently had a bit of luck on the horses. Their explanation was accepted without further comment. It's like having a secret bank account, thought Sandra. This is what life must be like for the rich. She recognised the girl slightly from Zumba.

From time to time, Sandra thought back to Ralph and the morning he had turned up at their door. But not often. As time went by, she found it easier to forget about him altogether. Though once, stopping to look at a particularly desirable pair of boots in a shop window she caught him smiling back at her in the reflection. It felt like a sign of approval.

He turned up unexpectedly in her favourite soap too, wearing his shiny shoes, so she stopped watching. She didn't tell Ray about these visitations.

They were pleasantly surprised to discover how many tradespeople and establishments welcomed cash payment. With a little judicious juggling, they were soon able to pay off their credit cards and no longer went overdrawn at the end of the month. Sandra could buy herself some little treats. They redecorated the kitchen. Ray traded his bike and considered buying a car.

Sandra began to tell herself that Rosalind had deliberately left the money for them to find. Maybe she was dying and wanted the house returned to how she remembered it. The details were vague and didn't quite explain Ralph's turning up. Perhaps he was some kind of con man. And why had they never come back to claim the money? None of it could be explained. It felt like an Act of God. Though she wasn't religious, she suggested trying a Service one Sunday, but Ray poo-pooed the idea.

They hadn't kept all the money to themselves. There was the monthly donation to the Donkey Sanctuary. Sandra hadn't hesitated to buy a set of tea-towels and a duster she didn't need off the youth on a scheme, and she'd given generously to the Salvation Army before Christmas. The plaintive trumpet solo always brought a lump to her throat.

*****

Sandra bought an evening dress for the cruise and some leather-soled sandals for dancing. Ray bought a suit. He'd never had a need to dress up so fancy before. Sandra felt proud as they strolled the decks in their new casual designer wear, exploring the ports and enjoying a champagne cocktail before dinner. It had been a wonderful holiday, they agreed as they clinked glasses on New Year's Eve with their new friends Sally and Pete from Kent. They promised to keep in touch when they returned to dry land.

*****

One day in early spring, Sally invited them down for a weekend. Ray looked forward to trying out the new second-hand BMW on the motorway.

After lunch in Pete and Sally's favourite restaurant, they strolled along the front. They sat for a while, looking out to sea, waiting for the Iron Man to gradually reappear as the tide went out. Sandra took deep breaths of the salty air, shielding her eyes from the glare, gazing towards the distant horizon. I don't think she will find me here, she thought, having recently spotted Rosalind in the vegetable aisle of the supermarket.

'This is heaven, Ray. We could live here.'

Perhaps we could do with a change, thought Ray.

Walking back along Beach Avenue they passed a neat bungalow with a For Sale board outside. Sally and Pete knew the agent slightly and were encouraging.

It seemed the owners wanted a quick move and they could view it the following morning.

'Oh Ray, this is perfect,' cried Sandra looking through the open window. 'Come and listen. I can hear the sea!'

They put their house on the market as soon as they got back. The next two months passed in a flurry of offers, counteroffers, surveys and solicitors. While clearing out the wardrobe, Sandra came across an empty grey cloth bag. She held it out to Ray who, without comment, threw it into a plastic bag with the other rubbish. In late summer they were able to move into the bungalow.

'Don't you think it was meant to be, Ray?' said Sandra, taking a breather before opening another box.

Ray, not wanting to tempt fate, just nodded.

The previous day he'd been tailed by a middle-aged woman who seemed to shadow his every step of the way home. He'd glanced round and quickened his pace as he reached Beach Avenue but she was still behind him, closing the gap. His heart had thumped so hard he thought it would leap out of his chest. 'Settling in?' called the woman cheerily as she passed him and waved before crossing the road. It had only been a friendly neighbour, but Ray didn't like the nervous twist in his stomach that stayed with him for most of the evening.

One afternoon in late autumn Pete and Sally informed them they were moving away to live near their daughter. They had a last farewell drink together; said their goodbyes and told each other they would be sure to keep in touch. We're going to miss them, they thought.

'Don't worry,' said Ray. 'We'll make new friends.'

Sandra pulled her jacket closer. The tide was high, and a cool breeze had picked up. Oily dark waves splashed heavily against the sea wall.

'No sign of the Iron Man today,' she said.

'He'll be back tomorrow,' replied Ray.

They bought fish and chips and made their way home. It was already dark. They turned up the heating and were settling in for the evening when there was a knock at the door.

'I'll get it,' said Ray.

At first, he saw nobody. A full glittery moon cast its light across the street.

'There's nobody here,' he called, going to shut the door.

Two men stepped out from the shadows

'Who is it, Ray?' called Sandra.

One man took a step towards him. The other leaned lazily against the porch studying his nails. Ray shivered in the chill night air. He could hear the steady rumble of the shifting tide nearby, but it might have been traffic on the motorway.

'I've been expecting you,' he said. 'For a while now.'

He fancied he heard the sound of faint laughter and wasn't sure where it was coming from. It might have been his own. The moon had vanished behind the clouds. He wondered when he would see it again.

'Have you come to look around?'

'Very generous,' said one, as both men stepped forward.

'We used to live here once.'

WHAT WOULD TRISHA DO?

M.S. CLARY

THE LAST TIME I WALKED DOWN ELSINOR AVENUE, I saw that Number 34 was up for sale.

The garden looked neglected. Dead leaves lay un-swept in the porch.

It's blowing from the west today. No matter how hard I try to spear these bits of litter, they whoosh off, like they're having a laugh. Sweet wrappings, old envelopes, you wouldn't believe. Shan't bother with that one now, it's blown over the fence. Just hope the Boss Man didn't see.

The first time it happened was definitely an accident. I'd had a recurrence of my bad back, that low-down pain that catches you when you bend. Dr Jones had put me on antidepressants. I told him I wasn't depressed, but he insisted. My load had got unbearably heavy with all the junk mail. Most of it seemed to be catalogues.

On my way back to the depot one morning, I noticed there was a bunch of letters still stuck at the bottom of the bag. It was too late to deliver them, so I took the bag home and put it under the stairs. I definitely intended to deliver them the following day.

A week later, I looked in the cupboard, and there they were. I came over a bit shaky, because in my fifteen years with the Post Office, I'd never failed my customers. I decided to take matters into my own hands and deliver only the important stuff. Birthday cards, credit cards, that sort of thing. The rest I stuck in a bin liner and shoved under the bed.

'How's it going, Jack?'

'Not too bad, Mr Howard.'

'I'd like to get this area finished by lunchtime, if possible.'

'No problem, Mr Howard.'

It should be time for a break soon. I try to do my best for Mr Howard. His job's not an easy one and he's been quite sympathetic about my back. Not like the old devil back at the depot. I swear he put me on a new round on purpose. An estate with lots of dead ends I couldn't drive the van into. I was having to carry everything on foot. It was then I really noticed the weight of the catalogues. Despite the antidepressants, I was getting depressed.

One morning, I decided to pop home for a cup of tea. Put my feet up, watch *Trisha*. She's good at solving problems. I did intend finishing the round later, but dozed off, and when I came to, it was time to get back to the depot to clock off. I was in a right dilemma. I looked at the bag and wondered what Trisha would have done. Me, I solved the problem by putting it with the first lot, under the bed. The strange thing was nobody seemed to notice. I thought there would be a lot of angry people ringing in, but nothing happened. I realised my customers weren't worried by the lack of post but, like me, felt released from a burden.

I had noticed there was a woman in Elsinor Avenue – Number 34 (you'll have guessed) – who was often in the garden waving her kids off to school. She was friendly, always smiling. I didn't care for the husband, and he never glanced twice as he drove away in his old Vauxhall.

One day, I realised I hadn't seen the car or the husband for quite a while. Something had happened. I started looking out for a letter from him and at last one came, with a Derbyshire postmark. Mr Smith had written to say he wasn't coming back, that he'd met somebody else. Some husband, eh? How could I let her see that. I decided to write to her myself.

Dear Evaline,

I am looking for work and will send for you and the children soon. I miss you. Love Tom x.

As an afterthought, I enclosed a ten-pound note. Then drove into town and posted it.

'How many more hours have you got with us, Jack?'

'About two hundred and forty, Mr Howard.'

'Better get going then, slowing down won't make them go faster.'

'Right you are, Mr Howard.'

I kept looking out for more letters from Mr Smith, but none came. I strolled past the house occasionally to see whether the Vauxhall had reappeared. I just couldn't forget that poor lady, waiting for another letter. I decided it was time to write again.

Dear Evaline,

How I miss your warm kisses. I'm longing to see you and the children. I am applying for lots of jobs, and we will all be together again soon. Love Tom x

(P.S. I'm looking for a new car.)

My back wasn't getting any better. Some days I hardly had the energy to deliver anything. Morning breaks with *Trisha* became a habit, and the pile under the bed got so big I had to start putting sacks in the bath. Eventually, I took a pile over to the tip. It was a relief to see it go.

One weekend, I was walking past Number 34 and saw Evaline in the garden. I waved and said hello. I told her not to worry, that Mr Smith would be home soon. But she looked away and hurried indoors. I rang the bell, but she didn't answer. It was after that visit, I learned she had called the police.

They found 100 sackfuls of undelivered mail. Even to me, that came as a shock. Because of my previous good record and health, I was sentenced to 400 hours of Service to the Community. That's how I come to be spending days on the roadside picking up bits of paper. You wouldn't believe what gets thrown away.

Sometimes, I dream of Evaline. She is smiling the sweet smile she once gave to me, and the children are singing some jingle off the telly. A soft breeze lifts her hair as we join hands and walk towards the park.

SOMETHING CRAZY?

NEIL HANCOX

'WHAT'S THAT SPACE FOR ON THE MANTLEPIECE?' MY WIFE asked.

I emerged from behind the paper. 'Oh that. It's for my Nobel Prize medal. You get to shake hands with the King of Sweden, a good dinner and a lot of money, as well as a medal.'

'The money would be useful,' my wife, forever practical, observed.

'I've been to several writing classes, had stories in five or more anthologies, published a book of my own short stories and won a couple of competitions. Bob Dylan won the prize for his songs.' I added as reinforcement.

'He is famous,' she replied, 'And that does help. Must be off, meeting friends for lunch.'

I nodded. The doorbell rang. At least I had remembered to put in new batteries.

'Hello.' There were three females standing there, looking rather woebegone. Two quite young, one of whom had a lamb in tow, and an older woman. She was dressed in long robes and wearing a crown.

'We are three characters in search of an author,' they said in one voice.

'You want Pirandello, he lives at Number 27, though you are three short of the required six.'

'We've been there, he's not in.'

'Touché. You can't stand around on the doorstep, come in.'

They trouped into the lounge, sat down and introduced themselves, Mary One and Two, and one queen.

'I'm Steve,' I said. 'Would you like coffee?'

'Please. One decaf latte.'

'A cappuccino.'

'And an Americano with cold milk,' various voices requested.

'I hope the lamb is well behaved,' I said. A head nodded in reply.

'Will there be any croissants?' two voices enquired.

'I'll see what I can rustle up.'

Drinks appeared, plus croissants, jam, butter and cakes. One young Mary, the contrary one, was gazing at our garden. 'It looks a bit of a mess,' she said. 'I could put it right for you and add some ornaments – silver bells and cockle shells are a favourite.'

The older woman had removed her crown. 'Not real gold or jewels,' she said. 'Those are kept in the vaults in Holyrood Palace, if my worthless husband hasn't already pawned them.'

The front door opened again. My wife popped her head around the lounge door. 'Hello,' she said, did another take and added, 'Hello, you three. Friends of yours?' she looked at me.

I explained and disappeared behind my paper, the safest place.

Over the next few days my wife organised things – new clothes, jobs, a place to stay. The young one with the lamb started work at the local vets and bonded straight away with hedgehogs, and the contrary gardener, well, gardened. She's good at mowing lawns and around here most folk are too lazy to do the job themselves. It's all cash in hand.

'We could call them the Three Hail Marys,' I joked with my wife. She was not amused as the Irish Catholic genes kicked in. Behind the paper again.

Only the queen, who, as you will have guessed, was Mary Queen of Scots, or MQS for short, stayed on with us. She readily took to jeans and a top from the charity shop and put the ersatz crown away.

A week later, as I was sitting at my PC wondering what to write, MQS appeared at my shoulder. 'You are an author,' she said.

I couldn't disagree.

'So why not write a series on kings, queens, and royalty? I could advise.'

That was it. *The Game of Thrones*, no that's been done, *The Crown*, ditto. *Half a Crown*, that would be a comedy, and I wanted to do proper drama. I don't think the Nobel committee goes in for funny stuff. So, we hit on *The Royal Houses of Europe*.

I've been tapping away for months now. MQS left me with plenty of ideas and then simply faded away. I'm onto series two, looking for a producer.

'Remember,' my wife called out. 'We've guests for lunch. Three hungry ladies.'

I peeked out from behind my paper. 'Make sure we don't have lamb.'

I didn't duck in time.

THE STOPOVER

NEIL HANCOX

STILL NINETY MILES TO GO. HIS CONCENTRATION WAS beginning to fade. Twists in the road started to surprise him. He noticed the sign, 'B&B' with a crude white arrow painted on a piece of board, pointing down a rutted track. With luck his car springs would survive.

The farmyard was British Standard: untidy, rusted bits of equipment pushed to one side or stored in a barn, mud because of the recent rain. Fortunately, the traditional dog was either absent or locked away. The farmhouse was red brick, old red brick, the windows were large, the individual panes of glass small. The building would be described by an estate agent as 'substantial'.

'Yes,' the woman said. He sensed hesitation in her voice.

'A single room for the night and some food.'

That could be managed if he didn't mind scrambled eggs and bacon twice. 'Excuse the apron,' she added. 'I was baking.' That sounded promising, he thought.

She led the way up the narrow staircase, with its bare treads, to the first floor. The room was old-fashioned. A brass bedstead, 'and a feather bed', the woman, now identified as Mrs Preston, said. 'There is plenty of room in the large wardrobe and the bathroom is just down the landing on the right. The door does lock, after a bit of persuasion, and it's a bath not a shower. Plenty of hot water.'

He thanked her. Better not put his case on the bed. It might stain the pristine white coverlet. He had nothing he needed to hang up in the wardrobe. If his wife had been there, it would have been different. The dressing table was 'busy'. At one end there was a large bowl and jug, for show now, but once used for washing the face and hands, he knew. The tilting mirror, which dominated the centre, was showing signs of its age with the silvering on the back deteriorating around the edges.

Nevertheless, it still reflected his weary face, much in need of the attention of soap and razor. The rickety chair in the corner, with the fretwork back, did not invite human use, though maybe it could sustain jacket and trousers. No more or it would collapse though old age.

The two pictures on the bedroom wall clamoured for his attention and appeared pleased when he viewed them. Old frames. He touched the imitation gold carefully, so as not to dislodge any. The smaller picture, at least three feet by two, showed a crowded melange of pressed flowers, much faded, though still in place. Probably, he thought, a work of love, or boredom, from a hundred and fifty years ago. The larger print showed two young girls in Victorian dress being chased by a playful dog. They looked happy and alive.

Mrs Preston welcomed him to the large kitchen – 'we never use the dining room' – with a range in one corner and a central isle piled with food, dishes and cooking paraphernalia. 'It's all fresh produce,' she said, 'straight from the farm. Except the bacon, but that's from a local supplier.' The earlier baking had proved fortunate for him. Excellent apple pie and custard completed his dinner.

She had lost her apron and pushed back her dark hair but compensated with the addition of glasses. Her husband, she said, was out at the market, or its aftermath, and her sons probably at college. They should be, anyway, though the local cathedral city held too many other attractions for the young. She sighed and shrugged.

He agreed with her diagnosis, more because of tiredness than belief, and managed to persuade his hostess to provide coffee rather than tea.

'We have a TV in the lounge,' she said 'but it's not working. It's difficult to get anyone around here to repair electrical things. Then, the programmes are not very interesting.' This time his agreement was genuine.

'I might sit and read,' he said. 'Preparing for the meeting I have tomorrow.' The lighting was good, something in B&Bs that was often not the case in his experience, and the settee comfortable. Nevertheless, profit margins, human resources policy and trying to second-guess market trends quickly palled and the feather bed beckoned.

With clean teeth and pyjamas, he settled into bed. The two young girls and the dog seemed to dance before his eyes. He was certain there was movement. Their names must be Katie and Emily. They had finished lessons for the day with their governess; English literature, a little French and maybe drawing. Tea was not for an hour or more. Rover wanted exercise and so they ran off into the field in front of the house where they lived with their parents and several other siblings. Feet might get wet, and hay and seeds would work their way into their long hair, but no matter. After tea and a story, bed, chatter, sleep.

He looked again. Was that a hint of darkness in the corner of the picture? Something tugged at a skein of his memory, but nothing would come free. Water, a stream? Tiredness won. His eyes closed and he started to snore.

The bright sunlight, slipping between the curtains, woke him up. It was early but he felt refreshed. In the picture the dog, Rover, was still chasing the girls. What would be their fate? Slowly he recalled an aunt, a distant one, eighty years or more in the past, two young children, sisters, water, ice maybe. The families erased it all from their collective memory: too many mundane things intervened, life had to continue. He hadn't thought about the incident for years. Now he knew what he must do. There was no logic to this decision, simply instinct.

'Good morning,' a bright, cheerful greeting from Mrs Preston; more of a grunt from a heavily built man standing by the range. Mr P., he presumed. More bacon and eggs and toast and butter appeared as promised and this time he took tea.

'Was everything satisfactory? 'she said.

'Oh yes, thank you, a most welcome stay.' He hesitated, 'One thing, it's an unusual request, but that picture in the bedroom of the two young girls and the dog, I would like to buy it.'

'Dated rubbish,' the man's voice came from the far side of the kitchen. 'Take it away and then we can redecorate.'

Mrs Preston stood, irresolute.

'I'll give you £50, cash,' he added.

'You must excuse the cobwebs behind the picture,' Mrs Preston said as she removed it, placing it in a large plastic bag with another over the top for complete protection.

The package was carefully wedged into the boot of his car. Where would he hang it? It was too old-fashioned for the décor of his house. The study perhaps. The fate of the girls and their dog would be safe there, frozen forever in time and happiness.

Adrenaline drained from his body. Had he imagined the whole episode, something in his family's distant past? No matter. A long journey, a boring meeting on which he must focus.

'What do you make of that?' the woman asked her husband, later, over lunch.

'Perhaps he was an antiques dealer. Anyway, there is a large tin of magnolia vinyl silk emulsion in one of the sheds, just the job for that room – freshen it up and do away with all the memories.' He squeezed his wife's shoulders. 'Start this afternoon if you like.'

WHAT'S IN A NAME?

NEIL HANCOX

'THAT'S HARRY'S CHAIR.'

The speaker was Tom, a hunched man with a mop of white hair, slouching in the chair next to Harry's. Despite the warmth of the residents' lounge he was wearing a woollen muffler.

The remark was addressed to an old lady walking towards the seat. Alice stopped, leant on her stick, and moved to an adjacent chair. She smoothed her floral dress as she sat down and extracted a pair of glasses from the pocket of her brown cardigan. She was new and must learn the pecking order. With her glasses balanced on her nose, she fumbled in the right-hand pocket of her cardigan and pulled out an envelope containing a small card. The other residents, apart from Tom, resting, reading, or just sitting, had ignored the remark. The chair, with a high back, side 'wings' at the top to stop the head falling too far to either left or right, and red upholstery showing signs of wear, appeared indifferent to any potential occupant.

Minutes later an old man, clad in regulation baggy, worn, corduroy trousers and supported by a walking stick, shuffled into the residents' lounge, his slippers hissing across the woodblock floor. He steered towards Harry's chair and lowered himself into position.

'Don't delay': Alice remembered the advice from her distant childhood. Introduce yourself now and get to know people. 'Why do they call you Harry?' she asked.

The occupant of the chair looked bemused for a minute, and then smiled. It was good to have a new neighbour.

'It's my name. I was christened Henry, but I don't like Henry, reminds me of all of them old kings, always chopping people's heads off. So, I'm Harry.'

Alice nodded. The answer she might have expected. 'My name is Alice,' she added. 'I'm new here.' She offered a card with a picture of flowers on the front and the word 'Welcome' to Harry. 'From my nephew,' she said, 'saying he hopes I'll be very happy here.'

She relapsed into silence, which soon descended into a rhythmic snore.

Harry scraped back the cuff of his cardigan and then the sleeve of his shirt, cursing the buttons in his way, and looked at his watch. Four o'clock, well, round about. That meant tea and a bite to eat. 'Teatime,' he said, 'is one of the four pillars of our existence.' Nobody took up the challenge of a debate, though his new neighbour opened an eye.

On cue Marja appeared. 'Hello everyones!' she shouted. No, she must remember that it was 'everyone'. Next time she would get it right. They had told her when she started that it was no good whispering in this place. All the old people here had hearing aids, but that didn't mean working batteries. 'And with your accent,' the manager had added, 'you could easily be misunderstood.' Marja recalled bristling. She had good English, learnt from the radio and TV, she knew all the swear words, and she was working on the way she stressed her speech. The money was not that good, though a lot better than she had earned at home. Cigarettes were expensive. She had already asked her mother to send some supplies; not enough to cause attention, just the occasional packet.

'Cup of tea!' she shouted again. No, she must remember, 'cuppas'. Come on, tell me what you like.' She went round with her notepad, cajoling, sometimes gently prodding a sleepy soul. The list was fourteen teas, one weak, one with soy milk ('It's good for your complexion,' the speaker said. 'You should try some.') ; one oat milk, ('I've read about it somewhere, I forget now, was it on the TV?') and two with the milk in first ('That's very important.').

The kitchen was chrome and polished work tops, with plenty of disinfectant. 'Get a bug in here,' Marja had been told,' and it will sweep through the place like wildfire.' Tea was brewed in two large aluminium pots, battered but dependable, the insides thick with a layer of tannin.

While a catering assistant scraped a product resembling butter, though cheaper, onto white bread and then added a thin slice of cheese, or fish paste, and cucumber, Marja lined up fourteen mugs. 'You have to let the tea brew, stew, or mash,' she had been told on day one and several times afterwards. Different words from different speakers. Very confusing. And be very careful about mixing up a 'masher' with a 'brewer' or 'stewer'. Certain things, Marja had found, could be divisive: people would not speak to one another for days over something so trivial. 'It's like football teams and politics or religion, except,' the speaker had added, 'most folk don't believe in either of the last two anymore. Reality TV is a better bet.' Marja had taken notice. The Brits could be very puzzling at times.

She filled each mug, half emptied one and added hot water, and finally poured honest cow's milk into each brew. She knew the drill. Big smile, 'Of course, Ada, it's oat milk straight from the supermarket.' She felt guilty about this deception, especially when she thought about her own grandmother. Maybe one day, when she was in the supermarket, she would buy a carton or two of oat or soy milk.

The trolley arrived with Marja serving, while a youth doing 'work experience' and evidently of the firm opinion that old age was well into the future and not for him, pushed. Several residents could manipulate the trays attached to their chairs, which swung round in front of them, a base for snacks. If not, that was the first job Marja did. Some tea was spilt, there were cries of 'Where's the sugar?', 'I don't like cucumber,' and 'What sort of cake is it? Not them rock cakes, they break your teeth.' With a quickly acquired skill Marja spooned, sorted, assured the doubtful and asked the young lad to go back for the cake.

Harry caught her wrist, gently of course, as she served him.

Patience, Marja thought to herself.

He gave her a big, toothy smile, hoping his dentures were free from the detritus of lunchtime cabbage. 'Where are you from, my dear?'

'Slovakia.' Would he understand?

He looked at her, sipped some tea and asked the youth, now bearing cake, for a slice of 'that chocolate thing'.

'I know my geography,' he finally said. 'Never heard of that place. It wasn't in my school atlas.'

'It's in centre Europe,' Marja explained. 'We used to be joined to Czech Republic. Now we is a separate country.'

'Oh aye,' Harry replied. 'Is it a landlocked country?'

Marja frowned.

'Landlocked, got no seaside,' Harry added. 'I mean do you go there for your holidays?'

The work experience lad had stepped into the breach distributing cake and offering top-ups of tea if needed.

'Our holidays were spend in mountains and under forests. There were lots of lakes where we could swim.'

'And lots of mosquitoes, I expect,' Harry added.

Before Marja could refute this slur on her country, Harry returned to his narrative.

'When I was young,' he began, 'my dad, mum and sister and I spent a week every year at the seaside, south coast. We used to stay in a boarding house.'

'What is that?' Marja interrupted.

'Like a hotel but not so posh. Every day, unless it was raining, we went down to the beach and hired a deckchair for Mum, where she relaxed, read her book and put sunscreen on our backs.'

Harry was in full flow now, not to be distracted. 'Dad took off his shoes and socks, rolled up his trousers and put a knotted handkerchief on his head. Sis and me, we were in our cossies in no time, down into the sea and then, after we had explored a bit, we had sandwiches and pop and started digging.'

Marja jerked her attention back to the present and forced a smile. 'Tell me more. Dig for treasure?'

'We were making a sandcastle,' Harry said. 'Two towers – that's what the buckets were for, moulding the sand – with a flag in either tower. Union Jack of course, none of this foreign nonsense, and a moat round the lot. Then we waited till the tide came in and fought to defend our castle from the advancing waves. We always lost, but it was fun.'

He stopped for more tea. 'If we were lucky and Dad was feeling flush, we might have an ice cream and once or twice in the week a fish supper. We kids shared a portion of fish and chips, and Mum would give us extra chips from her wrapper.'

There was a tap on her shoulder. The youth beckoned. 'Manager says it's time to go.'

'You tell me more next time, Harry.'

'Yes, I will. That's a proper holiday, though, none of this countryside stuff.'

'See you later, Harry,' Marja said as she left.

The manager smiled at her. 'I know you should interact with our clients,' she said, 'but don't get too distracted. You are due a day off,' she added, 'but I can arrange extra shifts, if you like. Next week you will be on the other wing. One of our carers is down with measles, of all things, and another has managed to get herself pregnant. I hope she realises the unreliability of most potential fathers round here.'

Marja removed her overalls and slipped outside for a smoke and a phone call to her sister back home.

*****

It was lunch time a week later. No residents had died, and no new ones had appeared. Harry was sitting at a table with three others, Alice, Tom and ... he kept forgetting her name. The soup, tomato again, was deposited in front of each person.

Alice smiled conspiratorially. 'It comes in tankers you know,' she said. 'Tankers full of soup, not petrol,' she added for clarification.

Tom nodded in agreement. 'That's a good conspiracy theory,' he said. 'They make a lot more sense than reality. Do you agree, Harry?'

'Don't know really. Reality is just plain chaos today.'

The one whose name they could not remember butted in. 'Pass the salt please. I know it's not good for your blood pressure, but I like to live dangerously. I wish they would give us a glass of wine now and then.'

Further discussion ceased as the soup bowls were gathered up.

'You are new here, aren't you?' Harry said to the young man serving them.

'I am Juan,' the man said, putting down a soup dish, to emphasise the fact with his hands. I am from España, Spain.' He gave them a toothy smile, though this time the teeth were permanent and not easily replaceable unlike Harry's.

'I'd put him in his twenties,' Alice remarked as Juan disappeared into the kitchen.

'It's stew and potatoes, plus cabbage,' Tom said as the next course appeared. Finally, in the debris of apple crumble and custard, Harry found an opportunity to grab Juan's attention.

'What was your name, again?' he asked.

'Juan.'

'One.'

'No— Oh, never mind, that will do.'

'Spain, eh,' Harry continued. 'You have a lot of olive oil there.'

'Yes.'

'So, when you have bread and jam for tea, you must put olive oil on the bread, instead of butter, and then the jam on top. Doesn't that taste funny?'

'We have butter, too in España,' Juan shrugged and smiled.

'And,' Harry continued, 'you call your country by that name, do you? I thought it was Spain.'

'Of course, that is the name you English give it.'

'That accounts for all the troubles in the world,' Harry explained as the friends ambled back to the comfort of the sitting room and their after-lunch nap.

'What does?' Alice asked.

'They don't know the proper names for where they come from, they ain't got any butter and they can't have proper seaside holidays.'

Outside, Juan lit up a cigarette.

'Hello,' a young woman said. 'I'm Marja.'

The pair shook hands, laughed and Marja accepted a cigarette.

'Let's get a drink in the village,' Juan said.

'Great,' Marja replied.

'I wonder,' she said, as they walked down to the pub that evening, 'those old people, they put their flag everywhere, all over the world in the past. See them now. How did they manage that?'

Juan took her hand. 'Let's forget them. Maybe they tell us in the morning.'

WRAPPING PAPER

NEIL HANCOX

THE TREE WAS EIGHT FEET OF SCANDINAVIAN PERFECTION, via the local supermarket and a field in Northants. The LED lights cycled through a succession of colours which were reflected off sundry baubles to produce instant enchantment. A certain stable had nothing on this. Underneath was a pile of parcels, their mysteries and delights hidden beneath thick newspaper – the *Guardian*, obviously.

Alex had more than his share of the impatience of youth. He prodded the gift, bearing the usual legend, and 'from Mum and Dad', smelt the newsprint and started to tear it off. Pausing, he asked, 'Why don't we have shiny Christmas paper like the rest of the world?'

'Because,' a tightly curled ball of dressing gown and shiny pyjamas topped with a screw of blond hair, thought by many to be both human and a sister, remarked, 'we are green.'

A politically correct cat, that was both black and white, sidled through the room in a disdainful way. 'That's one of my adjective allowance for today,' mother thought. But such thoughts quickly faded as her sensitive antennae for family matters picked up that this nuclear group was about to fission, as brother and sister glared at one another. Only Father, sipping his golden Christmas 'cough medicine', which induced serenity and somnolence, appeared unmoved – or, more likely, unaware.

A chance perturbation of the local universe avoided conflict, and Alex continued to rip paper from contents. Silence, horror, amazement. 'What's this?' He looked at the package: Lego, technical admittedly, but not the anticipated Xbox. The said item was hurled at the tree, which, despite its Chinese-engineered, multipoint support base system, crashed forward. The fairy, recently promoted to the top job, grabbed the star and abandoned ship in time to avoid the collision with the sofa. Father sipped, tears started in Mother's eyes, daughter scrolled – the stiff upper lip prevailed for a moment.

Father planted a scented kiss in the vicinity of his wife's ear and whispered, 'Motherhood. One day they will grow up.'

The psychic energy dissipated, the tree was righted (though the fairy was AWOL), more presents were unwrapped: extra and superior 'cough medicine' for the head of the household, black lingerie for the real head, and hair and beauty products for the other feminine element in the room.

A cat, still disdainful, strolled through the detritus of discarded packaging in search of peace, inner sustenance, who knows?

Elsewhere clever scientists were developing means of reading animal minds, admittedly with little success so far. Had they been more advanced, they might have found that a certain animal in a certain house wondered why certain young people were not put in a bath full of water and ... Then this thought was supplanted by the aroma of cooking meat, a celebratory meal, with perhaps duck pâté for a faithful feline.

THE BURGLAR

SARA BANERJI

JOSEPHINE LIES IN BED, HANDS CLENCHED, JAW tight. She doesn't cry any more. The thing inside her has burnt out, the lonely grief has turned it into a dry black clinker. She had had friends once. After Jim died, they fell away. She asked too much. She was too needy. They did not know how to comfort her. They did not have the time to comfort her.

Her thoughts were interrupted by the tiniest sound, a sound she had not heard since Jim died. Someone was coming into the house. Sounds so soft she could have been imagining them.

Then a creak on the stair boards. She did not imagine that! She sat up, hopeful. It must be Milly, the young cleaner. Even the grumpy little teenager was better than no one! She looked at the clock. Two in the morning! But even chaotic Milly wouldn't come at that time.

The bedroom door slowly opened.

A dark figure emerged.

A young man wearing a black puffer jacket and jeans edged cautiously in.

Josephine sat up, crossed her arms, and waited.

The young man stopped abruptly, as though he had had a shock. He was used to screams and leaping about. This woman's apparent indifference was unnerving him.

But all the same, he managed to growl out, in a tone that he hoped sounded threatening, 'Got cash in the house?' He said in a stronger tone. 'I don't want to hurt you.'

'Of course you don't!' she laughed. 'I don't want to hurt you either.'

He was starting to feel angry and frustrated. 'Where's the bloody cash?' he shouted.

She was smiling. He was trying to keep his tone threatening but his voice had come out a little shrill.

'I think,' she said cheerily, 'There might be some in my bag. On the chair over there.'

He crouched on the floor and began scrabbling among the contents of her handbag.

'Have you had supper?' Josephine spoke in the tone of one soothing a fretful baby.

The man kicked the bag's contents, sending lipsticks and powder puffs spinning across the floor. He opened the wallet and eagerly stuffed the few tens and five-pound notes into his pocket.

'Come to the kitchen,' said Josephine, 'I think I've got a bit down there for paying the gardener, Mr Penny. He's wonderful with dahlias.'

'Cut the crap, lady,' the young man snarled. 'Where is the jewellery?'

'There.' She pointed to the box on the dressing table.

He plunged his hands into the box and pulled out a handful of earrings and necklaces.

'A load of crap!' he said, tossing them back into the box.

'Most of those jewels were given to me by Jim, my husband, and he certainly would not have given me crap!' Josephine said indignantly.

'So, you got cash in the kitchen?' the young man said.

'Oh yes. Come on. I will make us a bite to eat as well.'

He followed her cautiously down the stairs. This must be some sort of plot; was she playing around with him till someone came? He needed to get this finished quickly.

But on the other hand, something about her gentle indifference was comforting him. He had followed her downstairs thinking how this unknown woman was the only person who had spoken gently to him since he had come out of prison. His own father had turned his back on him. 'I don't want my boss to find out that I have a criminal son,' the father had said. 'I might lose my job if they found out.'

'Come on, love, sit down,' she was saying as she cracked eggs in the frying pan. 'What would you like to go with it? A glass of wine or a beer?' She put a piled plate before him, saying, 'There, you eat that, and I will try and find that envelope of cash. It's £30 for the gardener. But I can get some more before he comes. Oh, and I don't even know your name! You can call me Aunty Josey.'

'Jim,' mumbled the young man through a full mouth.

CATASTROPHE

SARA BANERJI

BEN, THE NICE MAN NEXT DOOR, LOOKED over the fence as I was pegging out my husband's white shirt to dry. The peg slipped from my hand and the shirt fell onto the muddy ground. Instead of picking it up, I gave it a spiteful little kick.

'Dave's lovely shirt is getting mud on it,' said Ben, reaching out to rescue it.

'Serve him right,' I scowled.

'Sally!' Ben sounded shocked. 'Dave has gone and bought you, at huge expense, exactly what you asked for. An organic car! Because you said you hated plastic.'

'I did not mean a car made of mashed potato, Ben.'

'You can't get anything more organic than mashed potato,' Ben protested.

'The car is going bad, Ben. It's rotting!'

'Well, what do you expect, Sally? That's what happens to mashed potato.'

'And on top of everything else,' I grumbled. 'Betty Smithers, who Dave keeps saying is so pretty, her bloody cat raked its claws down my leg this morning.'

'It won't be doing that any more,' Ben said. 'Poor Carrot got run over this afternoon. I am going to ask Betty to give me its head.'

'What on earth for?'

'I'll put Carrot up with the rest of my trophies! Cat as trophy ...'

'It's not a catastrophe, Ben! It's a triumph!'

ME AND JEREMY

SARA BANERJI

'WON'T MR GREEN GET CROSS?' JEREMY SAID. He was always a bit more cautious than me. Probably because he was a year and a half younger than me. 'Cutting down all those trees. Remember how cross he got when you cut off a branch when I was climbing that tree?'

'You got stuck – I was saving you!' I said proudly.

'I could of easy got out by myself,' said Jeremy.

Mr Green had been furious. 'I been caring for this garden for twenty years. And all that time this garden ain't never had such a couple of destructive varmints like you two.'

Yes, Jeremy was right. Mr Green would get absolutely furious if we cut branches off his precious trees to make our tree tent.

'Perhaps we could just bend some of the little ones over us,' Jeremy suggested.

'Then there wouldn't be any leaves on them in case it rains,' I said.

We searched in the coppice for enough fallen branches, but Mr Green had tidied it. There wasn't a single one.

'I know!' I said, 'There's some trees in that field with the cows in. We could make our house there.'

'Where are you two?' called Mother from the kitchen. 'Lunch is nearly ready. Come in and wash your hands.'

'We are just doing something,' I called back.

'Come in THIS MINUTE!' she yelled.

We knew that yell. It had to be obeyed. Also, we were hungry. We dashed in. We did a bit of symbolic hand cleaning in case Mother was looking, and flung ourselves into the chairs.

'What have you two been up to?' asked Mother through her mouthful of mince. Her tone was more suspicious than curious. It was Tuesday, and that meant mincemeat. There was a war on, as we were constantly reminded, and meat as well as lots of other things like butter and bacon were rationed. As well as our gas masks, we each had our brown ration books. The joint of meat was roasted on Sunday, eaten cold on Monday, and minced on Tuesday.

'Making a treehouse,' said Jeremy. I kicked him under the table.

'You know. A little tiny thing for ...' he paused.

'For frogs,' I said quickly.

'What about a house for Lilly?' asked Mother, laughing.

'She's not called Lilly,' Jeremy protested.

'Oh, sorry. I thought she was. What's her name then?'

''Cos she might be a boy toad,' Jeremy said fiercely. 'Or anything,' he added.

When we were much younger, before we went to boarding school, Jeremy and I had been confused about gender. Nanny had bathed us together, dressed us together, but even though she put a sort of sacred stress on the words 'the *boy*' and none on 'the girl' (me), we had developed a theory, in a period when such matters were kept away from the ears of children, that the day would come when I would grow a little waggly tube like Jeremy's.

'Don't you go chopping Mr Green's precious trees again,' said Mother sternly.

'Of course not!' said Jeremy and I in unison.

We had another plan. We were going to chop Mr Barker's trees. His land adjoined our garden.

'And don't you dare go damaging Mr Barker's hedge again,' said Mother fiercely, as though she had read our thoughts.

We had made such a teeny hole through the yew hedge. We just couldn't believe Mr Barker had noticed it. His fury had been quite scary.

The good thing about yew hedges is that yews take ages to grow, so although our hole had got smaller and we had got bigger, we still managed to wriggle through, and there, on the other side, was a woodland full of fallen branches, and two fields away from Barky's house. We began to drag together the right-shaped branches, moist, with rich smells of sap and fungus, spilling slivers of bark to reveal sleeping beetles and little clings of tart moss. Jeremy and I, our hearts filled with happiness and creativity. His cheeks had gone red with heat and excitement.

'So are yours!' he responded, giggling and breathless.

As we peeled back wet leaves and pieces of rotting wood, creatures came crawling out. We had to get on our hands and knees to see some of them, they were so small. Struggling worms, a battalion of ants, woodlice with their smart grey armour. We let the creatures run over our hands, giggling at the tickle, wincing at the stings, and watched the way their legs went, and how they waved their antennae about. Sometimes, when we found a really exciting one, we would clasp our palms around it, and both of us sit, laughing and looking.

'Jeremy! Jeremy! It's got elbows! Look!'

'And knees.'

We managed to drag out three branches that looked right for the basic structure. We got them stuck into the ground after a lot of effort and hole-digging with Mr Green's spade – oh, he will get so cross if he finds out. We hoped to get it back in the tool shed before he arrived. We held the tops of our posts in a bunch at the top, and tied them together with some of Mother's macramé thread that I had stolen.

'Now what?' said Jeremy.

'Mm ... Yes, we've got to find a cover for it. Where could we get it?'

'In Mr Barker's barn!' said Jeremy joyfully. 'There's some big sheet things he puts under the hay.'

*****

'Oi! What are you little devils up to now? Stealing this time, is it?' He had caught us. We tried to run but he barred the exit with his arms. 'What do you want it for?' he asked.

'For putting over our stick house. In case it rains,' My voice came out a bit squeaky and trembling.

'Well, look. I got an old one here. It's got some holes in it where the rats bit it, but it should do you. I was just about to throw it out!' He bundled a great tumble of muddy canvas into my arms.

'Thank you!' I gasped.

*****

That night, Jeremy and I lay down on the piece of old carpet that Mother had given us, and went to bed, still wearing our clothes, in our new stick house.

It was so exciting that we could hardly get to sleep. The whole of nature seemed to be trilling and throbbing. As the night went on, the grasshoppers fell silent, and the voices of bats took over. Only children can hear bats, we had been told. Grown-ups can't hear them. An owl called from quite nearby. Some of the noises were a bit scary.

'You don't get tigers in England, you silly,' I told Jeremy when he suddenly sat up with a scream.

We fell asleep at last. Half waking in the night I could hear a rustling sound – of the wind moving the grass? Hares? Hedgehogs? Maybe foxes. Or was it the sound of Jeremy breathing?

As though he heard my thoughts, he murmured sleepily, 'I can smell fox!' We woke to the sound of birds waking. We no longer were people observing the wild world, we had become part of that world.

*****

It was while we were lying there that we got the idea for buying a bull.

'There's a notice about it in the shop,' I said. 'A bull calf for sale. Seven shillings – let's buy it!'

'We haven't got seven shillings,' Jeremy said.

But I had thought of a way. Jeremy and I made cakes. We told Mother the money was for giving to the Red Cross. She was terribly impressed, gave us all the ingredients and even told us how to make them.

We put the cakes by the front gate with a message pinned to the gate 'Cakes to sell for the Red Cross.' They were all sold in about two hours, and we got eight shillings and five pence for them.

Terribly excited, we gathered up the money and were setting off to the farm to buy our bull when Mother appeared. She snatched the money from us, grasped our hands, marched us to the Red Cross tent and made us hand the money over.

There came a write-up about us in the local newspaper. 'Sara and Jeremy Mostyn, nine and eight years old, baked cakes and raised nine shillings for the Red Cross. Bravo children!'

Mother was terribly proud. We were cross.

LOSS

SARA BANERJI

I HAVE NO VOICE. How can I comfort my love, who lies awake with a terrible longing?

Who says, 'I want! I long! I crave!'

Oh, speak to me – darling of my world, holder of my soul.

But I have no voice.

Who whispers so softly that I cannot hear it.

Tongues of birds, but they are too desperate.

And I have no voice.

The language of the motorway traffic is ugly and without emotion.

I blend my essence with the marshes where the bullfrogs croak.

I linger among lambs, soon to be murdered. But the baby bleating is not the right sound.

I find my soul among the trees when the wind goes through them.

I mingle myself into that sound that comes from the bottom of the throat and whisper, 'I love you.'

I try to wrap my spirit around you. But it dissolves before the lightest touch.

I wrap you with my transparent love. Can you feel me?

But you lie quite still, breast filled with fear, stiff with grief, and my spirit is not strong enough to comfort you.

ONE NIGHT STAND

VALERIE DEARLOVE

E-MAIL TO: Joshuarandyshite@gmail.com

02 August 2024 19:38

From: Tinanuthead@hotmail.co.uk

Hi, Joshua

Your phone must be broken, so sending you an e–mail instead.

Aren't your Dobermanns ugly? But, nevertheless, if they need walking, I am the person to do it.

While standing in the rain yesterday outside your country estate with those fancy electric gates, all six were excited to see me.

You said we weren't compatible. Well, I don't agree. I overheard the dare your Etonian mates set you, to chat me up at the bar. Went a bit further than that, didn't it, posh boy?

Well, my mother said I should hang onto you – she never usually likes my boyfriends, so I have decided I will be your *girlfriend*! What a laugh, as I had it off with your butler earlier that night at the club. Your butler loved my piercing, tattoos and rude jokes.

Changing the subject, I rang your barrister mum in court this morning for a chat, and your merchant banker dad yesterday.

I couldn't understand the gist of their conversations. Too posh for the likes of me, but they were shouting quite a lot. However, I am sure they will be in touch.

See Joshua, how I gel with your parents. Give me a ring as soon as you see this mail, I left my number in the post box at your gate. I'll be there this evening.

I have minced meat reduced at Asda, and leftover scraps from our Sunday dinner for your guard dogs. They miss me when I don't turn up.

Tried hard pushing and shoving your gates, unfortunately with no success at all. They wouldn't open, so I've eBayed 'electric gate fobs for Country Houses in Wiltshire post codes' – alas no luck so far but will keep trying.

Will email you tomorrow. Oh, forgot to say I have a law degree, and am Chief Assistant Lawyer to the Attorney General for England and Wales.

In Westminster I am friends with some renowned MPs, just in case you are thinking about messing me around, posh boy!

Love and kisses...

Tina x

PUSHING THE BOUNDARIES

VALERIE DEARLOVE

WAYNE AND SHARON WALK ALONG PUTNEY HIGH STREET, passing the offices where, as a baby Sharon would sit in her pram for hours while her mum cleaned office toilets, hurriedly moving from one office block to another.

As they enter the library, she thinks: *No books in my house, just confusion and chaos.* She sees mothers holding the hands of their precious children and remembers: *No bedtime stories for me as a child.*

In the library they both stand staring through the glass partition wall, pushing their noses close to the glass. Looking into the small room off the main hallway, they can see a table and chairs.

The teacher and seven other people enter the room.

My God, they look clever! she thinks, with their intellectual appearances, carrying books and laptops under their arms.

Wayne spurts up: 'You can't go in there, you must be mad, you won't fit in, you're out of your tiny mind. What makes you think you can go in there? You will be a total dickhead, out of your comfort zone, totally out of your tiny mind!'

'*Why not?* I want to *fit in*! I'm going in – why *them,* not *me*? I want to go in. You don't get it, do you? I want to write stories.'

'Aren't you nervous about going in there?'

'*Of course* I'm nervous! Why do you think I spent the whole morning on the toilet thinking "Should I put my head in the sink and drown myself?"'

'Well, I'm off to the *Cock and Monkey*. It's up to you what you do – see you at home.' Wayne picks up his anorak. 'Must go and clean out the ferret cage, and maybe I'll ask Maureen across the road if she wants to go for another bike ride.'

'Plonker – I hope you both fall off your sodding bicycles!'

Picking up her notebooks and pencil with clammy hands, she meanders into the room, sitting down carefully as if she could easily be broken in two. She's received with an enthusiastic welcome.

The class includes guidance on writing techniques, and much more. They take it in turns to read their own stories out loud – she loves to hear people read. They're wonderful, interesting stories, their *own* stories, written by them. How she wants to write stories! So magical. She feels included. Maybe one day she'll pluck up the courage to show them the comedy play which she's written. *Maybe!*

Being with these interesting artistic people feels cool. Feels *okay...*

There's tea and cake too, which reminds her of the saying: If you eat cake, you will get too fat to be carried away by kidnappers. Eat cake, stay safe!

The teacher says to the writing group: 'See you next week.' Then she turns to Sharon. 'You will come again, won't you? You fit in very well with the group.' She sits on the bus, feeling all the fear of the morning slowly pour away from her, but then out of nowhere hysteria takes over, in the form of uncontrollable laughter. She just can't stop, and the passengers on the bus think she's laughing with someone on her phone.

'This morning counted for something., I climbed the mountain, pulled myself out of my sodding box, did something special, pushed the boundaries,' she says to herself and smiles.

TEMPTATION

VALERIE DEARLOVE

'EVE, WE WILL BE CURSED! Maybe die of chronic thirst!'
Why did you pick that apple first?'

***

'I'm sorry, Adam.
But honestly, what a mess!
Although you look like you couldn't care less.'

***

'Eve, I'm scared, and angry with you,
One more silly thing, like you always do.
Think about what you've done for a bit
You're a silly twit.'

***

'I'll say I'm sorry, and that's it!
Why did I do what I shouldn't have?
I knew He would be mad.
The serpent bragged that we would gain
the Almighty's powers.
Life would become like Alton Towers.'

***

'Why didn't you just pick a bunch of flowers?'

***

'I was simply tempted, that is all!
I took my eye off the flying ball.'

***

'Haven't you got enough?
Why do you need more garden stuff?
Why can't you behave? I'm saddened.'

***

'Well, nothing awful has happened!
It's not gone dark, or windy, and were not in the buff!'

***

'You behaved badly, that's blinking enough.
When will you stop meddling?
Let's keep sheltering.'

***

'Let's pray, it may save the day.'

***

The Almighty appears, to say:
'You picked the fruit from the tree of knowledge...
How would you dare,
You stupid mare?'

***

'Will you curse us, Lord, and send us away and burden us with cares.'
Wearing fig leaves to hide our body hair?'

***

God picks up the forbidden fruit from the ground.
Examines it, turning it around and around.
'That stupid serpent, how this bothers Me.
He tempted you with fruit from the wrong tree!
Adam, you were also enticed twice the other day'.
'No excuse that you were bored.' Said the Lord'.

THAT DOG SHOULD STOP SWEARING

VALERIE DEARLOVE

THE HIGH COURT JUDGE WALKS PAST WITH self-righteous superiority, still on a high from the visit by his regular rent boy the night before. The dog tells him to 'Fuck off!'

The minted neighbour walks past. She goes through life without helping, or showing concern, for anyone. The dog tells her to 'Fuck off and buy someone a cup of coffee!'

The lady passes, with her distinguished golf club membership and far too much time, and a diary full of nothing, living off her dead husband's fat pension. The dog tells her to 'Fuck off and do something!'

The sad, hapless teachers walk by. They've marked their pupils' useful homework wrongly, or never marked it at all. The dog tells them to 'Fuck off!'

The professional teachers who've changed children's lives pass by. The dog says: 'I wish you were my teacher!'

A furtive person with a devious nature hiding his vile secrets walks by. The dog says: 'Fuck you!'

The girl walks by and gives him a sweet smile. The dog licks her.

The politician walks by with his briefcase and a swagger, thinking he will never be caught out. The dog tells him to 'Fuck off!'

People in their stereotype boxes pass by, pulling their academia along in their golf trolleys. The dog tells them definitely to 'Fuck off!'

The valued doctors and nurses walk by. The dog can't thank them enough.

The entertainers who have never entertained walk by. The dog tells them to change their act.

The transvestite walks by, feeling good today in his new dress and shoes. The dog says: 'Hi!'

The people with me me-me syndrome walk by. The dog tells them to 'Fuck off!'

The know-it-all braggers who aways refer to Google and contradict the academics, pass by. The dog tells them: 'You don't have to prove or validate that you know a lot.'

Art critics walk by, specialising, analysing, interpreting and evaluating art. How dare they judge! The dog says: 'Fuck you!'

A warmonger walks past. The dog gets a gun and shoots him.

For the people who are not quite wired up correctly... The dog is nice and encouraging.

The wheeler-dealers and drug dealers, the overthinkers and the dudes that are crude and rude the dog leaves for another day.

The dog, exhausted, walks away, thinking to himself: *Should I stop swearing?*

No, be yourself, dog!!!!!

THE CONVENTION, WRITING AND YOU!

VALERIE DEARLOVE

'PLEASE PUT YOUR HANDS TOGETHER AND GIVE a warm welcome to K. J. Rodling who will be talking to you on her prepared topic "Writing and you"!' shouts the small stout Yorkshireman in a brown suit.

K. J. Rodling enters the room and gracefully takes the podium.

'First of all, I am happy to be in Doncaster, *up the North*, so to speak. Love the accents, by the way. Looking in present sight, my audience here this evening resembles gifted foxes in this literary northern hemisphere. Hope you manage to afford organic vegetables.

'Remember, writers, you should write on an empty stomach, this is a known knowledgeable resource.

'Most important, writers, always keep lead in your pencil, and write from the thirteenth person – this accommodates the general public with autism and those who are dyslexic, and in that way, you will avoid a lawsuit, as legal bills are extremely high, and you could buy a designer handbag instead ...

'Take comfort from the fact that punters will buy your book, but won't read it, though it will end up on interregional coffee tables.

'Create no plot whatsoever, release all the wizards, demons and fantasy people from your mind and jingle jangle them in words, stars and snowflakes, plus the odd tipple of whisky.

'If you decide to include the delicate subject of global warming in your story, never research a blinking thing – let it be organically raw.

'Have no punchline that's crude and outdated, take off your codpiece, become liberated, remove your constipated faces, become undiscriminating podcasts. If you are happy, let your face know it!

'Accept that true facts are contradictory and will clutter your mind. You will never learn anything if the mind is cluttered with anecdotes and cockamamie, quirky, imaginable stories!

'Just write from the heart of the coal mine, get dirty, and I can't stress this more – *jump in the murky river*, follow the behaviour of your domestic pets! They know more than us! For example, the dog breeds to consider are Alsatian, Shih Tzu and Labradoodles. They are top of my list: their behaviour is crucial to your creative ability during this global unrest. Anyway, they are a nicer species than us.

'Thank you very much for having me, just off for a chip buttie when in Rome. Happy Creative Writing – after all, writing hasn't been too bad to me, has it folks? Laughing all the way to the bank, *me!*'

THE ORPHANAGE

VALERIE DEARLOVE

FEBRUARY 16TH, A TUESDAY MORNING AT 12.00 PM, in 1953, the day when I was out of that *God-had-forgotten place.* Conforming to my circumstance, I still smell furniture polish, boiled cabbage, beetroot and candle wax, and may feel melancholy bordering on the sadness of it all.

As I came up the wooden stairs that morning I glanced over at my bed, actually at the fourteen beds in that dormitory. When you cried, no one offered a kind word: crying was a shared pastime.

As I stood staring at my bed that day, I noticed brown paper all over my candlewick bedspread, with an accomplice, a large reel of string. I have seen this before, and then I never saw my friends again.

Sister Superior says to Joseph whose 14th birthday was on that very day, and poor little George was just five years old, 'Joseph, you and your brother George will be leaving us today. You will need to collect George from his classroom. Hurry, put all your belongings in that paper and wrap it up tightly.

I was quite materialistic I thought. I collected things, for example, pinecones from the garden, discarded snakeskins, now looking back, I was not as much being materialistic as just cherishing things from nature, old dead leaves, furry caterpillars, and woodlice. I loved dead flies with their legs standing straight in the air, and bird shit was my favourite, once, my mate thought it was loose pieces of chocolate and ate some.

I checked on my brother George at break times. He was having a harder time than I was, so every day I told him I loved him. I know it sounded soft, but I meant it. I would look at him, poor little bugger, those nuns never even bothered to dress him up properly. George was my sanity.

It is funny, but as a child in the fifties, I never questioned anything.

I remember the final few minutes standing in the courtyard with George. I remember thinking I haven't a single kind thought for these women, who hide behind their religious fancy-dress robes. I was standing imitating a statue, I wasn't really there.

They were supposed to represent God, love and kindness, and all that stuff, well, they sucked at it.

Now in later years I know being in that place for four years made me emotionally strong and very judgemental of fairness. Also, later in life I realised those bastards surely could teach and had granted me a good education.

As George and I stood in the courtyard, with our paper packages we resembled prisoners who had just been released from Her Majesty's Prison Wormwood Scrubs. Our mother appeared through a wooden door, looking far too well dressed to have taken four years of charity from this place. We were supposed to be destitute, homeless and poor people. What I did not know at that time was that our mother had just been released from a mental institution in the town, and that accounted for the absence of family visits.

My mother walked past us, and straight to Mother Superior. She lowers her torso and, on her bended knees *would you believe it?* kissed her hand. Isn't that what you're supposed to do with the Pope? Her posture was ridiculously subservient and embarrassing.

Mother Superior was not amused. Mother then turned to George and me and ordered us, 'You two, say thank you to these lovely sisters for all their kindness which they have bestowed upon you.'

I wanted to shout – these nuns had held George's head down the toilet because he wets his bed.

I wanted to shake her so hard, so she would know they burnt my fingers with a poker for making them a shit cup of tea; I wanted to tell her they have it off with church wardens in the vestry.

Walking down the road with Mother, she never spoke: communication wasn't her strong point. In fact, she hardly ever spoke to us, and we had to find out things for ourselves and from others.

I asked her where we were we going to live. 'Oh yes,' she said, 'George, your uncle and auntie want to adopt you and return to Israel. How do you feel about that?'

I said, 'That isn't going to happen, Mother.' I never called her Mum, that felt too close!

She wasn't listening as usual, 'Oh yes', she said, 'I got married again.'

*****

Mother speaks casually, 'You will call him Mr Warped -Smyth.'

We were told he was a doctor in psychiatry and he worked in a mental hospital in East London; we would live with him.

Then she lit a fag. Looking at her standing on the pavement I felt only pity: she had a different agenda from mine; from another planet, with no clue what was happening around her.

When I had been eight years old and having a weed-enhanced whitey, completely out of my tiny mind, slumped over a sofa in the living room, she had greedily finished off the rest of my weed and sat on the floor hysterically laughing, eating raw carrots. George was eventually found crawling up the road in his soiled, soaking nappy.

We stood huddled together under this impressive Tudor stone archway with inlaid wooden seats at each side of the door, maybe for visitors to sit and contemplate whether they were worthy or not. The large wooden front door was painted black, with black door furniture, and the house had many windows.

We rang the doorbell and Mr Warped-Smyth peered through a tiny opening of the door. Even through this small gap, I saw his face: he couldn't hide his disappointment. Was he going to let us in? Well, let us in he did.

What a fucking circus this was going to be! A 'Home, sweet home' situation there, not so very sure!

Mr Warped-Smyth had a sly look about him... His crossed eyes never looked you straight in the face, and his mannerisms resembled those of someone who was permanently in an identity line-up and never wanted to be recognised as the culprit.

Why wasn't Mr Warped-Smyth going to work? He was a professional, a doctor after all. He was Mother's pride; her loyalty was overwhelming; she forgave him for everything, and he even had a hyphenated name.

I investigated Mr Warped-Smyth, and discovered he was related to the great Earl of Northumberland and that accounted for his wealth. Devouring this new information, Mother was even more prepared to forgive him for his strange behaviour. She kept saying his hands and nails were clean.

Warped-Smyth scurried around looking sneaky, spending hours in the basement. If he did leave the house, it was always late at night, and he was constantly pressuring me to get out of his house. I wasn't ready to leave George.

On the late evenings when he did go out, he carried a suitcase. On one occasion I followed him. He went by train to Piccadilly Circus, where he had a large ground floor flat: I saw his name on the doorbell at the entrance.

I followed him to a pub where he picked up a woman and then took her back to his flat; I then left for so-called home.

In the basement I found papers of Mr Warped-Smyth releasing him from the same mental hospital as Mother. He was a resident, a patient exactly the same as Mother. What the f*** was going on? Now it made sense. I read his diagnosis – he was a psychopath with violent intentions.

He started dressing up as Mother in her leopard leotard, then a Boy Scout Master, a High Court judge, or just in a snorkel and flippers. Mother failed to explain this behaviour away, but it was the phrase 'violent tendencies' that was constantly in my mind.

Mr Warped-Smyth *never* actually married Mother, it was just a church blessing by a bent clergyman arranged and paid for. He needed the money and Mr Warped-Smyth needed a respectable front to showcase to the outside world, representing him as a respectable married man with a family, in a respectable neighbourhood.

He soon became nasty, dragging us, including Mother, into the garden and locking us out of the house all day, telling us to tidy the garden. We were without gardening tools, spades or forks.

He kept changing the locks and then changing them back again. He only had two sets of locks, so we soon sorted that caper out. He would switch off the electric, water and heating, thinking that would affect us. Well, we had been through worse. Then he wouldn't let us eat in the house, so we bought food from the corner shop down the road, and ate in the garden,

One day I found a dead cat in the dustbin in the basement, and then again, another dead cat. I remember Mother saying neighbours were losing their pets, even an Alsatian dog had gone missing, and yes, there it was, a very large Alsatian dog with his back legs and behind sticking out from our dustbin.

There were days I would walk to the shops for food and see sweet cats playing on the road and scare them away from the direction of our house, or even pick them up and place them somewhere else.

One day I smashed Mr Warped-Smyth in the face, he was a small man. I told him I was going to tell the police about the dead animals. He threatened to kill Mother, George, and me. Therefore, I kept quiet.

One Sunday when we were all locked in the garden, I decided to walk to the very end just because Mr Warped-Smyth had instructed us to leave that part of the garden alone, 'Stay up here near the house so I can see you,' he *would* say.

I walked down the garden and found a heap of freshly dug soil. I ran back and told Mother. She was having a fag and gazing up at the back windows, hoping Mr Warped-Smyth would soon let us back in.

The police came that next afternoon and arrested Mr Warped-Smyth on five counts of homicide – the bodies of three women and two men were found in the garden of the flat in Piccadilly– and for the cruelty to three dogs, five cats, and George's hamster.

'You married a mad-man, Mother, and a murderer. What else is in store for George and me?'

'He wasn't a bad man,' Mother would say, 'it's just Mr Warped-Smyth kills people and is cruel to animals!'

Never forget he was well connected!

SCREAMING QUEENS

SIMON HOWARD

'IF THERE'S ONE THING I CANNOT ABIDE, IT'S *BOGOSITY*! Your family are completely bogus, and all this religion's driven everybody *mad*! Do you know, I came to stay the weekend and I've been here for...'

This is a voice from my past, and it belongs to a man called Roger Fennell, who lived in my Aunt Diana's house in Oxford. I'd been listening to the same diatribe since I was a kid, and the only thing that changed was the length of time he'd lived there. 'I came to stay the weekend and I've been here for *two years*!' '...seven years...eleven years... fourteen years...eighteen years...twenty-one years... *twenty-seven years*! –' I watched my life slipping away as I listened to Roger telling of his misfortune at Aunt Diana's hands after she'd once plucked him from trouble.

'I crashed a car,' said Roger.

'He bounced a cheque,' said Aunt Diana.

His life had fallen apart after he'd had a serious back operation and couldn't work for a long time. It seemed that he might not walk either, but he was a driven man, Roger, so he did. A curious walk it turned out to be, though, as he swung his legs in front of him like an electrified flower-pot man. And so he ended up in trouble: possibly the car he crashed was one he'd paid for with a bounced cheque.

Besides being a widowed writer, Aunt Diana was a prison visitor, so she took him in for the weekend before his trial. He slept in the bedroom by her front door and remained there for the twenty-seven years until her death, frequently behaving like the drunken porter in the Scottish play, though he looked very English: as time wore on, he became a toothless parody of Dennis Price and made increasingly more futile attempts to keep abreast of the housework he was expected to do in lieu of rent.

'I'm not saying that your aunt's not a wonderful woman in many ways, because she is, but I must be *me*!' was another of his mantras.

During their twenty-seven years of co-dependency, they never once discussed Roger's homosexuality. However, on a few occasions she evicted naked young men he had brought home from the pub.

'The physical thing never meant much to me,' he used to tell me. 'I liked the *chase* more.'

Once Aunt Diana read me a poem by Walt Whitman called '*Good-Bye My Fancy!*', about the death of a loved one.

'Isn't that lovely?' she said afterwards.

'Yes.'

'Well, it's a pity it doesn't mean anything because he wrote it about a *man*.'

'The trouble with your family,' Roger told me regularly, 'is that there's no *love* in them.'

***

'The thing is, I'm not a *home* person, I'm a *pub* person,' was another of his refrains. 'My mother died when I was four. I was devoted to my father, but he married a ghastly old cow, and I couldn't wait to get away. I had to be *me*. And great fun I had being *me* too. I had a wonderful life in London. All pubs are gay bars, you know, in a sort of way. Then, of course, I led the most marvellous life in East Africa, selling office furniture. Oh, some of those Sikh boys... Ranjit Singh aged seventeen: when he took off his turban his hair flowed down to his beautiful *arse*!'

I would hear these stories in various pubs around Oxford. It depended on which one Roger favoured currently, and sometimes which one favoured him, as he was often banned for some frightful indiscretion.

'They understand me here, my dear,' he would say. One thing infuriated him, however: overt campness. 'If there's one thing I cannot stand,' he'd roar at me, 'it's *screaming queens* giving homosexuality a bad name! They bring it into *disrepute*!'

***

Her sacerdotalism being somewhat qualified, Aunt Diana liked priests to agree with her. Therefore, she didn't have much truck with the Jesuits. The Dominicans were out too, since a cousin of ours was one. Generally considered one of the great intellects of the Catholic Church, he was even thought by some people to be a saint. But he maintained that gay relationships were as valid as straight ones, so Aunt Diana never allowed him in the house. 'I always thought he was a bit of a Norman Hartnell,' she told me.

The parish priest, Father Tucker, was popular with her and, as he was a convert, she expected him to be more right wing than other priests. (Liberal Catholics always have to bear the burden of converts turning up on a regular basis and putting the enlightenment clock back, since they have to prove themselves more Catholic than anybody else.) I don't know if she ever discovered that he wasn't remotely right wing, or that he did a great line in *Ian Paisley and the Pope* impersonations. During one of Aunt Diana's dinner parties, he hardly batted an eyelid when Roger came in from the pub rolling drunk and greeted him jovially as 'Father Tucker, mother fucker'.

Popular too were the Oratorians, especially since the time Aunt Diana stayed with an extremely grand cousin whose house in the West Country was at least a quarter of a mile long. A door off the library led onto a balcony overlooking the chapel into which the Catholic villagers were allowed to file once a week for Mass. When Aunt Diana and her hostess went down the private staircase to the Communion rail, the Oratorian saying Mass – a weekend guest at the house – broke off from the rest of the congregation to give them Communion. Aunt Diana thoroughly approved of the feudal core inside English Catholicism.

Most popular of all with her, though, were the Benedictines. Whatever their personal beliefs, they generously allowed Aunt Diana to regale them with hers. The only time she was upset by one of them was when Cardinal Hume went on television saying something politically correct, sending her into a fury.

'I've never heard such rot!' she roared.

Making a mock sign of the cross, Roger moaned from downstairs: 'It's all this bloody north, south, east and *Holy Ghost*!'

***

Although Aunt Diana and Roger weren't prepared to discuss his homosexuality, she was intrigued by it.

'Do queers have smaller bits down below?' she'd ask my old school friend Raymond or me in her drawing room on the first floor. (Roger had taken a fancy to Raymond when he moved to Oxford at eighteen and became a barman in one of Roger's favourite haunts: *'I used to tell him there was a five-pound note lying on the floor.'*)

'*Fucking stupid cow!*' Roger would boom from outside his lair in the hall. 'Complete *bogosity*! Does she think the Sikhs have smaller bits down below?'

In those days he made sure that Aunt Diana never heard his outbursts, but on one occasion she did, after he'd returned from the pub even more drunk than usual. He called her a *bloody old cow*. Furious, she said she was going to throw him out of the house, and soon they both realised they were checkmated.

'I shouldn't have called her a bloody old cow,' he told me dejectedly.

'There's no gratitude in criminal circles,' said Aunt Diana, who started a new short story that afternoon, *The Ungrateful Crook.*

Using great diplomacy, I somehow managed to patch up their tattered relationship. Aunt Diana changed the title of her story to *The Repentant Queer*, and Roger rewarded me with lunch at t*he Horse and Jockey*.

'They also wait who stand and serve,' he boomed when the pretty barman brought our meal to the table. 'As a matter of fact, they understand me particularly well here.' Then he was back on the subject of Aunt Diana. 'Your aunt's always been very good to me. It's just that I can't stand *families*.'

Many years later Roger regularly called her a *bloody old cow* to her face, but that was after she'd become ill and couldn't tell day from night. Then she'd wander into his bedroom at all hours and take away his sleep. He had to wash her, change her clothes, care for her.

'I never thought I'd end my days dressing and undressing a *woman*!' he'd roar at me.

***

'Have I ever told you about the time I had an affair with a bandsman in the Household Brigade?'

I could feel my ancestors turning in their graves, as my family regiment was part of the HB. Roger was reminiscing about his East African days.

'He was a drummer. Nineteen. And his battalion had been sent out to play some concerts...'

Roger had been quiet for some time and was still in mourning for Aunt Diana, who had died six weeks earlier. He was now living in a flat for the elderly and had just sifted through a box of old letters and photographs. Images of boy lovers mingled with those of Aunt Diana on his table. He looked a bit drawn, though less tired than he had during the last days Aunt Diana spent at home, before she went into the care of kind nuns. Recalling the heady, sexy times in East Africa made him brighten up.

'We were asked to *entertain the troops*.'

'Did they understand you in East Africa?'

'Very well indeed. You see, I had to be *me*!'

'Did it ever go wrong?'

'Once. I made a mistake about a Scottish boy. I used to work with his father. Very dour.' He became quiet again. 'Then there was Graham, of course...' This was another story I had known for many years. 'He couldn't stay out of trouble. Terrible weakness for young boys. He was beautiful himself, but on a suicide course. Went to prison. That's why I returned to East Africa. Those were the days when all the queers went around saying "Are you musical?"' This part of the story was always accompanied by a camp, mocking voice: '"Are you *myoosical*?"'

He looked wistfully at the pile of letters and photographs. A young Sikh gazed out at us, his flowing hair hidden beneath his turban. A handsome bandsman beamed from under a sola topee.

'My drummer boy was bloody musical, but he wasn't camp.' Tears were forming in his old eyes. 'It's just something they pass through, unless they're Graham. You can't hold them – but, of course, I never wanted to. I couldn't have *lived* with any of them. I couldn't have been *me* that way. I needed the chase. Boys turn into men and marry, even if they're queer as coots. And the others become screaming queens, giving the whole thing a bad name. They bring it into *disrepute*!'

His eyes rested on a photograph of Aunt Diana. I remembered him following her coffin like a weeping, electrified flower-pot man.

'Do they understand you here?' I asked.

'I should think *not*! I've been here for six weeks and two days, and they don't know a bloody thing about me. And they're not going to! I shall continue to be *me* within the confines of this flat... I'm too old for any of that, anyway.' His eyes were still gazing at the photograph of Aunt Diana. 'Well, you'd better be getting along...'

We arranged to have lunch at *the Plasterer's Arms* the following week: either Roger or *the Horse and Jockey* was out of favour now. As I walked away from his flat, I thought: Roger, you might just be giving homosexuality rather a *good* name and bringing it into repute – however bogus he would think me for saying so.

He was dead within the year. Raymond and I made the arrangements for his funeral as we couldn't trace a single member of his long-lost family.

YOU'RE NOT LORD BYRON, ARE YOU?

SIMON HOWARD

'WHAT WE LEARN OF HISTORY IS DEPENDENT upon the prejudices of the historian.' A Jesuit told me that at school, but he didn't last long in the order. Later he taught philosophy at Oxford and carried an atheist's ticket.

This memory makes me think of a rippling sea. No, a lake! It's *Lac Léman*, and I'm at the Castle of Chillon, years ago, with my old school friend, Summers. In the dungeon is a celebrated graffito by Lord Byron. I read about his graffito in the guidebook. It actually boasted about it: 'Lord Byron wrote his name on a column in the dungeon in 18-dot-dot'. The castle was proud to have his signature. On a column, in the dungeon! *Lord Byron* or *George Byron* or *Byron* – I forget which.

Anyway, it was there, and the castle authorities were so proud of his signature that they'd stuck a little frame around it. A framed graffito, making it stand out from the others, which is helpful because the walls and columns are *covered* in graffiti. And, unless you read them all, this frame is the only clue to where Lord Byron's signature is. (You can almost hear the bureaucrat ordering it at the ministry: 'One graffito-frame, for the framing of Scottish *milord's* signature.') It's an important tourist item, this Lord Byron graffito: it makes money.

He put it there because he wanted to add his signature to that of François de Bonivard, who'd been held prisoner in the castle a few centuries earlier. Lord Byron, a celebrated graffitist, comes along, wallops his name on the column and moves on: it's a matter of respect. Next century the authorities stick a frame around it. What could be simpler?

The thing is, though, what do you do yourself when you visit? Perfectly normal, it seemed to me, to add my own signature – in a humble way, of course. I didn't know much about Bonivard, but I'd been a fan of Byron's since the age of fourteen, when the Jesuit told me he died of the clap in Greece.

My task was clear. With Summers' help, I found an empty patch of column at the bottom, round the back. I felt good about it, that it was the right thing to do: history demanded that I got involved and kept the cogs oiled. You have to know how to enter a historical moment, and the way to sieve its intensity. I'd had a healthy respect for graffiti ever since I saw the Emperor Septimius Severus's name gouged into one of the two Colossi of Memnon years earlier, while Yousuf the donkey boy made a very improper suggestion to me.

'Why not?' he reasoned. 'All the Frenchmen do.'

I beat a hasty retreat and didn't really get a decent look at Septimius Severus's handwriting.

Now, at Chillon, I took out my knife. And, here I was, humbly adding my name to the throng in Chillon, when I was distracted by an extraordinary tutting sound. *'Tutttttttt!'* it went. You wouldn't believe it was possible to get the sound of so many *t*s into one syllable, with hardly a trace of a vowel. *'Tuttttttttttt!'* The force of it made me turn round. It echoed through the dungeon and flew about like a bat. *'Tuttttttttttttt!'*

A middle-aged couple were standing in the shadows, scowling at me. Half-lit as they were, I felt they could have been from anywhere in Europe, disapproval personified. One of them had made the sound: impossible to say which, as a sound like that knew no gender. But it had a cosmopolitan ring to it which said: *'You and Summers are vandals.'* Summers rose to the challenge.

'It's all right,' he said, charmingly. 'Lord Byron did it.'

One of them replied, I forget which, in a North of England voice:

'Well, you're not Lord Byron, are you?'

This had a terrific logic to it, and I wondered if Lord Byron had experienced the same thing when he'd gouged *his* name on the column. Perhaps a passing Walloon had gone *'Tutttttttt!'* at him.

'It's all right,' Lord Byron would have said, 'François de Bonivard did it.'

'Well, you're not François de Bonivard, are you?'

Perhaps it even happened to Bonivard as he lay there in chains, scraping his name onto the column. He probably outraged a fellow prisoner who was due for execution next day. Maybe someone even had a go at the Emperor Septimius Severus, or perhaps Yousuf the donkey boy's ancestor tried to get him to do something improper up against the Colossus, saying, 'Go on, all the Phoenicians do.'

History's a curious thing. I don't know much about it. What I do know is that without it, and people like Lord Byron, that Swiss bureaucrat would never have had to put in a request for a graffito-frame. It was probably the most exciting event of his career. And I, who have spent a lifetime chasing after the memory of emperors and poets, would have had far less to think about on my travels while dodging people like Yousuf the donkey boy with varying degrees of success.

ANGLO-TUSCANS

A Tale from the Italian Hills

SIMON HOWARD

'Where you are is of no moment, but only what you are doing there.'

Petrarch.

'One must forgive one's enemies, but not before they are hanged.'

Heinrich Heine.

POSITIVE THINKING

'I LOVE MY FACE!' shouted an American woman from the CD player beside Belinda Duguid's bed. Her voice dripped enthusiasm.

Belinda quickly looked around the empty room before sheepishly repeating what the American woman had just said.

'I love my face,' she whispered.

'I love my nose!' said the voice.

Belinda was unconvinced, so she only mumbled the refrain.

'I lovemynose.'

She was lying alone under the mosquito net draped over her large old double bed, trying to shut out the sound of crickets chirruping below in the garden. Like most English people, and unlike the old Tuscan peasant couple who'd lived here before her, Belinda had left the windows and shutters open, hoping against hope that a tiny touch of breeze might ease her discomfort on this hot July afternoon. It had merely helped to increase the heat in the room throughout the morning.

'I love my mouth!' said the voice.

'I love my mouth.'

'I love my chin!'

'I love my chin.'

'I love my body!'

Oh, I do want to, thought Belinda.

'I love my navel!'

'I love my navel.'

'I love my vagina!'

'Oh, really!' Belinda said out loud. 'The *Americans*!'

She wasn't fond of Americans anymore. Not since the success of Frances Mayes' *Under the Tuscan Sun* had made all the prices rise in the shops in and around Cortona, the beautiful hill town a few kilometres away which could be seen from several other hill towns in this part of Tuscany. A glass of wine now cost four times what it had three years ago, she believed. It was almost impossible to park in the town, and the roads were sometimes blocked by *charabancs* of American tourists making their pilgrimage to glimpse the author's house, now – at the end of the twentieth century – a more important sightseeing destination than the *Duomo* Museum which housed its famous *Annunciation* by Fra Angelico.

In fairness, Belinda thought, no one had been more surprised by her literary success than Frances Mayes herself but, nevertheless, life in the Cortonese hills had become tougher for everyone except the shopkeepers and bar owners – and the estate agents, of course, several of whom seemed to come, for a reason Belinda could never understand, from Essex. There were times when her idyllic life in Tuscany owed less to Signorelli and Fra Angelico and more to Romford and Braintree than she liked to admit.

She sat up and looked at the CD cover. It was called *New Ways to Positive Thinking.*

The Americans always use shock tactics, thought Belinda. That's why she'd given up *EST* years before. (Her fads went back a long way.)

At one *EST* gathering, she'd been persuaded to sing *One Currant Bun in the Baker's Shop* to an audience of three hundred strangers at a large church hall in London. It took her several years to live down the embarrassment, and even now – on hot, sticky Tuscan nights – she sometimes relived the shame lying here, perspiring on this huge empty bed, under this same protective mosquito net.

Suddenly she was disturbed by the sound of a *motorino* skidding on the gravel outside, followed by a crash and a voice crying 'Ohfuckinellnotagain!'

'I love my toes!' said the American woman's voice on the CD. She'd been travelling down her imaginary leg while Belinda was thinking about the Americans and her own humiliation through *EST*. At least Tony had been around in those days, though, to help her through life's minefield.

Hurriedly, Belinda got up from the bed, pushed aside the mosquito net and switched off the CD player before rushing downstairs, thinking: *What can she have done this time?*

In the kitchen stood a beautiful young woman with her arm in a sling and bits of Elastoplast dotted about her tanned forehead. Scabs covered her bare shoulder, and blood dripped onto the tiled floor from a fresh wound on her knee.

'Julia!' shrieked Belinda.

Julia hiccupped back at her.

'Bloodyrottenroad,' she muttered, fumbling around in a torn shopping bag. 'I'm afraid we can't have a *frittata* because all the eggs broke.' She hiccupped again. 'But I could probably scrape enough off the drive to make a *carbonara*.'

She hiccupped once more in celebration of her culinary escape.

***

'I love my ass!' said the American woman's voice vibrantly.

Oh, I really wish I did, thought Belinda. *I really do. Ass* seemed so inappropriate; *buttocks* much more real.

She was back on the huge empty bed after lunch, veiled by its mosquito net, though the mosquitoes weren't usually about at this time of the day. The *carbonara* had been surprisingly good, and though she'd detected a tiny piece of grit, and possibly some bark from one of the cypress trees, Belinda had forced herself to think positively about it. She always tried to be as encouraging as possible to Julia, whom she worried about much of the time and had taken on as cook for the summer. Julia was the younger daughter of friends in Oxford, where Belinda lived when she wasn't staying at her Tuscan farmhouse – her *Casa Cimabue*, to which she'd come early this year to complete the first draft of her fifth book on Italian design, the epic *Marble Patterns in the Marbleless Churches and Chapels of Tuscany.*

'I love my cellulite!' proclaimed the American woman.

A loud crashing sound from the kitchen made Belinda push aside the mosquito net once more and run from the room as the American woman's voice pursued her down the stairs.

'I love my wrinkles!' she called.

In the kitchen Julia was pulling a shard of glass out of her lovely hand.

''Snothing,' she mumbled drunkenly.

'Julia, dear...' said Belinda, unsure how to deal with this not uncommon situation, or even what to say next. Her mother was a very old friend, so Julia was almost a daughter to her. But the truth of it was that Belinda's own youth had been so terribly different from this wild and beautiful young woman's – it was a youth which seemed to revolve around alcohol and injury, and a lot of both. She felt almost grateful when she heard a car drawing up and went outside to see who had come.

'Signora!' cried old Alberto, stepping out of his *Cinquecento.*

White as bread, Alberto nevertheless spent much of his time out of doors tending, among other things, Belinda's two hundred and forty-three olive trees. In exchange for a few flagons of oil, which she stored in an outhouse called the *capanna*, Belinda allowed him to harvest and sell the crop. An English visitor once estimated that Belinda's thirty litres a year cost her one and a half million *lire* in those pre-*euro* days.

However, she was determined to support local enterprise, play her part in the affairs of the village, and ensure the health of her trees. She refused to shop at the Co-op (*Coop* in Italian) in the growing sprawl of Camucia, down on the plain, which she believed was putting people like Alberto out of business, even though English neighbours reported seeing Alberto shopping there himself.

Belinda bought all her household provisions from Giancarlo's shop in the village, where she kept a tab all summer long with Giancarlo's indecipherable writing on it. (Alberto and Giancarlo were implacable enemies, which explained why Alberto shopped at the *Coop*. Belinda had a vague idea that one of them had been a Fascist during the war, and the other a Communist, but she couldn't remember who'd been which.) At the end of each summer's visit, she and Giancarlo would go through the mountain of indecipherable receipts together till Giancarlo wrote down an astronomical total in surprisingly clear handwriting. Year after year, Belinda was too honourable to question the figure. And every year in recent times, she wondered how Tony might have dealt with the situation.

'Signora!' cried Alberto, beaming his white-faced smile. *'Tutto bene?'*

From the tiny car he took an oil flagon and a couple of bottles of his undrinkable home-made wine. People in the village said this opaque muck was the cause of his deathly complexion. As he strode towards Belinda waving his offerings, the American woman's voice wafted down from the open bedroom window.

'I love my nipples!'

Belinda suspected that Alberto secretly loved hers, and she was grateful that he couldn't speak a word of English to tell her so. Another crash sounded from the kitchen.

''Snothing, really!' shouted Julia from the shadows.

Then a second crash told Belinda that the shelf holding the saucepans had collapsed, presumably after being fallen against by a beautiful drunken body.

***

Older than Troy. That's what they say about Cortona. It's been in perpetual occupation for nearly five thousand years, or so the claim goes. And there have been various occupations along the way. The most recent is by the foreign incomers and tourists and Frances Mayes' devotees. Before that it was the *Wehrmacht* and the *SS*.

'A lot of women were raped during the Occupation of Italy,' says Deborah, an English tourist drinking her expensive glass of wine and nibbling on a free *crostino* at one of the many new bars on the *Via Nazionale*.

'Not only the women,' says her French companion, François, a retired diplomat.

'And it's said you can see a paint skid-mark on the wall at the *Palazzone*, where Signorelli fell off his ladder and died doing his last fresco.'

'Eh bien...!'

*****

LIVORNO!

Belinda and Julia were driving to Pisa to pick up friends from the airport. Julia was sitting in the back of the car so that she could stretch out her bandaged leg. Belinda was confused by the road around Camucia which had been altered since last year. Unlike the lovely hill towns, the sprawling new urban complexes of Tuscany had no beautiful churches or *palazzi* to navigate by, and all looked the same to Belinda. She got lost every time she visited the outskirts of Sinalunga or Arezzo or even the outer reaches of Florence. Camucia, though not large, was impossible.

Added to that, it was a bank holiday, a *festa nazionale*, though she couldn't remember which one was being celebrated. Belinda was knowledgeable about the Renaissance, but not so good on contemporary Italy. Also, she'd been foolish enough to drink more than one glass of Alberto's revolting wine last night.

She couldn't decide whether to take the *autostrada* via Florence or the *superstrada* past Siena. She asked Julia's advice, principally to keep her involved in what was going on, as a kind of therapy, but got no answer. When she looked in the mirror, she saw that Julia was fast asleep and felt concerned. She couldn't help noticing that Julia always seemed to fall asleep if she hadn't had a drink for about twenty minutes.

Then she spotted two women getting into their car outside a shop. One was middle-aged and the other about twenty, probably her daughter. Belinda thought they looked friendly, so she pulled up and asked them in faltering Italian the best way to Pisa.

'O Pisa!' they shouted enthusiastically, then had a heated discussion together about the *autostrada*, the *superstrada*, the *festa nazionale*, *Firenze*, *Siena* and several other things, as far as Belinda could tell. She tried her best to understand them, but soon became hopelessly lost. At last, the middle-aged woman, smiling kindly, told Belinda to follow their car.

She drove behind them out of the town and along a winding country road for several kilometres. For the whole journey the mother and daughter kept up an animated conversation inside their car, which swerved from one side of the road to the other as they looked at each other, rather than the road, and waved their arms frantically. Several times Belinda thought they were giving her signals to turn left or right, but they were just being Tuscan.

Eventually they stopped opposite a big old house and beckoned Belinda to follow them inside. She left Julia asleep on the back seat – an elegant, injured mound of rising and falling plaster and bandage. Grateful to be out of the heat, Belinda followed the two women into a dark hall. A map lay on a round table.

'Babbo!' called the mother, picking up the map. Even Belinda recognised this as the familiar word for a father, though she had no idea whether it was used outside Tuscany. *'Babbo!'*

There was no reply, so they started to walk through the large house. *'Babbo!'* the mother called into one room after another. *'Babbo!'*

Eventually they entered the last room on the ground floor and there they found him: a frail, gaunt old man sitting in an old leather armchair, gazing into space. Belinda thought he looked as though he was in a trance. His daughter and granddaughter glowed with optimism when they saw him.

'Babbo! Per arrivare a Pisa, che strada deve prendere – Firenze o Siena?'

The old man continued to stare into space.

'Autostrada o superstrada per Pisa, Babbo?'

'Eh?' said the old man at last.

They shoved the map under his ancient nose.

'Babbo! Per Pisa – Firenze o Siena?'

The old man's glazed eyes wandered over the map, and then his stare settled on the far wall. The women leant forward to receive his verdict.

'Babbo...' they whispered expectantly.

Belinda was not hopeful, but she tried her best to think positively. Suddenly the old man looked up to heaven, then down at the map again. His frail old body gave a little tremble, and his lips began to move. His daughter and granddaughter strained to get closer to him. At last, he spoke in what Belinda considered a gaunt, proclaiming voice.

'Livorno!' he said.

'O Babbo!' shrieked his daughter, glowing with pride. Her own daughter also glowed beside her.

'Livorno!' shouted the old man again. *'LIVORNO!'*

Belinda worried that he might give himself a heart attack if he went on shouting *Livorno!* like this. Hurriedly she looked at the map, and it confirmed her worst fear. Livorno was beyond Pisa, further along the coast, and being told to drive towards Livorno didn't in any way help her to decide between taking the *autostrada* towards Florence or the *superstrada* past Siena. Life in a foreign country could sometimes be so difficult. Especially Italy. She bade farewell to the delicate old oracle.

'Molto grazie, Signore. Arrivederci.'

The old man was by now gazing into a corner of the ceiling.

'Arrivederci,' he said frailly.

The two women escorted Belinda through the various dark rooms and hall towards the blazing heat of the summer morning as the old man's voice rang out behind them.

'*Livorno! LIVORNO!*'

'*Grazie, Babbo!*' his daughter called over her shoulder.

She tried to make Belinda take a cool drink, but she declined politely in her heavily English-accented Italian:

'*E molto gentile, ma –*'

'*LIVORNO!*' wafted down the corridor and into the hall where they were standing. '*LIVORNO!*'

'*Grazie, Babbo!*'

***

Belinda stepped into the road, where she found Julia standing beside the car, trying to improvise another sling around her other hand, which was dripping bright red blood in the sunlight.

''Snothing,' she said, smiling sweetly, 'bloodydoorbangedshuttoo-quickly.' She hiccupped.

You really should try to love your body a little more, thought Belinda. God knows, enough *men* do – especially around these parts, where Julia was never short of admirers – even if they were a little alarmed by the excesses of her drinking.

Belinda got into the car and started the ignition while Julia arranged herself on the back seat, spilling only a small amount of her blood onto the floor. Soon she was fast asleep again.

Botticelli or Simone Martine? Belinda wondered as she tried to force herself to make the decision about travelling via Florence or Siena. It was the only way she'd be able to choose. Everything was so much more difficult without Tony. He'd have known which route to take, even if he wasn't so good at telling a Piero from a Raphael.

Verrocchio or Duccio? she asked herself. Lorenzetti or Giotto, Pisano or Brunelleschi? It was enough to drive you mad. Even here in heavenly Tuscany.

***

A lizard rested under the shadow of a flowerpot filled with basil. Ants scurried across the stone path outside the kitchen, carrying away crumbs from a loaf and other kitchen scraps dropped by Julia as she cleared up after lunch. Upstairs, three middle-aged Englishwomen lay, sated, on Belinda's huge bed under the mosquito net.

'Are you absolutely certain it's safe for her to cook in that condition, Belinda dear?' asked Marjorie Lovejoy.

'Oh yes, surely...' said Belinda uncertainly.

'As long as bits of her don't start dropping into the sodding *pasta*,' said Hermione Ember, who was always one for blunt statement.

'She drinks so,' said Marjorie.

'Obviously trying to forget,' said Hermione. '*What*, I wonder?'

Belinda saw her opportunity to say something positive.

'She seems to fall asleep if she hasn't got alcohol inside her.'

'Then she should become a bloody teetotaller and stop trying to kill herself,' said Hermione bluntly.

Belinda pushed the *play* button on the CD player's remote control and waited to be annoyed by the American woman's voice.

'I love my life!'

'I love my life,' echoed Belinda and Marjorie. Hermione remained silent.

'I love my work!'

'I love my work!' boomed Hermione. She was Belinda's literary agent.

Do I love my work? wondered Belinda. *I certainly* ***should*** *do.* What could be better than spending the whole of your adult life studying and writing about the Italian Renaissance, staying several months every year in Tuscany, knowing practically all the churches and chapels between here and Montalcino – and between here and the other side of Florence? Between here and the far side of Siena?

She'd studied every inch of some of these churches. If only she'd studied the Italians' language as thoroughly, but she hadn't, and she felt ashamed, comforting herself with the thought that, for all their love of talking, the Italians are basically defined by their visual sense.

That's why the thrice daily *passeggiata* is so important to them, she told herself. It doesn't just provide an opportunity to catch up with local gossip but gives people the chance to show off their latest *Prada* handbag, *Ermenegildo Zegna* shirt or *Gucci* shoes. So, people who thought you had to speak the language fluently to understand the Italian character were wrong. You had to know their great art: their *duomos*, their Michelangelos, Titians, Caravaggios and their wonderful frescoes. And Belinda certainly did.

Not only did she understand the spirit of the Italian Renaissance, she even knew the exact measurements of some of its great masterpieces, down to the last millimetre. What could possibly be better than that? Well, having someone to share it with, of course, and Tony had tried so hard, even though he wasn't what you'd call arty. More mechanically inclined, really. Into digging dams and wells and terracing. That sort of thing.

Marble Patterns in the Marbleless Churches and Chapels of Tuscany. Her latest book. It was only a working title, but it helped to keep her eye on the ball. It was a catalogue and description of all the surfaces painted to look like marble: the green and white *Apollino* from Euboea, which the Romans took with them as far as Colchester; *Rosso antico* in various shades of dark red, a name taken up by Josiah Wedgwood to describe his red stoneware; the oranges and yellows and off-whites and other variations or hues developed by masters and lesser painters to emulate the look of marble in churches where marble wasn't to be found – or had been once, before it was stolen by invading armies.

Yes, surely she enjoyed – *loved* – this work, which bonded her, Belinda Duguid, to the aims and ambitions of those Tuscans who set out to define their culture and to change the world's. *Surely*. It was certainly a *sort* of love. And then she started to worry about Julia again. Does *she* love her work? *Oh, dear, I feel so responsible...*

'I love my orgasms!' declared the American woman.

I can't remember, thought Marjorie.

'I never loved any of mine!' shouted Hermione.

'Oh, I very much enjoyed some of mine,' said Belinda – at first surprised, and then appalled, by her own candour. She feared a return to that *EST* frame of mind when she so foolishly sang *One Currant Bun in the Baker's Shop* to those three hundred strangers. She shuddered at the thought.

And then she remembered the time she'd spent here at her *casa colonica* with Tony: all his plans for the property, and his crazy inventions. Once, before Alberto had taken over the tending of the olive trees, Tony had designed and built an olive-picking machine. It was his pride and joy, and he named it *Leonardo* to please her.

The entire neighbourhood turned out to see it one October morning at the start of the olive- picking season. Don Ettore Caballo the parish priest blessed the machine, while his faithful terrier *Pasticcio* sired yet another litter behind the *capanna* with one of his parishioners' mongrels. Alberto broke a bottle of his undrinkable wine against the engine while Giancarlo announced to everyone that this was the best thing to do with the disgusting muck.

The whole congregation tensed as Tony's great invention approached the first tree. It spread its long tentacles, grabbed dozens of olives and hurled them half a kilometre across the fields and down the hill. That was its one and only outing for years. Later that day, drunk on Alberto's vile brew, Tony and several villagers wheeled the olive-picking machine into the *capanna*, where it would have stayed forever had it not been destined to make one more public appearance during Tony's lifetime. It was used on a starry night to help a man of God.

An English Jesuit, an old friend of Belinda and Tony's, was driving away from the house after enjoying an excellent dinner prepared by Giancarlo's wife Ines, the best cook in the area. The *Brunello* had flowed freely that night as well, since Jesuits always like the best of everything. Instead of going forward as he intended, Father Peter Hewitt, SJ shoved his gearstick into reverse by mistake and sent his car flying off the terrace into the branches of one of the larger olive trees below. Fortunately, it was a sturdy old tree, so the Rev Hewitt's vehicle remained suspended aloft and didn't crash to the ground, as Belinda feared it might.

Word went around the village in no time, and soon a crowd had assembled around *Casa Cimabue*.

Cosa c'è? What's up? What to *do*? Nobody could work out how to get the car down, till someone had the brilliant idea of trying Tony's olive-picking machine. A group of men crowded into the *capanna* and uncovered *Leonardo*, which was by this time full of rust, and poured *benzina* into the tank. They wheeled it out, and Tony cranked up the engine till it croaked back to life.

Shuddering and spluttering, *Leonardo* approached the tree below the terrace and gently plucked both car and Jesuit from its branches before placing them safely on the terrace. Forever afterwards Tony's contraption was known as *la macchina divina*, and Father Peter Hewitt as *il padre volante*, the flying priest.

'I love my attitude!' shouted the American woman.

'Huh!' sneered Hermione.

'I love my determination!'

'I love my determination,' said Marjorie quietly.

'I love my superiority!'

'Mmmm...' they all mumbled.

A bang outside let them know that Julia's *motorino* had skidded on the gravel and crashed into the *capanna* housing *la macchina divina.*

'Aaagh!' wafted through the bedroom window from below, followed by a silence which suggested that Julia might have knocked herself unconscious this time.

All three rushed from the security of the mosquito net and downstairs to investigate.

*****

LOST HOUSES

Balancing a tray on one splayed hand, Belinda gently knocked on Julia's bedroom door with the other.

'Uuuuuhhh...' sounded from inside.

Belinda opened the bare old wooden door and stepped over the threshold cautiously, as though she were entering a foreign country, or possibly landing on a distant planet. White bandages showed behind the whiteness of the mosquito net. Most of Julia's lovely hair was hidden by a large one wrapped around her head, and other bandages covered an arm and a hand. Bloodstains speckled the pillow with vivid red. She had a closed black eye, but the other one slowly opened and focused on Belinda.

I'm going to love your body, thought Belinda, *even if you won't, and I'm going to save it from* ***you****. Now that's positive thinking.*

She placed the tray on the bedside table, then sat down on the bed and began to put *porcini* soup into Julia's lovely mouth.

'Julia dear, I thought we might go and spend a few days by the sea when you're feeling a little better. Nice sea breezes and everything...'

Since the complications of the trip to Pisa Airport, Belinda had become aware that she didn't know nearly enough about coastal Tuscany. She clung to the hills and their beautiful towns for comfort, and perhaps it was time for her to learn a little more about contemporary Italy. Seaside towns often tell you a great deal about life as it's lived now, she thought, though she shuddered at the idea of Blackpool conveying to foreign visitors anything at all about English culture. However, a trip to the seaside would be a good way of discovering more about the arcane workings of Julia's mind.

There you are, she told herself – *the power of positive thinking.* She felt quite elated.

'Mmmmm...' said Julia.

The CD started playing loudly from Belinda's room.

'I love my health!' shouted the American woman.

'I love my health!' Marjorie and Hermione shouted back.

'I love my money!'

'Jesus Christ!' boomed Hermione.

I wish I had some, thought Marjorie, though she wasn't nearly as poor as she suspected. It gets a lot worse than that, the poor could have told her.

Hurriedly Belinda jumped up from Julia's bed and ran onto the landing.

'Dears!' she implored them. 'Think of poor Julia.'

At that moment a car drew up on the gravel outside, and almost immediately a dog barked. It was *Pasticcio*. Belinda rushed downstairs and opened the front door in time to see him urinating against the *capanna*, where he had sired one of many litters all those years ago. Don Ettore was climbing out of his car, beaming at Belinda.

'Buongiorno, Signora!' he called to her, before saying proudly: 'Good morning.'

Belinda knew that Don Ettore was learning English in order to increase his flock from among the foreign newcomers. He was spoilt for choice really: now there were British, Irish, American, Dutch, German, French, Belgian, even Australian people everywhere, and several other nationalities too. And all of them living in *case coloniche* which the locals had long ago found too old and uncomfortable to inhabit anymore. They'd all moved into comfortable new housing developments in horrible places like Camucia.

For the first few years that Belinda and Tony occupied the now renamed *Casa Cimabue*, its previous owners, an old peasant couple forced to move out by their greedy offspring (who pocketed all the money paid by Tony), made an annual pilgrimage to see the old place and inspect the olives, tutting as they hobbled between the trees – till one year they were killed in a car crash on their way home to Camucia. A little *Madonna* beside the road marks the spot.

Don Ettore wasn't too fussy about whether the newcomers were Catholic or not and welcomed them all to Mass and church events – from the school play to the many concerts he encouraged in the little church grounds. He even laid on an annual *festa degli stranieri*, a party for foreigners at which the locals would force huge amounts of food on them, and Alberto poured out endless glasses of his foul wine for the unsuspecting newcomers in the hope that they would buy cases of it the next day. Don Ettore had been giving Holy Communion to Belinda for years without acknowledging what he must have heard or at least suspected: that she was a faithful member of the Church of England.

''Ow is the invaleed?' he asked Belinda, waving a bag of peaches at her.

Before Belinda could answer, the American woman's voice blared from the open bedroom window above.

'I love my sexuality!' she shouted.

'Oh, shut the fuck up!' boomed Hermione back at her.

Then she must have somehow interfered with the CD, because it started playing manically, making it sound like a stylus had got stuck in the groove of an old vinyl record. The American woman's voice said the same thing over and over again, faster and faster, like a mad mantra:

'I love my clitoris I love my clitoris I love my clitoris I love my clitoris...'

Close to despair, and feeling far from positive, Belinda hurriedly ushered in the devoted priest to see her drunken, self-mutilating patient for whom she felt so responsible – and whose mother, Diana, her oldest friend, Belinda was keeping very much in the dark about her daughter's youthful alcoholism.

***

Most of the pieces of furniture at *Casa Cimabue* were lovely old Tuscan chests and tables, wardrobes and chairs, washbasin stands and cabinets – bought over the years in Cortona and Florence antique shops or at the market held in Arezzo over the first weekend of each month. But one corner of the house remained resolutely English.

A small room leading off Belinda's study – her *sanctum sanctorum*, her *boudoir* (she didn't know what the Italians would call it) – was stuffed with little reminders of home. Leatherbound copies of Jane

Austen, the Brontës and Thackeray, back issues of *Country Life* and *The Field*, old *Private Eyes*, a 1920s croquet set, several Noël Coward records, a collection of opera programmes from Covent Garden, Tony's *Wisdens*, his yellow and red *MCC* tie and his cricket bat: all vied with each other for space on the floor and on the bulging shelves.

And covering every inch of the walls, so different from the great oil paintings and frescoes of the Italian Renaissance, were nineteenth century English landscapes in watercolour, and prints of great and lesser English and Scottish country houses, several of which had been in her or Tony's family.

Whenever the Tuscan sun became too unbearable, or the mosquitoes too delinquent, or the locals' tricks too complicated, Belinda retreated to this small haven and pretended she was back in Wiltshire, Knightsbridge, Yorkshire, Oxford or Perthshire – whichever she had most need of at the time. She adored Tuscany but thought it wrong to believe that you can't have too much of a good thing. You *can*.

In the public parts of her lovely house, she was prepared to compete with all the other foreigners to be more Tuscan than the Tuscans, but in this sacred little spot she was going to be as English as she liked – or at least Anglo-Scottish, which Tony was, though she had a feeling the Scots spelt his surname *Duiguid*. (God knows, she had enough trouble getting people to spell it even the English way, and here in Italy it was practically impossible.) But her thoughts were rambling, and she was beginning to lose her thread. She wanted to concentrate on the holiday she intended to spend with Julia by the sea.

She would leave Hermione and Marjorie behind at the house. Secretly she would lock the door of the *sanctum sanctorum*, of course, and hide the key somewhere safe. They could drive the little run-around *Fiat* she kept as a spare car, and they'd probably be just as happy without her, pottering around antique shops and galleries and, especially in Hermione's case, the many bars that had opened in the town since the success of *Under the Tuscan Sun*.

In fact, Belinda would probably have been a hindrance because Hermione frequently liked to stay out late, haranguing the locals wherever she went – even if she was sometimes surprised when Continentals of one kind or another took offence at some of her remarks.

Belinda was quite pleased that Hermione kept most of her travelling to within Europe, as she suspected the Moslems, for example, however hospitable, might take great exception to some of Hermione's forcefully expressed views on most controversial issues.

Funny, thought Belinda, *the people you're fond of.* She remembered an interview she'd read years earlier with the novelist Timothy Mo, in which he said you sometimes get on much better with people whose political opinions are very different from your own, and can't stand the ones whose views are close to yours.

The trip. She must refer to the *Blue Guide* (not the *Rough Guide* as Julia's contemporaries would do). They'd better head in the direction of Grossetto. How could she know so little about the west of Tuscany? How could she speak and read Italian so badly, after all these years? Not that her heart wasn't in it. It was. The trouble was how terribly easily you could get by in Tuscany with just English, and how lazy this made some people.

In the early years she'd hardly ever mixed verbs with nouns, usually spilling out a stream of either one or the other, operating a sort of linguistic apartheid. For ages she'd been meaning to sign up for an Italian course but had never got around to it. Apart from that, she just wasn't terribly good at languages. Even her cleaner Maria, Giancarlo and Ines's daughter, spoke to her in English. (Maria only cleaned for foreigners.)

She thought about her own character, or at least what she knew of it, since she would never have claimed to be very psychologically self-aware. Belinda knew she was a bit old-fashioned. In truth, she believed she was like a misunderstood character in a nineteenth-century novel: Anne Elliot, perhaps, or Elinor Dashwood, or Jane Eyre. Or Mrs Rochester? *Don't go there... That's the trouble when you start trying to place yourself in literature – at first you think you're Juliet,* thought Belinda, *and you end up as the Nurse.*

And what of Tony? Not quite Captain Wentworth, it's true, nor Colonel Brandon, and certainly not Mr Rochester. Perhaps the sweet, kind, loyal Fred in *Brief Encounter. That would do,* she thought. *You can't beat kindness. And you certainly can't beat loyalty.*

How appropriate: Fred's wife – the heroine of the film played by Celia Johnson – was called Laura, the name which Arezzo's famous son Petrarch gave the great heroine of his poems, inspiring Europe's lyric poetry forever after. Belinda, who'd conveniently forgotten that Petrarch spent most of his life in Provence, had read some of the poems, but only in English translation. She reckoned that her appalling Italian was so vastly inferior to a decent translator's there was no point in her even trying to read the originals.

She looked at the prints of English and Scottish houses and thought about the lives of her and Tony's ancestors. One picture in particular caught her eye: that of a huge pile in the North of England which, for Belinda, represented everything she would ever know about loss – more, even, than no longer having Tony around.

This great house was the darkest ghost in Belinda's past. So dark that it had been the setting of a celebrated case many years earlier, when Belinda was forced into the spotlight of publicity and notoriety by the death of her parents – and the latest, worst piece of behaviour that her once-gilded, delinquent and far older brother David had ever perpetrated. At the time Belinda was about the same age as Julia, but so very different from her in every way...

*****

ENGLISH THANATOPSIS

Somewhere in the frozen northern garden, beyond the dark trees, a wounded peacock screamed in anguish. Massive pyramids of box stood like a great wall, black against the moon and trembling when the wind shook their bulk, as though the peacock had brushed past them and set up a chain reaction while staggering by, trailing its blood in the frosty grass. They seemed to shake with anger, like the Furies...

Beneath the porch of the huge house, across its mighty threshold, lay the body of a well-bred gundog, broken almost in two by the force of a shotgun blast. Belinda imagined stepping over the poor creature and entering her old home, crossing the hall before opening the door of the drawing room where her aristocratic parents lay butchered by their only son who, in his own view, had judged and executed them for the crimes they had committed against *him*.

***

All passion spent, his *royal moment* passed, David Landor was seated in a crimson armchair, sipping whisky from a heavy glass. In his distorted mind he could already feel the weight of outraged loyalty forming ranks against him: the Establishment, whatever that was; his parents' tenantry; the aristocracy; the outraged morality of every class; the press; the police... the list would be endless. The tabloids, to use one of their own clichés, would have a field day. *Everyone* would, of course, except him. He listened to the wind rustling in the box hedges which ringed the house.

A dark-haired man of 34, David had the air of one who has known great buying power during his life. He'd also known the loss of it, which was part of the problem, and, through the many failings of his personality, had devised poor remedies for this. Wearing one of his best Savile Row suits, his old school tie and a fine pair of simple gold cufflinks, he raced down from London in a Porsche borrowed from a friend. It was the staff's night off, and the teenage Belinda was travelling in Italy with her friend Diana.

As he sipped the whisky, David saw, through the cut glass at the bottom of his tumbler, his father's face looking surprised. The pattern of the glass broke up the old man's features and seemed to separate his silver-topped head from the rest of his body. David lowered the tumbler again, noticing that the head and body were still divided. Then he remembered how the force of the shotgun's blast had lifted the head from the trunk, shattering the neck and most of the shoulders.

Emerging from the crater where Mr Landor's collar had been, his Guards' tie lay in tatters across his blood-spattered breast.

Taking another sip of the excellent whisky, David shifted his view and, as he looked through the golden liquid smearing the glass while it trickled down again, saw his mother impaled on the corner of a seventeenth century walnut chest, with her womb blown out.

Not for the first time in his life, David began to feel what people called the consequences of an action. As he thought about it, he tried to swallow but found that his throat was completely dry. A gentle shudder rippled through the whole of his body, making his organs tighten. More than at any time since his childhood he felt the overwhelming loss of his innocence. The process had begun long, long ago in this great house.

Adjusting his starched white cuff and its beautifully simple cufflink, he stood up and poured himself another glass of whisky. Holding the decanter by its neck between his middle fingers, he grasped the stopper with the forefinger and thumb of the same hand, for a moment simply feeling their weight. Then he dropped the decanter onto the mahogany table, making a crashing sound – though the glass was too strong to break – and thrust home the stopper with a thud. The noises resounded in his ears for a while, since they were the only traces of sound in this enormous, empty house.

The peacock was silent by now, presumably dead somewhere in the garden. When even the memory of the sounds had passed, David slapped his hand against the table and listened to the echo ricocheting off the far corners of the huge room. He looked around at his ancestors' portraits on the walls and the several family photographs in silver frames, including one of Belinda doing her best to hide the fear that life would defeat her.

***

'Now, we don't know very much about the Etruscans,' said Anna, the English tour guide, to her small party of British and American enthusiasts and tourists crammed alongside her in the little tomb on the outskirts of Camucia. 'Note the tomb's house-like form...'

Everybody studied the roof-shaped ceiling.

'These tombs are the most we have, apart from some wonderfully realistic statuary, painted vases and the marvellous metalwork you'll see in the museum later this morning. If you look at this wall-painting, you'll get the biggest clue, really.'

They all moved forward to inspect the picture on the wall.

'We can't decipher their hieroglyphs, though we *can* make out their phonetic structure. The language isn't Indo-European, and the experts haven't decided whether they originally came from Lydia or somewhere else in the east, or from the Italian mainland itself. They were probably the first rulers of Rome.'

'I read somewhere that the Etruscans were very direct when discussing sex,' said Hermione, fixing Anna with a ruthless stare.

The guide looked back at her cautiously, not quite sure where this was going.

'What do you mean, exactly?' she asked.

'Well,' said Hermione, making sure that the entire group was paying attention, 'if you turned up unexpectedly at your friends' house while they were *in flagrante*, the slave answering the door wouldn't say "Oh, sorry, the master's busy pruning the roses," or "The mistress is holding a mothers' union meeting in the drawing room," or use any other sort of euphemism…' She glared at her rapt and wary audience, defying them to turn away. 'He'd just say, "My master and mistress can't see you now because they're too busy fucking."'

A shocked intake of breath passed around the group, the loudest coming from the American contingent who were only in this Etruscan tomb to fill in time before taking the *charabanc* tour past Frances Mayes' house and other *Tuscan Sun* sites later. If she hadn't already been inside a tomb, Marjorie would have liked the earth to swallow her.

'Oh, Hermione, dear,' she groaned. 'I think we'd better go and pick up some wine from the *Coop*.'

And with a firmness usually unknown to her, she marched Hermione out of the tomb – leaping, as she hoped, more than two and a half thousand years in twenty seconds.

***

The consequences of an action. And the sequence of events and feelings which had led up to it...

Sitting down again, David recalled the highlights of his shoddy life: the points of contact, which were rare; and the loss of it, which was not.

He had always been considered aloof, even when he was behaving wildly at parties. There was a separateness about him, as though the damage had started early in his life. Or was his isolation inevitable, as some people thought, due to his privileged position?

In this room he had celebrated winning his places at Oxford and Sandhurst before joining the Guards. Both family and staff had toasted the dashing young man with the perfect career ahead of him. And in this room he had suffered the vigil of shame which followed his being cashiered from the army. Here his parents read his Colonel's letter.

'This is a disgraceful case,' it said. *'You have abused the trust of everyone in the battalion – officers, NCOs and guardsmen alike – and shown yourself to be utterly unfit to hold a commission in HM forces. There is no longer a place for you in the regiment...'*

Humiliation indeed. In certain sections of British society you can't fall any further than that. And Belinda, as David's only sibling, couldn't have fallen much further either, or known greater embarrassment. She would be almost grateful for the *EST* rumpus later, to help her bury just a little of her shame.

In this vast room so much news of his various disgraces had been received. He remembered the years of high life: staying for months on end at Claridge's; treating Europe like a playground for him and his glamorous set, the Mediterranean as a lake; living in a kind of paradise.

Followed by the fall: the prison terms he served after the perfect life had crumbled, when his promise had finally been denied forever. In reality, he had been seeking the same goal in both worlds – in the public life of his first, privileged existence, and in the shame of his downfall – *joy through oblivion.* Once, visited in a high security psychiatric hospital by Belinda, he had tried to explain this to her, but it was a concept too far – just too foreign for a simple, trusting mind like hers.

He recalled his school days, when his enormous income had often bought the indignities of others. Love had fought its first battle there and been defeated by him so completely that it never dared to take him on again. At sixteen, a beautiful boy called Alex loved him, an emotion that David saw as weakness, and one that he would never let himself suffer from. One moonlit night, he abandoned the weeping, pleading Alex kneeling naked in the shower room. Later that night the miserable boy hanged himself from one of the cisterns.

***

'*Signore!*' shouted Alberto as he spotted Marjorie and Hermione inspecting the shelves of wine in the huge Co-op.

Then he somehow made tut-tutting gestures simultaneously with his old mouth and skinny arms, seeming to upbraid them for buying wine that wasn't his own disgusting muck.

'Oh, bugger off!' said Hermione, beaming at him with what she imagined to be her sweetest smile as she loaded bottles of *Chianti Rufina* onto her trolley.

She knew he couldn't speak English, but her smile, far from charming him, appeared to frail old Alberto as a deep-felt curse. Subconsciously, he called upon old Etruscan gods to defend him from this brutal woman whose friendship with the *Signora* was a mystery to him. She was like a terrible spirit conjured up in the groves of ancient Etruria – or perhaps the enemy virgin-warrior Camilla who was eventually killed by the Etruscan Arruns' javelin.

Hermione, sensing her triumph over Alberto, continued to pillage the shelves. She ignored the expensive bottles of *Brolio*, and both the *Antinori* and *Frescobaldi* labels (including the delicious *Nipozzano*), the Montalcino Brunello and *Rosso*, the *Ruffino*, the *Ricasoli* labels, and threw in more *Rufina*, plus a few bottles of *Colli Senesi*.

Alberto watched in white-faced horror as he calculated the loss he would make on missed sales of his home-made brew. In common with most Tuscan men, who normally show reliable taste in their appreciation of wine, he had an overwhelming blind spot about his own wine-making ability.

***

For the first time in his life David, sitting here with his murdered parents in front of him, felt the terrible loss of love. Actually felt it, the loss of the thing he had never experienced in any of his many affairs with women. He couldn't remember any of their faces. Not one. Not a single girlfriend, whore or mistress appeared before him now as he sipped his whisky. Instead, only blurred shapes drifted around his memory.

He thought about the buying power he had known. Waves of it, appearing now almost like a tidal sea rushing towards him. And the terrifying stillness when those waves had calmed, the buying power removed – leaving him stranded and empty. The courses of action he had taken then, and their awful consequences. While he felt the rhythm of this sea at work within him, sitting here in the vast drawing room, what seemed like a single piece of driftwood bobbed towards him as he lay there on the shore...

Gradually an image became clear, and he saw the boy David, aged ten, weeping, his earlier hysteria having been spent and replaced by despair. Drenched in water, he was crouching at the top of the cellar steps, replaying the solicitor's words in his mind.

'...and, in addition to all this, the residue of my estate, I also leave to my grandson David for his immediate use the sum of ten thousand pounds, knowing that his parents will advise him sensibly on how to spend it...'

Buying power. This was his first opportunity: his grandfather's enormous fortune to look forward to, and a huge sum for a ten-year-old's immediate use. This was the first money of his own, and it provided him with a chance to *give*. He could buy presents for everyone. He suggested it at once, but they all declined, saying no to young David. *'No, no – of course not,'* they said. *'It's all for you. Spend it on yourself, like Grandfather wanted...'*

He felt hemmed in, trapped, claustrophobic. They wouldn't let him give, and he wondered if that meant he could never be free. He thought with both the fog and the clarity of a ten-year-old, and he felt that there was no chance of crossing the huge divide. Something snapped within, and he was lost forever. *'I want to buy things for you!'* he screamed hysterically. Uncomprehending, they were desperately concerned about the boy. *'David, you mustn't,'* they said. *'Now stop it. We don't want anything. Just calm down...'* The talking failed, and David became more hysterical. In the awful panic, he heard his mother utter one last word to Jenny, a worried housemaid.

'Water...'

Jenny made for the door, but David ran after her.

'Jenny, let me buy you a nice new coat!' he screamed, tugging at her apron.

She pulled herself free and vanished through the doorway. Dizzy, David turned back to his parents, pleading.

'I don't want the money! I want to spend it on you! Please let me – *PLEASE!'*

Jenny rushed back into the drawing room with a jug of water in her hands, followed by the cook and a kitchen-maid. David's father took the jug and threw the water over his son, who started to choke amid his sobs. He saw everyone staring at him and cast his eyes down...

'...will advise him sensibly on how to spend it...'

The words seemed to scrape inside his brain as he sat, drenched and sobbing, on the top step of the cellar stairs. He thought about an injured rabbit he'd tried to drown in the lake three years before, when he was seven, hoping to put it out of its misery. He remembered its ears pressed back against its exhausted body, the corners of its mouth turned down and the eyes too tired and afraid to move. Blood from its wound ran with the water in the lake. David was panicking and close to tears.

'Oh, please die,' he pleaded. 'For God's sake, die. You're so hurt. Just die, please don't suffer...'

Quietly he let himself slide down the stairs one step at a time. He could hear the voices of concern on the other side of the cellar door, which he had locked. Gradually the voices became fainter, until at last an absolute silence hung over the dark cellar, a silence which seemed to clothe and even caress him – and which soon began to feel completely comfortable and familiar, like a parent.

He started to play down there in the darkness, and knew it was a world he'd never leave, a silence from which he wouldn't return.

*****

UNDER THE ETRUSCAN SUN

Someone else who'd managed to fool himself about an imagined wine-making ability was Terence Jarvis, the owner of a neighbouring *casa colonica*. He'd discovered the area in a former incarnation, when he came out to investigate a fellow Brit's suspicious insurance claim involving stolen Ferraris.

Soon he abandoned his life as an insurance broker, and his home in Epsom, where he'd spent most of his unexciting life, and moved into *Casa Magnifica* – though *Casa Stereotipata* might have been a more appropriate name for it. Now he kept himself going by doing up fellow Brits' houses. He'd carried out some of the less complicated jobs at Belinda's home, but she didn't feel comfortable employing a non-local.

Like Belinda, he wasn't very good at Italian, but enjoyed brewing his own wine which, unlike Alberto, he never passed on to anyone else – free or otherwise. And, very unlike Belinda, he wasn't a fan of the *passeggiata*, which he considered over-indulgent to the Italian ego. He was often seen reading a newspaper while the *Gucci* and *Ermenegildo Zegna* floated past him on the *Via Nazionale*. He went there to see what was going on in England, as the bar supplied him with free British newspapers while he drank their cheapest wine. The information was only two or three days old, after all. Local children did their best to distract him, without much success.

Now he gazed in horror at the sight and sound of Hermione as she experimented with the resonance of *'too busy fucking!'* on the totally bemused, non-English speaking Albanian woman at the sales till. Marjorie was praying they'd be back at *Casa Cimabue* and drinking the wine within twenty minutes, even if it meant breaking the speed limit along the winding hillside road.

Terence had been shopping for his sweetheart Ortensia, who'd been widowed two years earlier. Later, he'd be having dinner with her and her three children, who liked to try out their English on him, and sometimes translated for him and Ortensia when there was a danger of the lovers misunderstanding one another. And with their cosy family dinner, Terence and Ortensia would drink the wine produced by her late husband not long before his unexpected death.

***

Seated in the crimson armchair, David sipped his whisky, drumming his nails against the table beside him. Steadily he altered the rhythm, so that all four fingers and thumb hit the mahogany at the same time. In his hazy mind the tapping became the sound of an axe cutting into oak, somewhere in the wood...

David was eleven, walking down a path between the vast trees. At the centre of the wood, where several paths converged, stood the woodman's son, John, who was the same age, and one of life's victims. In his grubby hands he held a dying starling.

'Let me see,' said David, who was curious and wanted to share the experience with John.

Fear and resentment blazing in his eyes, John turned and fled with the injured bird, certain that David would kill it. David started to chase him along the path but, even as he ran behind him, focusing on John's dirty clothes, he didn't really know *why* he was chasing him.

Suddenly, into the path stepped the woodman, Bowen, axe in hand, ready to protect his son. When he saw that it was David chasing after John, he lowered the axe and stared at him. Even at the age of eleven David knew that Bowen's look of resentment went far beyond the immediate and the personal. But it also gave the aristocratic boy a sense of power: he felt like he was riding a strong horse, restraining massive force through the reins, and cutting the beast's mouth with the vicious bit as he made it obey him.

He held their stares for a while, then turned and ambled back along the path, not exactly happy, but certainly more knowledgeable about the status quo.

Putting down the cut-glass tumbler with a bang, David got up and walked over to a Georgian bureau. He opened a drawer, took out a scrapbook and began to read a cutting.

'HIGH SHERIFF'S WOODMAN JOINS POLICE. John Bowen, until recently employed as head woodman on the estate of the county's High Sheriff, Mr George Landor, is to join the police force. Mr Bowen, 21, grew up on the Landor estate, where his father, the late Mr William Bowen, was woodman before him...'

David slammed the scrapbook shut and closed his eyes.

***

The sound of whipping echoes around the farmyard. In the shadows of an old barn John, aged twelve, is stretched naked across the arm of an old plough, crying and biting his lip as David flogs him with a piece of shredded bamboo. Blood streaks his buttocks, and splinters of bamboo lodge in his ripped young flesh. A bit of bamboo flies off, and David bends down to pick it out of the sawdust scattered on the ground. Then, holding it in his hand, he approaches John's grubby, shaking flesh and cuts three deep lines in his arm.

'That's my mark,' he says, almost caressing John. 'It means you're my property.'

John pisses himself with fear. David unzips his trousers.

***

As the crickets chirruped outside, Belinda cautiously opened Julia's bedroom door.

'Julia, dear – are you nearly packed?'

Bandaged Julia was sprawled across a creaking chair, drinking from a wine bottle, with her feet on the unmade, bloodied bed. (The cleaner, Maria, always approached this area with caution, and preferred to tidy up when Julia was out on one of her *motorino* escapades.)

'Nearly.' She gulped down more wine. 'Do you re-remember when Mother was pregnant with Lucinda?' she asked slurrily.

Belinda thought back to the joyful days leading up to the birth of her friend Diana's first baby. She and Tony went round to her house in Oxford every day, finding many different ways to help.

'Yes, it was so moving –'

'She told me that Granny kept going on at her about how im-impor-portant it was to have beautiful thoughts...' Julia burped, and Belinda braced herself.

'Your grandmother did like to think positively.'

'Well, Lucinda turned out beautiful, all right...' another burp, 'but *hideously unhappy*!' Julia took a mighty swig from the bottle. 'Granny never said a bad word about anybody-dy – she even claimed that Hitler must have been a charming baby!'

'Julia, dear – are you ready to go to the seaside?'

'Grandad was a funny one, wasn't he? One day he climbed onto the roof to mend it, took a swig from his fl-flask and fell off. He just got up and walked away. It should have ki-killed him.' *Glug*.

Belinda didn't want to dwell too long on family memories in case Julia started asking questions about the Landors. She was being more chatty than usual – *almost as chatty as the crickets,* thought Belinda.

'Shall we set off in twenty minutes, dear?'

Julia gave another burp, then asked: 'Is the wine in the car?'

***

David opened the scrapbook again and read:

'PC PROMOTED SERGEANT...'

He smiled, remembering the three marks he'd cut into John's arm. Then he noticed, inside the drawer, a loose cutting from *The Times*.

'HIGH SHERIFF'S SON ORDERED TO KEEP OFF PARENTS' ESTATE,' it read. *'A High Court judge today ordered a former Guards officer to stay away from his parents' property...'*

David stared at the cutting for a few moments before closing the drawer and sitting down again in the crimson armchair. He picked up the telephone and dialled a number. A voice answered. David spoke calmly.

'Hello, could I speak to the Chief Constable, please?'

As he waited, he was struck by a small irony. His father, as High Sheriff, had been responsible for the comfort of visiting circuit judges.

'Hello?' said a new voice at the other end of the line.

'Hello, Sir James,' said David. 'David Landor, here. Look, I'm afraid something bad has happened at the house... Yes, I'm at home... I know, but I am anyway. Now, the thing is, you'd better send some people over. It's my parents... Yes, they're dead... Yes... I won't go into it now. I'll wait here...'

He listened to the Chief Constable who, once he'd recovered from the initial shock, became a model of efficiency – which David, as a former soldier, greatly appreciated. He'd been dreading the idea of keen young police officers bearing down on him, unrestrained. He had confidence in Sir James.

'Good. I'm most grateful, Sir James. Sorry to cause you so much trouble. I'll just sit here and wait...'

David replaced the receiver and poured himself another glass of whisky. He didn't have to worry about getting his story right, as he was going to admit everything. He looked around the room again and walked over to a tall window. Drawing back the heavy curtains, he saw that dawn was breaking. A glowing light was starting to cut across the sky. The wind had dropped, and the surface of the lake glistened. He drank his whisky and waited for the sound of sirens.

At last, he heard them far away. Leaning his forehead against the cold glass of the windowpane, he realised that his life had really ended many years ago – long, long before he had moved out of this house as a young man, when Belinda was just a child growing up so timidly within it. Then she longed for his occasional visits, before the court case which resulted from his growing violence against their parents.

Appearing through the gateway at the top of the avenue were two gleaming white police cars, their blue lights reflecting on the surface of the lake. He wondered what the officers would think as the house loomed so massively ahead of them. When they pulled up outside the great porch, he saw Inspector John Bowen lead his men up the stone steps, past the dead gundog, towards the front door. He moved away from the window and met them in the hall. Seeing John inside the house once more made him feel a sense of peace, almost a return to misinterpreted innocence.

Later, when he was driven away by the CID for questioning at the police station, he looked back and saw John standing at the top of the steps, in possession of the old place, and was quite content to leave the house in his care. The police car enveloped him and shone like a white avenging angel as it drove along the avenue. More police cars and an ambulance approached from the other direction, and the lake reflected a sea of spinning blue analeptic light as David Landor was taken away to be held, perhaps forever, within England's protective bosom.

***

The pyramids of box stood quite still, paler in the early morning light, which cut across them sideways. Between each one hung fresh cobwebs in which drops of dew were illuminated like beautiful pearls. The Furies had left, and the great hedges were now at rest. Beyond them, undiscovered so far, the peacock lay stiff on the frost-hard grass.

And Belinda Landor, at that time a timid girl of nineteen – no-one, including herself, would have called her a woman, young or otherwise – returned prematurely from Italy but never entered the house or garden again. She received a lot of advice and care, understood nothing, and buried herself forever after in the treasures of the Italian Renaissance. People who didn't know about the celebrated case would never have guessed that someone as seemingly uncomplicated as Belinda could possibly have known such darkness in her earlier life.

From time to time she visited her much older brother at his new home in Broadmoor. The scenes she witnessed there often reminded her of those in Signorelli's *Last Judgment* in the *Duomo* at Orvieto.

*****

ITALIAN SECRETS

Belinda hadn't told Julia why she'd changed her mind about Grossetto and decided they would visit the famous resort of *Forte dei Marmi* on the Tuscan coast. It wasn't just that this was the place where smart people go – Cannes rather than Blackpool – but she was also fascinated by the name: it meant *'Fort of the Marbles'*, and Belinda, given her fascination with marbles – or the lack of them – couldn't help believing this held some sort of healing power that might change Julia's catastrophic life.

She sat gripping the steering wheel as Julia weaved her incredibly unsteady way towards the car, with Marjorie several yards behind her, carrying the stained suitcase. Maria hovered nearby with a mop and bucket and change of sheets, ready to blitz Julia's bedroom once she was certain she'd left.

Hermione bellowed from an upstairs window: 'Don't kill too many Eyeties on the way, Belinda! If you do, hide them in the fucking boot!'

Belinda grimaced and waved up at her through the driver's window as Marjorie put the suitcase in the boot. Once Julia had tumbled onto the back seat, she said: 'Do your seat belt up, Julia – *clunk-click...*'

'That's what they all say to me!' shouted Julia, making Marjorie and Belinda jump. *'Clunk- click! Clunk-click!'*

Marjorie closed the door and went round to Belinda's window.

'Good luck, Belinda dear,' she said. 'Lots of love to you both. Have a wonderful time!'

'Don't lose your fucking marbles!' yelled Hermione from above.

Belinda feared she might fall asleep that night hearing those words ringing in her troubled ears.

***

The Cortonese children had discovered a wonderful new way to irritate Terence. Giuseppe, owner of the bar where he sat outside reading the free papers during the *passeggiata*, had installed a device which projected the image of a dancing bear onto the pavement. By jumping up and down, the kids could rattle the device and get the bear to dance across Terence's newspaper, seriously distracting him. They could even make it upstage the *Ermenegildo Zegna* and *Gucci* passing by.

Terence was determined not to be beaten. The *passeggiata* is as much about ignoring people as acknowledging them, he told himself, while he read a gossip columnist discussing a relationship:

'A – What's he do? B – Product manager. A – What's the product? B – I don't know. We didn't get that deep.'

At the next table, François, the French diplomat, said to his English companion, Deborah: 'I had to introduce the Minister of Agriculture to the Pope. He pulled a medal out of his pocket and gave it to *Il Papa*, who said: "*I* usually give out the medals."'

The bear danced across Deborah's glass of *Colli Senesi* as she listened, and the Etruscan enthusiasts walked past with their guide, Anna. The last two were engaged in a heated discussion about another member of the group. One of them complained:

'She's such an opportunist, if you said you were going to Antarctica, she'd ask you to bring back a couple of penguins.'

And then a child – a tiny girl in a red dress and white cardigan – marched along with her family and gave a regal wave to everyone as she proceeded grandly along the *Via Nazionale*.

That ego's developing much too fast, thought Terence.

***

After the *passeggiata*, Terence was driving up the hill to Ortensia's house. He'd decided to propose to her that evening, having been inspired by the wedding announcements in the *Daily Telegraph*. The road wound and wound in true Tuscan style, but Terence wasn't the sort of person to see that as a metaphor – or would he have called it a simile?

He wanted children with her, although she already had three – two girls and a boy – but did he want English or Italian children? What would *she* want? Would she insist on Italian, or would she like half-and-half? Would he want them to be bilingual? Since his Italian wasn't good, would they keep secrets from him? He hadn't experienced complications like these in Epsom. But he hadn't been a married man in Epsom.

Suddenly a huge black dog dived out of the bush beside the road, making him swerve, and the tyres screech – and the car, out of control, careered down the hill, off the road. He wasn't a particularly good driver – and driving in Tuscany was a lot harder than driving in Surrey at any time. He was astonished at the speed with which he descended through the landscape. And he just caught a glimpse of the little *Madonna* marking the spot where the old couple who'd owned *Casa Cimabue* had been killed.

***

Belinda sipped her morning coffee as she sat at an outdoor café table between the mountains and the sea. And she thought about the marble that had been extracted from those mountains, which were in the same range as Carrara. She'd got over the strain of yesterday's journey via the outskirts of Florence and Lucca, and Hermione's warning about not losing *her* marbles. She hadn't worried about *autostrada* or *superstrada*: she'd just followed the signposts. Julia had slept practically the whole way, after downing a bottle before they'd even reached Camucia. It wasn't only *lack* of wine which made her doze off.

Belinda also thought about some of the celebrities associated with *Forte dei Marmi* – particularly Aldous Huxley and Henry Moore. It was probably just as well that she didn't know Thomas Mann had stayed there. He was too dark a force for Belinda, though Henry Moore's statues were borderline.

She leant back and enjoyed the air of the place and the aroma of her coffee, confident that Julia was safely asleep in her bed at the hotel. Gradually she started to examine the other people enjoying their morning beverages, but she did it with Belinda-like discretion. Then she saw a face which began to make something click in her memory, but she couldn't be sure what it was.

The older man at the next table looked almost familiar, and he seemed to be going through a similar process as he pretended to examine a shop front across the street. Had she seen his picture in a newspaper? Was he on TV? Had she met him or known him vaguely, once upon a time? What *was* it?

'Excuse me,' he said quite nervously, in a faint Yorkshire accent, 'are you by any chance Belinda Landor that was?'

An alarm sounded in Belinda's brain, and she jumped. How long was it since anyone had called her that?

'Er...'

'I'm so sorry, I meant to say Belinda *Duguid*. Please forgive me. I was just travelling back in time...'

'Er, yes... Who –'

'I'm John Bowen. I was your father's woodman when you were a child.'

How polite of him, she thought, *not to say, 'and I arrested your brother for murdering your parents when you were nineteen.'*

'I recognised you from articles I read about your books. I'm a bit of a fan.'

'Oh! You joined the police force, didn't you? Are you still in it?'

'Just retired. Chief Superintendent...'

'Congratulations.'

'I'm on a bit of a sabbatical till I become an adviser next year. May I join you?'

'Of course.'

John Bowen got up and moved to her table, and they both found themselves talking and talking and talking – and drinking several cups of coffee over the next two hours. Belinda even had two glasses of *grappa* and learned that he had become fascinated by Tuscany through her books. She'd never encountered a fan before, or drunk *grappa* in the morning.

***

When a *poliziotto* came and told Ortensia that Terence had been badly injured in a car accident the previous night, after he'd swerved to avoid a dog down the road, she screamed.

'That's where my dead husband's dog was killed when I ran it over last year! It's come back to haunt me.'

The *poliziotto* looked shocked. He gulped.

'Are there no other black dogs around here?'

'No. Everyone says they've seen the ghost of it at exactly that spot. It's haunting us!'

Terence and his car had only been discovered that morning by a farmer as he fed his goats. Ortensia didn't know why he'd failed to show up for dinner, but assumed it was work-related. Now she got her children to telephone *Casa Cimabue* and ask, in English, if she could leave them with Marjorie and Hermione as the *poliziotto* was going to drive her to the hospital.

***

Belinda and John, still immersed in conversation, were wandering around the town. He listened to her reminiscing about Tony, and she learned that John had a failed marriage and, like her, a lack of children. They both thought the pier didn't live up to its English counterparts, and they weren't as impressed by the Grand Hotel as they'd expected to be. The Belgian royal family, who stayed there a lot, must have been easier to please than other royals, Belinda thought. One of them was even born there.

'I think the *grappa's* kicking in,' she giggled.

John laughed out loud, delighted that they'd hit it off so well after such an enormous length of time, although he'd followed her career with a sort of secret intimacy.

As they glanced back at the pier, Belinda thought there was something familiar about a figure leaning against the railing – the second time that experience had occurred today. Thanks to the *grappa*, for a moment she felt she was seeing two people, then it became one again. Yes – it was Julia!

'Hi, Julia, dear!' She was surprised at how loudly she called out.

Julia continued to gaze out to sea, so they went over to her. She seemed very contemplative and, for the first time in a very long while – could it be possible? – *sober*... She spoke before Belinda had a chance to introduce her to John.

'I've been reading about film directors who stayed here,' she announced. 'Visconti and Malaparte...'

Belinda had seen some of Visconti's films, but she'd never heard of Malaparte.

'Malaparte swapped his fascism for communism, and his atheism for Catholicism,' said Julia.

The sea air seemed to have had a remarkable effect on her. Belinda couldn't believe it, as she imagined it should have taken days to clear the alcohol out of Julia's body. She introduced her to John, and the three of them started walking through the town. As bracing as it all was – and, obviously, therapeutic – Belinda was already feeling a little homesick for Cortona and the hills. She thought it would be nice to show them to John Bowen.

***

Ortensia's children seemed mesmerised by Hermione. They had never come across anyone – or any*thing* – like her in their young lives. They'd neither read about someone like that in a book, nor seen it in a film or on TV. And they had certainly never heard an adult say *'fucking'* as though it were just a normal adjective.

Usually chatty, they found themselves being rather silent at *Casa Cimabue*. Then, when their imaginations felt tested to the maximum, she introduced them to the sound of *New Ways to Positive Thinking* on the CD player. Was this some terrible premonition of what the twenty first century would be like? After all, it was approaching fast.

'I love my vagina!' was particularly hard to take. The two girls said it was worse for them, even in a foreign language. The boy insisted it was far, *far* worse for him, and he started to pray in Italian.

***

In the hospital at Castiglion Fiorentino, Ortensia was prepared to wait all day and night while surgeons operated on Terence. She felt the children would be well cared for by the two Englishwomen. After all, any friends of Belinda's must be completely reliable. She telephoned *Casa Cimabue* and was surprised how unchatty her son, Edoardo, was.

She didn't know that Castiglion Fiorentino was the hometown of Roberto Benigni who had, only a couple of years earlier, directed and starred in *Life is Beautiful*, in which a father spares his little boy the truth about the concentration camp they're in. Edoardo would have liked to be spared the truth about the one he was currently in. Every time he heard Hermione's voice, he saw a picture of Satan. The imagery came easily because he'd recently been introduced to *The Divine Comedy* at school. He was also reminded of the she-wolf threatening Dante in the wood. He and the boy in the film both needed a Virgil to help them out.

***

Anna was leading her group through the streets of Castiglion Fiorentino, pointing out Vasari's *loggia* and telling them that traces of Etruscan civilisation were found there comparatively recently. She didn't know that Hermione was planning a visit to the area, to pay tribute to the mercenary John Hawkwood, whose *Castello di Montecchio* was nearby.

The Americans who'd joined her from their *Tuscan Sun* expedition were elsewhere, discovering more of *Tuscan Sun* Tuscany. One of her own group shared some exciting news:

'Frances Mayes has had enough of all those people turning up and invading her privacy. She's selling her house!'

Anna was convinced it wasn't true.

***

Belinda decided to waste no time. She proposed that she, Julia and John should drive along the coast and gradually make their way back to *Casa Cimabue*, where John could stay in her English *sanctum sanctorum*. Then they would take daily exercise together – long walks – under John's guidance. They'd climb a hill or two a day.

***

From within the oxygen tent across his hospital bed, Terence accomplished the thing he had been rehearsing since he'd come round from the operation:

'Ortensia,' he whispered through the bandages and plaster cast and plastic, 'will you be my *moglie*?'

'O!' shouted Ortensia. *'O...'*

The children would be spending much of the next few days at *Casa Cimabue*.

*****

THE PATH TO PARADISE

Belinda was very pleased to see that John and Julia were getting on so well, often chatting away together as they explored various beaches in western Tuscany. She felt that Julia was now a shared burden. But she had yet to learn that John had been in Alcoholics Anonymous for twelve years, and his converting Julia would eventually take on the *whole* burden.

When they returned to *Casa Cimabue* three days later Julia was already saying: 'I'm Julia, and I'm an alcoholic,' quietly to herself. John explained the situation to Belinda who, at first, feared it might be like the *EST* world. He reassured her by telling her all about his own life-changing experience, and the nightmare of being an alcoholic senior police officer.

He was far too polite to suggest the main reason for his alcoholism was the abuse he'd received from her brother during his childhood.

He was never going to say: 'I'm John, and I'm an alcoholic because your brother bullied and molested me when I was eight to eighteen...'

They were surprised to see two alarmed-looking little girls heading towards them as they parked in front of the house. Belinda hardly recognised them as Ortensia's daughters at first. One took her hand, and the other John's. Julia headed inside with her suitcase.

When she entered her room, she found Edoardo cowering behind the bed, hiding from the she-wolf/Satan.

'*Mi scusi* – will you please be my *Virgilio*?' he asked her, determined not to venture out again until he was sure of her protection – and that they were *one*.

'Did you kill any fucking Eyeties?' yelled the voice he feared as it welcomed back their hostess.

John Bowen had encountered a lot of rough diamonds in his time, but Hermione took even him by surprise. He was astonished to find someone like her in Belinda's world. Belinda proudly introduced him to Marjorie and braced herself for the Hermione response.

'A copper, eh?' she roared. 'Not a bent one, I hope!'

Even Belinda realised there was an inevitability about that line.

***

On their walk next day, Marjorie came too – and Edoardo clung to Julia's hand the whole way, up and down the two hills, surprising Julia by how reassured it made *her* feel. In the afternoon they drew the nearest hill together in sketchbooks supplied by Marjorie, and he told her what he knew about *The Divine Comedy*. She agreed with everything he said about Hermione but thought her definitely more Satan than she-wolf.

Julia promised she'd come on Hermione's proposed visit to John Hawkwood's castle. And what a curious outing that turned out to be. Hermione had persuaded the bar-owner Giuseppe to contact the owners for her, and she was determined to let everyone know a thing or two about the world they occupied.

Belinda and John went in one car with Julia and Edoardo, and Hermione and Marjorie took the frightened sisters, Rosetta and Alessia, in the little *Fiat*.

However scary John Hawkwood was with his army of mercenaries, Hermione made the locals feel that the English gene had increased its capacity for violence tenfold in the six hundred years since his death. She charged past a group of them, determined to inspect the fortifications.

'I suppose the local estate agents boast that he came from sodding Essex – as most of *them* do!' she announced loudly after parking the car and approaching the *Castello di Montecchio*. 'Open up in there – the British are coming, and the Eyeties too!'

'O! Rosetta, Alessia, Edoardo – le mie ragazze!' Their mother, Ortensia, had come down from the hospital to greet them.

The girls rushed towards her and threw themselves into her arms, but Edoardo held onto Julia's hand. Gently, she pushed him towards his mother, muttering to herself: 'I'm Virgil, and I'm an alcoholic.' John looked at her and smiled. Belinda was impressed.

'Come on, the young!' shouted Hermione. 'In we go... Never mind all the frescoes and marble, Belinda – write something about these walls, and how your marbleless churches wouldn't have been built or survived at all without the power of the fucking mercenaries!'

***

Exhausted by their outing with Hermione, they all gathered later in the hospital, where patients were being fed meals brought from home by their families. To Belinda it felt like a culinary competition for the sick. And she was mystified how anyone could hope to recover if they were being given home-made wine.

Ortensia led the children into the ward for a quick wave at Terence, who waved back from behind his plaster and plastic.

'Miei figli...' he whispered.

Ortensia would share the good news of her engagement with them at a later date.

'Hope you're not loafing about in there, Terence!' shouted Hermione from the corridor.

Belinda, John, Marjorie and Julia looked at each other; then at the walls, doors, windows and, finally, the floor – knowing that Hermione was worse when she felt the presence of an attentive audience.

***

The face looked like God the Father. Or was it a Greek philosopher? A Roman emperor? A poet? It couldn't be Virgil, because it seemed to have a beard. Edoardo wasn't sure. He'd only just woken up, after falling asleep on the other bed in Julia's room, and was looking at a smear of paint on the side of a chest of drawers next to him. The room had been decorated some months earlier by Terence, and the smear gave an indication that he wasn't one of life's perfectionists. But Edoardo couldn't know that. He was gripped by the face, and what it might be telling him.

'Time to go walking, *mio Dante*,' whispered Julia, who was feeling almost stoned by the effects of a life without drink.

She opened his shoulder bag to check the clothing situation and was astonished to find it full of used wrapping paper, empty cans and bottles and *God knows what?* she wondered.

'What's all this?' she asked.

'I didn't want to hurt their feelings,' said Edoardo. 'They'd be very sad if I threw them away and left them all alone – *tutto solo*.'

'Really?'

'Yes. Everything has feelings – *sentimenti...*'

Julia was starting to wonder which of them was Dante, and which *Virgilio*.

***

John Bowen realised he had a mammoth task ahead of him: the resurrection of the late Tony's olive- picking machine, *Leonardo*. He saw no reason why it couldn't be made into the pride of the region and put to use later that year when the olives were ready for picking. There was still plenty of time to work on it.

With the help of Hermione and Julia, as well as Belinda and Marjorie, it was wheeled out of the *capanna*. He handed out brushes and cloths and got everyone, including the children, to rub away at the considerable amount of rust.

'Rub on, Macduff!' yelled Hermione. 'Brush the fucking rust and dust off!'

Belinda would never get used to Hermione's language, but the children didn't wince or cower as much as before. In Tuscany, they reasoned, you adapt to the ways of newcomers.

At exactly midday John switched on the engine. Along with the walks, it became a daily job which he relished, fiddling with its many resurrected parts.

***

'I think the *passeggiata* is the most sensible idea humanity ever came up with,' said John, 'because it forces you to be a part of society, however much you want to hide from it. You *have* to join in.'

They were all sitting outside Giuseppe's bar as the *passeggiata* flowed past them – *Prada, Ermenegildo Zegna, Gucci,* children's overdeveloped egos, the dancing bear, regal waves, *tuttomondo*...

Two smart *carabinieri* passed by, chatting quietly to each other, their left elbows permanently cocked to prevent their swords from dragging on the paving stones. It was impossible to hear what they were saying, unlike the next passers-by, a local man and his German wife who were happy to share their thoughts:

'Her father found us *in flagrante*!' he shouted. 'He behaved like a gentleman. An Englishman. He invited me to leave the house immediately!'

'Ha!' shrieked his wife.

The *passeggiata* had provoked a new thought in Marjorie, but only because it made her wonder about things *more*. There was so much to look at – so many parts of human behaviour to study... Was Belinda suffering from what Marjorie had decided was an English condition – almost a disease? The need to *explain* everything. Or at least everything one was *able* to explain: marbleless patterns, if not the Landor family.

She didn't know how she'd ever be able to discuss this condition with her dear friend.

'Where's the bloody *Daily Telegraph*?' shouted Hermione.

***

'The lictors were originally Etruscan, and they carried the *fasces* before the magistrates in Rome.' Anna was leading her group along the *Via Nazionale* during the pre-lunch *passeggiata* next day. They'd just been visiting the Etruscan Museum at the *Palazzo Casali.*

Julia and Edoardo had come into Cortona after their walk, and having left John and the others to continue the work on *Leonardo*. It was the weekly market, and they were going to do some shopping. Julia also found it useful to test her battle with alcoholism as she watched others knocking back their wine and *grappa* at this time of day.

Edoardo was intrigued by Anna's description of the ancient lictors.

'Uno momento...' he said to Julia, and he rushed into the tobacconist's shop nearby. He emerged waving a little Union Jack and then led her along the *Via Nazionale*, holding it aloft and calling out *'Edoardo il littore!'* to his fellow shoppers as he and Julia headed towards the stall selling nicely aged *pecorino Toscano*.

You're Edoardo, and you're definitely my littore, thought Julia.

Neither was aware that they were passing a plaque commemorating another *fasces*-holding lictor who had been born in Cortona. A pilot in Mussolini's air force, he'd died in his early twenties, flying on Franco's side in the Spanish Civil War. *He* wouldn't have had time for Edoardo's antics and beliefs – especially the ludicrously anti-fascist notion that everyone, and *everything*, counts for something in this world.

***

I think the most sensible idea humanity ever came up with was ***God***, thought David Landor, as he sat looking out of his window in Broadmoor, Crowthorne. *It's a human construct, and we would have been mad not to invent it.*

He noticed a blackbird looking at him from the branch of a nearby tree. It appeared to be judging him, he decided, this *Turdus merula*, before hurling a biscuit at it through the bars. The blackbird was off its branch in no time, grabbing the biscuit in mid-air.

Later it would see off a large kite from its territory in Broadmoor – the *Turdus merula* winning over the *Milvus milvus*. David had been reading about animals which fly, but the drugs he was prescribed sometimes made him misread information on the page. He was really looking at a crow, one of the *corvidae* family living around Broadmoor. And he was yet to learn that the collective name for these new Furies in his life was a *'murder'*. A *murder* of crows...

*****

TUSCAN DREAMS

Belinda was aware that her dreams in Tuscany were very different from her Oxford ones. She thought it must have something to do with the food and the air. Her nightmares were another matter, though. How would the village cope with Hermione at Don Ettore Caballo's summer *festa degli stranieri* in the garden beside his church? There would be visitors from the whole area – of many different nationalities.

The local children, including Moroccan Moslems, would perform a play. All kinds of homemade food would be on sale, and Alberto's olive oil and disgusting wine on offer, as he explained in Italian that it must always be bottled at the new moon. People of every political persuasion were expected. But what if Hermione decided to be at her worst, given the size of her audience? Belinda confided her fears in her new rock, John Bowen.

'Let's see what the day brings,' said John, with a look of optimism in his eyes.

Belinda felt reassured, then astonished, when Hermione entered the kitchen for breakfast with a croaking voice.

'What on earth's happened?' she asked.

Hermione croaked back at her. Belinda couldn't understand the answer – but, more to the point, she could hardly *hear* it. She looked over at John, who was standing in front of the window, with the morning sun giving him a kind of halo through the glass. She would never know how this masterstroke had been pulled off. Would she have to reinterpret her understanding of *the* ***strong*** *arm of the law*?

***

Pasticcio attempted to shag every foreigner's dog as Julia and Edoardo busily placed their *pecorino Toscano* onto toast to make delicious *crostini*, which they would offer to the crowd. Edoardo carefully put the paper which had wrapped the cheese into his pocket, to avoid its becoming lonely in a rubbish bin. Boldly, he thrust the plate at Hermione, who grabbed two of the *crostini* and rammed them into her mouth, making a sound which he chose to translate as *'molto grazie'*. Julia winked at him.

***

One of the definitions for *crow* given in David's copy of *The Shorter Oxford English Dictionary* was: *'One who keeps watch while another steals.'* And the American name for the purple grackle was *crow-blackbird.* He wondered whether the entry had been done by W. C. Minor, the American surgeon and murderer who had compiled so much of the dictionary while living at Broadmoor, where he cut off his own penis with the knife he used as he worked on the ironically named *dic*tionary.

When he examined a picture of the grackle in his bird book, he thought his drugs must be taking over completely. It was like looking at a crow/blackbird/jackdaw while on loads of acid. He thought he was having paranoid delusions like Minor – the colours in its feathers were alarming! Even the grackle seemed to be on acid.

'Nurse!' he shouted.

Three of them entered his room. Safety in numbers was the rule on this wing.

***

'Love keeps you warm,' Edoardo was explaining to the unable-to-swear-back-at-him figure of Hermione, who had collapsed onto a deckchair.

'Wha-a-oad-o-u-ing-ollock-*sss*!' she whispered croakily.

The garden was full now, and Edoardo and the other village children were getting ready to do their play, *Six Characters in Search of God*, which Anna, the tour guide, was directing. She hadn't let the children or Don Ettore know she was both a Catholic and an atheist.

'Stand by everyone!' she called out.

'Tenetevi pronti, tutti!' said several voices.

Drums rolled, guitars twanged and voices squeaked as the show began.

Edoardo's sisters Rosetta and Alessia approached the nearest audience members, who were a mixture of nationalities, proclaiming: *'Benvenuti, tutti!'*

Smiles all round, followed by various scenes from the *New Testament* with one of the Moroccan boys, Mohammed, playing Jesus turning water into non-alcoholic wine.

Cheers, thought Julia.

***

Next day Marjorie woke up convinced that she had shingles. She was certain because she'd had them some years earlier, and she knew that the people who get shingles are ones who care about other people's problems. Hermione would *never* suffer from them.

When she told Maria, she yelled *'O – fuoco di Sant'Antonio!'* and insisted that they contacted Helena, a local healer who was the seventh child of seventh children. She'd even healed Don Ettore when he had them a couple of years before.

Helena came over to *Casa Cimabue* and made several signs of the cross over Marjorie's side and back and told her to take vitamin B, rub in anti-inflammatory gel and keep a raw potato against her skin at all times, held there by gauze.

Spying it later, Hermione, with her voice restored, said: 'Looks like a fucking collapsing colostomy bag!' then roared with laughter.

Marjorie consoled herself with the thought that at least *fuoco di Sant'Antonio* sounded more dignified than shingles.

'Got any scabs?' yelled Hermione.

Marjorie decided to spend the day in her room, though she frequently heard Hermione's mocking voice calling out to her: 'I love my sodding shingles! I adore my scabs!' Then: 'If your shingles meet in the middle, you die!'

Think positive, she told herself. *I love my fuoco! I love my potato!* Eventually she fell asleep, feeling certain that she was being Virgilioed by Helena and St Anthony.

***

Mohammed's grandfather was praying towards Mecca in the garden of their little house next to the church. They had been lent it by Don Ettore as part of his ecumenical drive. The church bell chimed while Julia and Edoardo led Hermione past it, determined to keep her away from Marjorie. She opened her mouth to share her thoughts with the praying Moslem when a mosquito flew inside it and bit her over-used tongue. It was unusual for a mosquito to be about at this time.

'Aaaaggghhh!' came out, followed by silence. Even the birds nearby seemed unable to make a sound for a few seconds.

Mohammed emerged from the house and beamed when he saw Julia and Edoardo, who invited him to join them on their walk.

The four of them ascended the first hill of the day, and the wildlife looked warily at the silent Hermione as she marched past.

Mohammed announced in Italian: 'I want to be a policeman...'

Hermione poked Edoardo to make him translate.

'He wants to be a *poliziotto* so he can arrest you,' he announced with a smile.

She looked as though she'd erupt but, when she opened her mouth, the tongue was so large that Julia thought they'd better get her to a doctor in Cortona. Even Hermione saw the point of that.

***

The four of them sat outside the doctor's surgery, having walked all the way to town. A teenage boy was also waiting. Edoardo asked him why he was here. When he answered, Mohammed giggled discreetly, then Edoardo translated for Julia and Hermione.

'His dog bit him on the *culo*...' The boy told Edoardo something else. 'After the doctor has treated his *culo*, he'll buy some ice cream.'

Mohammed piped up in Italian, and Edoardo translated again: 'Is red wine ice cream for grown-ups?'

Julia thought hard about that one, and Hermione's tongue looked ready to explode.

***

The pre-lunch *passeggiata* was in progress.

'And I heard her saying,' announced an Anglo-Tuscan woman, echoing the words of one of Anna's tourists on a previous *passeggiata*: '"She's such an opportunist, if you said you were going to Antarctica, she'd ask you to bring back a couple of penguins!"'

'Charlatans are big on patriotism,' said someone walking in the other direction, 'because they can't be trusted with loyalty to a particular individual...'

Hermione fumed, though not literally – as she couldn't get a cigarette past her enormous tongue. Edoardo, Mohammed and the teenager contentedly licked their ice creams, and Julia pondered the huge changes that had come into her life.

Recently she'd been reading about the importance of the olive in the history of the classical world: olive trees made up the landscape; olives were what cleaned the body, did the cooking, kept the home warm. Life was impossible without them. The Greeks regarded them as the fifth element.

Back at *Casa Cimabue* Marjorie was thinking that her dose of *fuoco* was the easiest anyone had ever had. Healing by the seventh child of seventh children had come about.

And Belinda thought that her own post-Tony life had been saved by her new *Sant'Antonio*, John.

***

The summer ended. Marjorie and Hermione returned to England, both restored to their former selves. Terence left hospital and married Ortensia. Rosetta and Alessia helped him make wine, which they didn't share with the neighbours – and the two of them remained Italian, though more Anglo-aware.

Julia stayed on and joined Anna when she took autumnal visitors to see Frances Mayes' house and the magnificent marbleless churches of Tuscany, and Edoardo often went with them. Mohammed marched behind the *poliziotti* and *carabinieri* during the *passeggiata*, ticking off the town's naughty children as he went.

At olive-picking time, John drove *Leonardo* into the groves and plucked the fifth element from their trees with a flourish. Alberto looked alarmed as he realised his reign was coming to an end, his call on the *olivi* gone. Belinda had never been prouder of anything in her life or felt so incredibly positive. As the millennium approached, she realised that she and John were the perfect Anglo-Tuscan couple.

When she wrote to David about her happiness, he wondered whether *Anglo-Tuscan* would ever make it into *The Oxford English Dictionary*. It might – after all, he was making a few contributions himself, à la W. C. Minor, fellow murderer and neighbour separated by time.

Maybe he'd even make it to Cortona one day. After all, Minor got back to America eventually and died, without his penis, in the Retreat for the Elderly Insane. His impact on Europe had been very different from Frances Mayes'. David's could be very, *very* different from Belinda's.

AUTHOR BIOGRAPHIES

ANNE HARRAP was born in Yorkshire and went to university there but has spent most of her life in the Thames Valley (with a short break of a few years in Paris). She studied languages and still enjoys trying out new ones. She contributes to two writing groups in Oxford including short stories, verse and playwriting.

CATHERINE HURST lives in a small village in north Oxfordshire. She has been a member of the Walton Street Writers for many years. Originally from London, her career began at the BBC followed by becoming a radio producer for London's commercial entertainment station Capital Radio. She particularly enjoys the craft of short story writing. When not writing she enjoys being outdoors gardening and walking where ideas for her stories begin to form. She is married with two children and one grandchild.

CHARLES BIDWELL (84) was brought up on an Irish farm and spent much of his working life as an EC Lawyer, struggling with 'Technical Regulations as Hindrances to intra-Community Trade' amongst other fascinating topics. His books *Maastricht and the UK* (1993) and *Help from Brussels* (1994) are hardly a laugh a line and he hopes that his contributions to *Côte Tails From Oxford* are rather more enjoyable. He is also collating some of his short stories for re-publication under the working title *Who Are We Neutral Against*—a fictionalised retelling of an operation in 1942 by a group of retired British Army officers in Dublin to smuggle British airmen out of a detention camp in the Republic and across the border into Northern Ireland.

HAROLD ROFFEY was born in London. He is the author of *Missed Opportunities* (2018), *I'm Frank Johnson* (2020), several newspaper articles and many short stories. He has worked as an industrial engineer, a consultant to many companies, some based in ex-Soviet countries. He has served as a director of a few companies and is the co-founder of an international software company. He lived in Zambia and South Africa for many years and now resides in Oxford with his wife, a retired lecturer. They have two sons.

J. M. KENNEDY writes fiction, poems, and children's books, and finds life provides endless inspiration for creative writing. She grew up in Hampshire, moved to Oxford for her degree, then worked in Canada, returning to Oxford almost fifteen years ago. When not reading, writing or thinking about stories, she enjoys knitting, and volunteering at The Story Museum.

JANE SPIRO has been a language educator in multiple international settings, including Hungary, Mexico, Japan and India, becoming Professor of Language Learning and Teaching at Oxford Brookes University in 2019. Her publications include two collections of stories for language learners, two collections of poetry, a novel, and a poetry/story 'smörgåsboard' about refugee journeys based on family histories. She has also written many resources for creative language teaching, including two books with Oxford University Press about language learning through poetry and story.

JENNY BURRAGE has enjoyed writing stories since she was eight years old at primary school. Now she has fun with sketches and poems as well as writing for Walton Street Writers and Oxford Inc.

KEITH McCLELLAN was an English teacher and later a head teacher at a comprehensive school, and has now been retired for some years. He has written and directed plays for his pupils and directed one of them on Kenyan TV. Since retirement he has attended writing courses, joined three writing groups and published a novel, *The Bootlegger's Widow*, and a biography of his father, *Public Library Pioneer*. He is currently planning the publication of his memoir.

M.S. CLARY has practised social work in London, Oxford and Miami. Has won prizes for short stories, and published two novels, *A Spell in France and Three Albert Terrace*. She has worked in fashion, and enjoys fiction, art and film noir. Visit www.msclary.co.uk.

NEIL HANCOX recently published a collection of his short stories – *A Selection of Short, Sometimes Very Short, Stories*, under the name N.L. Hancox, available from Amazon – and has contributed to a dozen or more anthologies. He lives in Abingdon, is married, and has two children and two grandchildren.

SARA BANERJI was brought up by her mother, Ann Mary Fielding, a best-selling novelist in the 1950s, to believe her life would be a failure if she did not publish a novel. Then, as her father was dying, he said, 'I have made a mess of my life.' So, determined to make her life a success and her father's life matter, Sara wrote her first novel by hand. Her husband typed it out and she sent it to Faber and Faber (the only worthwhile publisher (according to her husband). It did not occur to her that they would not publish it. After all, how many people had the energy to write 300 pages by hand? In her innocence, Sara scoured the papers for reviews before the publishers had even responded. Weirdly they nearly did publish. Eventually, *The Wedding of Jayanthi Mandel* was accepted by Victor Gollancz. Since then, she has had ten more novels published by HarperCollins. They are all still available with Bloomsbury. Sara has also published three of her own novels independently. "When I am writing", she says, she lives in her created world and experiences her characters' joys and sorrows.

VALERIE DEARLOVE (née BARDELL) is an illustrator, author and artist. Two of her paintings once hung in Ealing Film Studios – and one in the Montmartre district of Paris. Her parents met and married in Alexandria, Egypt during the Second World War. Her father, who was due to play cricket and football for Yorkshire, excitedly brought his Egyptian trinket wife to England! In the 1950s, when Valerie was twelve, her father died, leaving the family destitute. Her mother tried to place her three children in the Nazareth House Roman Catholic orphanage, Oxford. They were refused, because they weren't orphans! But her life in fiction had begun...

SIMON HOWARD has been a screenwriter, director, lecturer, journalist and writer of all sorts. He taught film and drama at Prague Film School and the universities of Westminster and Roehampton. He still does drama sessions with kids visiting from Ukraine. For several years he worked as writer and script editor for Just Betzer, producer of *Babette's Feast*. His latest film project is as writer on the Indian documentary *Risk Takers* about people living dangerous lives in Mumbai. He has been a special adviser to the National Army Museum. His novels *Cupid's Hypodermic*, *Rough Cut* and *World's End* are available on Kindle. So are his poetry collections *Children of Manu*, *Living Inside Strangers*, *Poems for Translation* and *The Accidental Post-Modernist*. He splits his time between Oxford, India and a few other places – especially Tuscany.